"What about you? Ever been in love? Married? Almost married?"

Something changed with that question, and as soon as Marcus looked in Addie's eyes, he regretted asking. She'd been happy, enjoying sharing her life with him. But now there were shutters in her eyes that fell just as he got a glimpse of the pain.

"Once upon a time," she whispered. "I believed in the fairy tale for me." She fell silent. He didn't ask anything more; he didn't want to twist the knife that she obviously felt.

They'd reached the white picket fence surrounding her yard. He almost asked how a girl who lived in a house with a white picket fence could live in it alone, but he didn't.

"Thanks for walking with me," she hastily said and pushed the gate open, just as hastily closing it between them. "Enjoy the rest of your evening." This time she rushed into the house, not looking back, not even to wave goodbye.

Why did he feel so disappointed?

Dear Reader,

The hardest part of writing any book, for me, is the ending. I want to make sure I get it right so you, and I, feel the satisfaction of the happy ending that is romance.

But each book's ending is also a moment to say goodbye to characters I've lived with, intimately, for months. In the case of my A Chair at the Hawkins Table series, for years.

Addie Hawkins has been with me since page one, since the Hawkins siblings first lost their mother and gathered around that dining room table to remember her. The joy I feel at finally giving her the happy ending she deserves makes saying goodbye easier. I hope you love Marcus as much as Addie and I do, and enjoy the final chapter of the series.

In this case, however, it's more than a goodbye to these characters. It's the last of the Superromance line. This has been my literary home for over ten years and eight books. And as a reader, for many years before that.

I have to thank so many people. The editors for letting me finish this series. That means so much to me. My fellow authors, who have given me friendship and guidance. And mostly all of you Superromance readers, who bought, read and love my stories and characters as much, if not more, than I do.

I'll never forget any of you, and I hope our paths cross again. Please visit my website at angelsmits. com for the latest developments in the next stage of my writing journey. I'll look for you there—and on the bookshelves of the future.

Angel Smits

ANGEL SMITS

—

Addie Gets Her Man

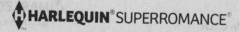

HARLEQUIN® SUPERROMANCE®

Recycling programs
for this product may
not exist in your area.

ISBN-13: 978-1-335-44929-0

Addie Gets Her Man

Copyright © 2018 by Angel Smits

This edition published by arrangement with Harlequin Books S.A.

For questions and comments about the quality of this book, please contact us at CustomerService@Harlequin.com.

www.Harlequin.com

Printed in U.S.A.

Angel Smits shares a big yellow house, complete with gingerbread and a porch swing, in Colorado with her husband, daughter and Maggie, their border collie mix. Winning the Romance Writers of America's Golden Heart® Award was the highlight of her writing career, until her first Harlequin book hit the shelves. Her social work background inspires her characters while improv writing allows her to torture them. It's a rough job, but someone's got to do it.

Books by Angel Smits

HARLEQUIN SUPERROMANCE

A Chair at the Hawkins Table

Last Chance at the Someday Café
The Ballerina's Stand
The Marine Finds His Family
A Family for Tyler
Seeking Shelter
A Message for Julia

Visit the Author Profile page at Harlequin.com for more titles.

The entire A Chair at the Hawkins Table series has been about siblings. And I'm lucky to have two very special ones of my own.

This is dedicated to Jeff Strong and April Wilkerson. I love you both, and am so glad you're a part of my life. Thank you.

And to Ron. You always believe.

CHAPTER ONE

ADDIE HAWKINS STOOD next to her car, letting the remaining heat of the day wash over her. The Someday Café's parking lot was nearly full, and from here, she could see the lobby was overflowing. Standing room only. Hopefully, they weren't violating any fire code.

Addie was so proud of Tara. Her little sister had grown into a competent, beautiful young woman. Tara's diner had nearly been destroyed in last month's flooding. But she'd survived; she'd rebuilt, and tonight was the grand reopening.

Taking a deep breath, Addie turned to grab the baker's box from the backseat of her car. Her special chocolate chip peanut butter cookies were nestled inside. It was a peace offering as well as a grand opening—uh, reopening—gift.

Tara had asked for the recipe, but Addie hadn't been ready to share it then. She still wasn't. This was a compromise.

"Please tell me that box is for me." Her brother DJ's voice came from behind her.

"Not a chance." She smiled and almost took

pity on him when she turned to face him and saw his smile fade. "These are Tara's. You might be able to sweet-talk her out of one."

"One?" He grimaced. "That's lame."

They walked toward the entrance together. "Where's Tammie?" Her sister-in-law was in the last trimester of her pregnancy, and she hadn't had an easy time of it.

"She's already inside. Tyler——" He grinned as he mentioned his son. "He was ready to come over around noon, so we compromised. They were here about an hour ago." His grin was indulgent and satisfied. The man was head over heels in love with his wife, with his whole family, and Addie was pleased to see it. They'd been through a lot to be together. DJ hadn't even known about Tyler until he was eight, and once they'd found each other, a madman had nearly stolen everything. But here they were now, happy and their family expanding.

"Everything okay?"

"Yeah. Doc says she's right on schedule." Was that a sweat breaking out on his brow? It was no secret that this whole having-a-baby thing was freaking out the former marine. Addie bit back a smile. The day they'd found out it was going to be a little girl, he'd nearly passed out in the doctor's office. Tammie and Tyler still loved sharing that tidbit of information with everyone.

DJ hurried ahead and opened the door. Voices, the sound of clattering dishes and the delicious aroma of Tara's cooking flowed over them. "Do you see Tara?" she yelled over the din.

DJ was taller than most everyone in the room, but he shook his head. "Wyatt and Emily are in the back corner. At the big table. Should be a little quieter over there," he yelled and led the way through the crowd. Addie gripped the box, praying she wouldn't drop it.

Getting through the room was a challenge. Everyone knew Wyatt and, of course, Tara, so by association the rest of the family were part of the community, as well. "Hi, Addie," "Hi, DJ," rang out half a dozen times.

As she moved, Addie glanced around. Everything looked great, just like it had before the flooding, before the raging river had torn through, destroying most of Tara's hard work. Thankfully, they'd managed to save all the furniture.

Tara had purchased several old wooden tables when she'd first bought the worn-out diner. The big three-leaf dining table where Wyatt was seated looked newly cleaned and polished. The mismatched chairs that sat at those tables looked just like Mom's after six kids had gotten through with them. It was a wonderful eclectic mess, just as Tara had planned.

A wave of homesickness washed over her, but Addie swallowed it and kept walking.

As usual, she took stock of who was here. Her older brother, Wyatt, called it her mother-hen mode. Just then, as if catching her in the act, he shot her a wink. Like always, he sat at the head of the big table while the others talked and ate.

Tammie looked great considering she was within days of delivering the newest Hawkins to the world. Wyatt's wife, Emily, was beside her, and next to her sat Mandy, her other sister, holding little Lucas on her lap. His tiny hand smacked the wooden tabletop, eliciting a giggle from his pudgy cheeks. Hard to believe he was nearly a year old.

Even Jason and Lauren were here. She'd known they were flying through on their way home from Lauren's European tour. She wondered if it just so happened that the ballet tour ended the same time as the grand reopening, or if they'd worked something out with her management company. Considering Jason was Tara's attorney, anything was possible. Either way, it was great to have them home.

Tyler sat at the other end of the table, imitating his father's gestures as he explained something quite intense to the little girl in the next chair. He was definitely ruling the roost. The boy had brought so much life to the entire Hawkins family when he'd come into it last year.

Addie watched the little girl for a long moment. This must be Brooke. Addie moved cautiously toward her. Morgan, Tara's...what the heck did you call a man dating your sister who was six foot two with body-builder muscles and a tough exterior? *Boyfriend* seemed too tame.

This was Morgan's daughter. Tara had said the girl was a bit skittish around strangers. Tyler seemed to be doing well with her, so Addie didn't want to upset either of them.

"Addie!" Wyatt called when she reached the table. "I can take that box for you." The twinkle in his eye told her he knew exactly what was inside.

She laughed and swatted him, winking at DJ. "I might have brought you some of your own, so leave those for Tara's customers."

"Oh, yeah, score." He and DJ high-fived, and Addie let the warmth of their enjoyment wash over her. Everyone in the family loved her cookies, and she didn't dare come to a family function without a batch—or two.

The fact that Tara wanted to sell them in her diner only made Addie's heart swell. These cookies were still the one contribution she made to this ever-growing family. It was her gift to them, what held her place in their hearts.

With all the new spouses and children, Addie often felt like an outsider in this big family. She missed their needing her.

She'd been so young when Dad died. Mom had fallen apart, and it had taken months for her to get back on her feet. As the oldest, Addie and Wyatt had taken on the job of caring for all the littler ones. She'd become more mother than sister, and she'd never really been able to go back.

Finally reaching the table, she set the big box down. As soon as she found Tara, she would pass the cookies off to her—at least now, she wouldn't drop them.

It might be quieter here in the corner, but it still didn't allow for much conversation. Just then, Wyatt caught her eye and waggled his eyebrows while he tilted his head to his right.

There was a reason she never got picked first to play charades. "What?" she mouthed to him, not sure what he was doing. He did the whole contortion thing again, and she shrugged, confused.

Someone tapped her arm, and Addie turned to see the little girl, Brooke, standing beside her. She crooked her finger for Addie to bend down.

"He's talking about the lady with the ring," she said.

"What lady with the ring?" She looked to where Wyatt sat next to his wife, and frowned. Of course Emily had a ring. And Tammie had her hand resting on her belly. Her ring shone in the light. It'd be impossible to forget her and DJ's big country wedding last year.

Mandy sat next to her, holding Lucas on her shoulder, patting his back as he snuggled close, sleepy-eyed now. Her hand moved—and sparkled.

"Oh…oh!" Addie rushed around the table, having to shove only a couple of people out of the way. Without thinking, or hesitating, she took hold of Mandy's hand and pulled it toward her. "When did Lane change his mind?"

Mandy laughed. "He never changed his mind. Turns out he just wanted to wait until he could do it right."

"Did he do it right?"

"Oh, yeah." Mandy grinned, and if it wouldn't have disturbed Lucas, Addie would have pulled her little sister into a big hug.

"I want details as soon as we're someplace I can hear them all."

Mandy nodded and resumed patting Lucas's back. Her ring winked so brightly, Addie wondered how she'd missed it. Wyatt gave her a thumbs-up across the table.

Like proud parents, she and Wyatt shared this moment. Addie knew he was thinking the same thing she was. That it would be so nice if Mom were here.

Before she got maudlin, she looked toward the serving counter. Tara was here—somewhere. A giant white banner that read Grand Reopening hung over the doors to the kitchen.

The swinging café doors had been a service-able silver color before the flood, but had taken on some damage. Tara had told Addie she'd had to paint them. The vivid pink was perfect, glinting in the light as Tara poked her head out.

"Wish me luck," Addie called to no one in particular as she grabbed the baker's box and headed toward the kitchen. After wading through the crowd again, she finally reached the doors and, well past formalities, pushed them open with her shoulders. Some of the crowd's noise was muffled back here.

She froze. Tara was definitely busy—with the help, it seemed. Morgan had her wrapped in his arms, and Tara was returning his kiss with everything she had. Addie blushed, then cleared her throat as loudly as she could.

Tara pulled away, her cheeks flushed. "I was just helping Morgan with his—uh—apron." She finished tying the white strings around the big man's waist.

Morgan laughed and reached for the coffee carafes on the burner nearby. "Gotta earn my keep," he said as he turned through the doors with a familiar swagger.

"Thanks," Tara called after him.

"I'm not asking what the thanks was for," Addie teased and set the box on the prep counter. "Here's a double batch of cookies." She said it as nonchalantly as she could.

"Oh, Addie. Thank you." Tara stopped what she was doing and gave Addie a hug. "You're the best."

"Order up," Earl, the short-order cook, called through the pass-through, pulling Tara back to work.

"I know you're busy. We'll talk soon. Promise." Addie left the kitchen before she distracted her sister any more.

Customers were slowly trickling out, contented smiles on their faces, as the waitresses seated another wave. Addie knew the staff, as well as their harried expressions. Staying out of their way, she headed to her family's table.

"Addie?" She didn't quite recognize the woman's voice that called out to her. Addie looked around until she found the sheriff, Dutch Ferguson, and his wife, Elizabeth, seated at a table a row away. Elizabeth waved.

Addie shivered as she looked at them. She couldn't ignore the older couple, and to be honest, she loved them dearly. But so much came with them. Memories. Shadows. Pain.

Elizabeth had never recovered from that long-ago night. Even now, in this boisterous, laughter-filled restaurant, a sad aura surrounded her. Addie gave the woman a hug, and felt the thin bones of her shoulders. "Hello, Elizabeth. Dutch."

Addie felt an obligation to them. They'd almost been her family, after all. Their son—Cal's image came painfully to mind—had been their only child, and her first love. He'd been so young. So handsome. So long ago. She swallowed the pain that threatened to choke her. *Almost* didn't count, except in horseshoes and hand grenades, her daddy used to say.

Addie looked at Dutch, and while his smile was broad, it didn't quite reach his eyes. *Uh-oh.* She made a mental note to stop by their house before she returned to Austin to make sure they didn't need anything.

"It's good to see you, Addie." Dutch gave her a brief hug. "Can you join us?"

"Sure, for just a minute. How are you doing?" As she sat, she aimed the question at Dutch, knowing he'd be the one to answer. Elizabeth seldom spoke. The last couple of times Addie had visited with her, she'd noticed changes. Subtle, but probably more obvious to her since she wasn't around Elizabeth all the time.

She recalled Dutch's words from that day. "She's slipping further and further away."

"We're doing fine," he answered, smiling at Elizabeth. "Aren't we, hon?"

"Yes. Yes. So nice to get out."

"Tara's done a fine job with this place." Dutch smiled. A big, gruff man, he was exactly what Addie had expected of a small-town sheriff. He'd lived his entire life in Haskins Corners, and he was as much a staple here as this diner.

"Yeah, things were a little uncertain there for a while. The floodwaters were pretty wicked."

"Water's evil," Elizabeth whispered, a venom in her voice that Addie understood. She looked at Dutch. He frowned, and the brief shake of his head told her not to follow that line of conversation. Addie was more than happy to leave it.

"Looks like everyone's here." Dutch nodded toward the big table in back. "Lots of change in the Hawkins clan."

"Yeah." Addie glanced over her shoulder at the overflowing table of her siblings, then laughed. "And then some. The family is growing so quickly." She hated the wistfulness in her voice. Addie chose not to analyze that too much. "I'd better get back."

"Come visit when you can," he offered.

Elizabeth looked up from her meal and smiled. "Yes. Come visit."

"I will. I promise." She gave them each a hug, holding on to Dutch just a bit longer, as if maybe he could use a little encouragement. Being Elizabeth's husband couldn't always be easy. But he obviously loved her. He patted Addie's hand that rested on his shoulder in silent thanks.

Addie glanced at Elizabeth and saw so much of Cal in her. Same color hair—except now Elizabeth's dark hair was going gray. Same eyes. Same jawline.

Sometimes it hurt to look at Elizabeth.

Right now, Addie didn't want to remember. Even the good times they'd shared hurt. There weren't ever going to be any more. Thankfully, time had dulled the edge of that knife, and she could bear the hurt. Almost.

Suddenly, a strong arm slipped around her shoulders, and she yelped. Wyatt's familiar hug surprised her. "Stop fretting, Ad," he whispered in her ear.

"I'm not—fretting." She frowned at him.

"Yeah, you are." He gave her a brief kiss on top of her head. "But we love you for it." He guided her to the table, where the waitresses had brought several plates of appetizers. Addie grabbed a potato skin that should taste amazing. It tasted like dust. She didn't have enough energy left to enjoy the flavor.

Dutch and Elizabeth got up from their table, and Addie watched as he guided his wife to the register. While he paid the bill, Elizabeth looked around, confused, then finally took Dutch's arm. Relief covered her face as he guided her outside.

"Addie." Wyatt stared across the table at her. Just as he recognized her mother-hen mode, she recognized his dad mode. They'd spent way too much time taking care of their younger siblings.

She closed her eyes for an instant. "I'm fine, Wyatt," she said, opening her eyes again and meeting his concerned gaze.

"I saw the way you were looking at the Fergusons. I know you've kept up with them over the years." He paused, and she dreaded what he'd say next. "It wasn't your fault, Ad." The last she didn't really hear, but rather, she saw the words form on his lips.

She shook her head. "I know." She hadn't even been there when…when the accident had happened. She'd tried for years to second-guess what might have happened if she had been there.

Wyatt leaned back in the wooden chair and considered her. She almost wanted to stand up and walk away. Instead, she smiled. It wasn't as if everyone hadn't done just that, at least once, over the years.

"Look—" She leaned forward and put her hand on his. His skin was so rough and calloused from working with the horses. She rubbed her fingertips over those hard-earned scars. "I care about them. I care about all of you." She waved at the table full of the Hawkins clan.

"You're done, sis," he said softly. "It's time you

looked after *you*. You helped raise everyone. Lord knows you were the main caregiver for Mom up until the end. And I know you'd take on Elizabeth Ferguson out of some weird sense of obligation to Cal." He shook his head. "But I'm telling you not to. Let Dutch handle it. You need to have your own life." He leaned back, with the look of decision on his face that told her he considered the situation settled.

"Really?" She frowned and looked at Emily. "Did my brother actually say all that?" He wasn't known for being a big talker.

"Yes. And he's right," Emily said.

"Now you're ganging up on me?"

"No, we're not." Emily squeezed Addie's hand. "Everyone's grown now. You've earned the chance to build your own life."

Addie stared at them. They didn't understand, and she didn't have a clue how to explain it. She'd never focused on herself, not since—not since Dad died. She'd grown up on that day, and she'd gladly taken on the role of nurturer.

The idea of giving that up made her panic as she looked at the faces around her. She'd helped them get here. She was proud of that, proud of all of them.

Her eyes stung. Everything was slipping away. What was she supposed to do now? She needed to be needed, needed someone to care for—to watch over, to want her attentions.

But her family didn't need that from her anymore. And yes, Dutch could handle Elizabeth.

She'd had a chance at her own life, had dreamed of her own family, once upon a time. But fate hadn't been on her side, and she'd lost that chance forever.

MARCUS SKYLAR RUSHED across the street, knowing full well that he was jaywalking and only slightly caring. He was late for class, and considering he'd given his students a lecture on timeliness last class, he didn't dare show up late. They'd never let him off the hook for that one.

Campus was still alive with activity even this late in the day. He was running down the stairs in Richardson Hall, his wingtips slapping against the steps, when his phone rang. He tried to ignore the incessant noise, but he recognized that ringtone. It was Ryan. His thirteen-year-old son wasn't someone he could afford to ignore. Not without Carolyn's help to intervene.

He let the memory of her waft through only briefly. "Hello, kiddo. What's up?" He shouldered the phone as he shoved open the hall door.

"We're out of jelly."

"Uh, okay. I'm in class for the next hour. We'll discuss it later."

"Peanut better tastes like crap without jelly."

"Watch the language." He tried to keep his surprise out of his voice. The boy was definitely changing lately. He'd have to deal with that at some point. "I'll be home in a couple hours. I gotta go." He hung up and stepped into the classroom.

Most of the seats were full, which gave him a sense of gratification. Many of his colleagues complained about the number of empty seats in their classes.

Marcus wasn't sure if his class in military history was full because of the political climate and social awareness, or for some other reason. It didn't matter. He'd take it. "All right, everyone." He set his briefcase on the desk. "Let's get started."

"That was a close call, Prof," Mitch, one of his most challenging students, said from the third row.

"Yeah, but it's not because of my procrastination," he pointed out to the young man who usually fell into that camp. "Teach my thirteen-year-old how to go grocery shopping, and maybe we'll discuss your grade."

The class laughed, and Marcus launched into today's lecture. It was on one of his favorite subjects, and he had to be careful not to get lost in his rambling. Vietnam was a black mark on this country's history, and still a tough topic to sell in some circles. He'd been hired specifically to share his knowledge on the collision of the government's promises and society's demands.

A collision intimately familiar to Marcus, as his father had been caught up in it. A nightmare Colonel Skylar still wore on his highly decorated chest.

Finally, the hands on the utilitarian clock hit the end of the hour, and Marcus wrapped up the lecture. He was putting his notes in the briefcase when a young woman came up to the desk. "Professor Skylar?"

"Yes, uh, Natalie, right?"

"Yeah." She grinned. "I have a question about our paper."

"The final project?" He emphasized the difference. There were many things besides papers that they could choose to do. Papers were the easiest for most students. They were used to doing them. He let his hopes rise that she was asking for permission to do something else.

"Yeah. I was wondering." She looked down at the desktop. "Uh, I don't think I'm very good at this history stuff."

"Why not?" He didn't want to come off sounding condescending, but he didn't see why she couldn't do it.

"It's hard." She finally looked up. "I was thinking about my topic last night. I was, um, hoping I could do something on fashion."

He stared at her. "Fashion?" He slowly closed

his briefcase. "Fashion of what? The era or of—" he tried to choose his words carefully "—Vietnam during the war?" Was there such a thing? "The 1960s themselves?" There were a lot of options.

She didn't look at him. Her topic intrigued him, mainly because he hadn't heard this one before. "Okay, explain what you're thinking." He leaned back, crossing his arms over his chest.

"Both." She finally looked up, excitement sparking in her eyes.

What the heck? Wasn't that his goal—to inspire these kids to at least pay attention?

"Fashion *is* a social statement. In the 1960s, it was a *huge* statement. And Vietnam had its own society. I want to compare that with what we had."

Marcus looked at her, attempting to ascertain if she was trying to pull something over on him. He wasn't new to this teaching gig, just new to this college. "I'll give you some leeway. Since the topic's a bit different, I want to meet with you halfway through to make sure you're on track."

"Oh, thank you, Professor." She rushed forward and tried to give him a hug. Marcus knew better and hastily put up his hand.

"Whoa! Just do a good job. That's thanks enough."

"Okay. You won't regret this, I promise," she repeated, then hurried out of the classroom. Marcus paused, taking a deep breath before slowly walking toward the door himself.

Everything was so different here, and while Natalie was part of the strangeness of this new world, she was a small part of it. He told himself he would adjust, he would figure it out.

Nothing was even remotely similar to the world in which he'd expected to live out his life. Carolyn's death— He froze, the memories slamming into him. No, he wouldn't let the hurt cripple him again. He'd fought too hard to escape the grief. He forced his feet to keep moving.

The job he'd loved, had thought he'd gain tenure with, had vanished too quickly when he'd fallen apart. He'd nearly lost Ryan, the thirteen-year-old waiting at home for jelly to make his peanut butter taste less like crap.

This move, this new position, had to work, had to save him and what was left of his world. It had to. What the hell? He'd read and grade *any-thing*—even a paper on the fashion of 1960s Vietnam—and give the student a fair grade, if it meant keeping his son, and giving Ryan the life he needed and deserved.

CHAPTER TWO

MONDAY MORNING CAME way too soon. Why, again, had she taken this job? Addie sat at the principal's desk that, six months ago, she'd thought was the epitome of the best career move she'd ever made.

Teaching had always fulfilled her. After Mom's funeral last year, though, she'd needed something to fill up the emptiness inside her. She knew some of it had to do with losing her mom, but not all of it. Not really.

So, she'd thrown herself into pursuing her long-held plan to become a school principal.

Now, after spending hours staring at budgets and accounting columns—that still didn't balance—she was rethinking everything.

Frustrated, she returned her focus to the papers in front of her. Somewhere, the calculations were off, and she had to figure out where. Maybe she should take it down to the eighth-grade math class…see if they could solve it?

Or she could go to the teachers' lounge and get a nice cup of tea. Caffeine sounded lovely right about now. She stood. Maybe a break would help.

Lindy Dawson sat at the break room table working on lesson plans. Addie smiled. She and Lindy had started teaching here the same year. Their friendship was one of the best parts of this job.

"Hey, Ad." The petite brunette leaned back and put down her pen. She rolled her shoulders. "What's on your exciting schedule today?"

"The usual." Addie sighed. "I can't get this month's budget numbers to balance."

Lindy had been the one person who hadn't supported Addie's job change. In all honesty, she missed the day-to-day contact with the kids, and Lindy had known that would happen.

"You having second thoughts? About the job, I mean."

"No. Just—" Addie sighed. "I don't know. Something seems off."

"Here?" Lindy tilted her head toward the hall. "Or at home?" She grinned at Addie, a shit-eating grin if Addie ever saw one. "You did go out to the ranch this weekend—to the land where everyone falls in looooove, right?" Her voice went a bit singsongy.

"Cut it out." The slightly annoying detail that all of Addie's siblings—*younger* siblings, all five of them—were married or seriously involved with someone wasn't lost on her. She chose to ignore the fact that she hadn't gone on a date in months.

"What?" Lindy laughed. "Got anything you'd

like to share?" She waggled her eyebrows, teasing. "Any juicy details of some wild weekend?"

"Funny." If Addie didn't know Lindy so well, if they hadn't shared nearly every deep, dark secret over ice cream and wine, she might be upset with Lindy's nosiness. She knew it was well-intentioned. Lindy was as close to her as Addie had ever been with either of her sisters. "No, nothing to share." Even Addie heard the disappointment in her voice.

"Maybe that's the problem." Lindy closed her notebook, and gathered up her things. "Give yourself a break. It's budgets. Nobody dies."

"Are you sure?" Addie flopped down on the couch. "We could all freeze to death if the heating bill isn't paid, you know."

"Nah, I'll just make everyone run around the building to warm up. Besides, we live in Texas, remember? Warm most of the time." Addie groaned as Lindy stood and shouldered her backpack. "One more swim practice before regionals." Lindy laughed as she headed toward the door. As the gym teacher and swim coach, Lindy always finished her day with swim class.

"Do you ever get tired of it? Want to change to another subject or something?" Addie asked.

"Nope." Lindy opened the door. "Watching teens in an environment where they can't posture and primp gives me hope for the human race." She laughed.

"You're sadistic."

Lindy just grinned back. "I know. Admit it— it's what you love about me."

Addie knew her friend also loved when she could teach kids the skills to save themselves. The rest was just a cover for the soft heart that resided inside.

Suddenly, loud voices came from the hallway. "What's that?" Lindy asked as she peered into the hall. Addie wasn't far behind. Jess Martin, the biology teacher, came out of the science lab the same time they stepped into the hall.

A crowd stood near the lockers. Raised voices bounced off the walls. There was obviously something going on. As Addie and the teachers got closer, kids on the outside of the circle stepped aside and away. They knew trouble was coming.

"Hey," Lindy called, wading through the group. Jess followed. He was taller and bigger than either of them, which might give him an advantage to see what was going on. By the time Addie reached the center of the crowd, Lindy had pulled one boy back and Jess had hold of another.

The first boy had a bloody nose—the second would have a pretty good shiner tomorrow morning.

"Everyone back to class," Jess instructed. After

the kids all groaned a bit, they trudged away, discussing the fight.

"You two." Addie pointed from one boy to the other. "My office. We'll call your parents. Lindy, get the first-aid kit." They didn't have a school nurse. They shared one for the entire district, but she was really here only when they were giving out vaccinations or holding a special event. Most crises were handled by the administration, or the teachers.

Lindy was better at first aid than the rest of them, since gym class tended to be the place *everyone* got hurt.

The taller of the two boys, the one Jess had by the arm, just snickered and shrugged. She recognized him—Nick Haldon. He'd been in her office before, a couple of times. She remembered his parents, as well. The Haldons were decent people, but the father seemed absent in the boy's life. Meeting with the pair was never a pleasant experience.

The other boy was smaller, but not by much. He didn't have the perpetual smirk on his face. If nothing else, he looked a bit shocked, perhaps scared. Was he afraid of her? Of getting in trouble? Of his parents? She looked at him for a minute, knowing she'd have the answer soon enough.

She led the way to the office, with Lindy bringing up the rear, and seated the boys far away from each other in the reception area. The receptionist, Gina, was there to make sure they didn't take off. Lindy took care of the bloody nose the best she could, but there was no getting the blood out of the boys' shirts.

Addie groaned. Visible evidence—blood, specifically—set parents off, with good reason, but that would only make it worse. Probably for them all.

Once the bandages and ice packs were in place, Lindy put the first-aid kit away, and Jess headed to his class, leaving Addie to deal with the two boys. She stood looking at them for a long minute.

She'd start with Nick. At least with him, she knew what to expect. "You—" she pointed at the new boy "—stay here until I call you. Nick, come with me." She headed into her office.

Seated, she looked across her desk at Nick. If he'd been in her office multiple times already, how many times had he been here with her predecessor?

His shoulders were hunched, and he held an ice pack to the bridge of his nose. It wasn't broken. Lindy had assured her of that. But Addie had to admit, the new kid—she really needed to figure out his name and use it—had a pretty good left hook. She wondered where he'd learned that.

"You want to tell me what happened?" Nick wasn't going to answer, but she'd give him the benefit of the doubt.

"No." His voice was muffled by the ice pack.

"I'm giving you the opportunity to come clean. But I understand that you might be in too much pain to talk clearly." She really needed to work on her penchant for sarcasm. She blamed her brothers and their own various busted lips and noses for it. "If so, you can sit in the outer office and wait until your parents get here."

She walked him to the separating door and had him sit, then turned to face the other boy. He had his own blue ice pack shoved against his right eye. Nick could slug pretty good himself. "Come with me," she told the other boy.

She didn't wait for him any more than she'd waited for Nick. She sat while he got comfortable.

"You want to tell me what you were fighting about?" She tried to keep her voice even and her face neutral.

"No."

"You know, someone's going to tell me what happened." She wouldn't even have to use the good cop/bad cop routine, though Lindy would be disappointed. She loved playing the bad cop.

"Nick won't tell."

"Oh, I'm not worried about Nick. I've dealt with his type plenty. No, the other kids who were standing around watching. They'll eventually tell me."

He looked at her, his eye wide as if that had

never occurred to him. How had he gotten to eighth grade and not realized his fellow students were not always to be trusted?

There was definitely something about the boy that intrigued Addie, and she wasn't exactly sure why. "What's your name?" she asked softly. Since he was a newcomer to the school, she didn't have a clue what to expect from this boy, unlike Nick.

"Ryan." He didn't say anything more, and she waited for a long minute.

"Do you have a last name?"

"Yeah." Another long silence, and in the one eye she could see, she saw his thoughts. She was pretty sure he was actually considering lying to her.

"Lying's a bad idea, just so you know."

"Uh… Skylar."

"Thank you, Ryan." She leaned back, knowing that Gina was even now pulling his file to get his parents' phone numbers. Addie pondered how to approach him.

Westbrook Middle School wasn't huge. When Addie had been growing up, she'd gone to school here. Back then, attendance had nearly overflowed halls. Now, with an aging population in the area, and the new system of charter schools and choices that weren't around when Mom was raising them, the headcount was lower.

There weren't many new kids each year, so

Ryan Skylar was notable in a sea of the same faces each year. Something about him interested her, and maybe it was because she'd spent way too much time staring at budgets.

She tried again. "Do you want to tell me what happened?"

He shrugged. "Do I have to?"

She fought back a smile. "You don't have to, but it might make things better for you. Ms. Hanson is calling your parents, and I'd like to be able to tell them you were cooperating with me."

He shrugged, and that single uncovered eye looked at her. If she'd ever seen pain, it was in that one brown eye. It jolted her. So strong. And almost familiar. She shook her head and sat forward again, crossing her arms on top of the budget papers. "You know, I grew up with three brothers. And a couple sisters. There's not much you're going to get past me."

He looked down, studiously examining his tennis shoes. She waited for him to look up again.

"I'm an only kid," he said softly.

"There are times I would have liked to be that." Flashes of all the craziness in her family flitted through her mind. "Does that have something to do with the fight?"

He shrugged again, but still didn't look at her. "Bet your house wasn't quiet."

"Uh, no." She laughed. "Not very often anyway." She gave him a couple of minutes, but she needed to find out what happened. "We're calling your parents—"

"You gotta call my dad," he interrupted.

"Okay. Is there a reason?"

"Mom." The boy took a deep breath. "Mom passed away…"

Well, she'd muddled into that one. "I'm sorry." Addie felt the knife in her chest for the boy, and from her own recent loss of her mother. That's what she'd seen in his gaze. Grief. It resonated with her. She knew how much it hurt. Faded memories of her father, and the resulting emptiness, were still too real.

"Then we'll call your dad." She cleared her throat, not sure what was stuck there. "What do you think he'll say about your getting into a fight?"

The boy looked down at those tennis shoes again. "He's not gonna like it."

"What do you think he'll do?"

He seemed to think about that a minute. "Probably cut down my computer time." The sadness in the boy's voice expanded to fill the room. She fought a smile. At least now she knew what was important to him, and she felt another stirring of curiosity.

Gina stood in the doorway and Addie looked up. "Yes?"

"His father's on the way. Nick's parents aren't answering."

So, what else was new? She really didn't want to deal with the Haldons, but there were some things about her job that were unavoidable.

"Unless you've got something to tell me, you can take a seat in the lobby until your dad's here."

The boy hesitated but finally stood. She had to admire him. He might not like Nick, but he wasn't going to rat on him. She watched him walk out and slump down on the chair—farthest from Nick.

She pulled the budget papers together and sorted them. She wasn't going to make any more progress for now. Even if she did, parents would only show up and disrupt her. She didn't know how long it would take for them to get here.

She glanced at the clock. Another hour and the day would be done. Hopefully, Gina could reach the Haldons before it was time for the boys to head home. She couldn't let them go before speaking to their parents, and she didn't want to stay any later than she had to.

"Addie?" Gina said from the door. She had the cordless receiver in her hand and a smirk on her face. "Mrs. Haldon is in Atlanta at a conference. Mr. Haldon is at work. They're looking for him."

"So, who are you talking to?"

"The housekeeper. She wants to know if she should come get Nick."

"Housekeeper?" Addie stared. "No. His father needs to come get him."

"I'll let her know." Gina left, and for some strange reason, Addie found herself feeling sad for both boys. Neither of them had the support they needed, that they should have.

Just then, a man Addie had never seen before came rushing in. He wore neatly pressed dress pants and a blue button-down shirt. His thick chestnut hair looked awry, as if he'd been running his fingers through it. Repeatedly. "Ryan?" He headed straight for the boy.

He knelt down, uncaring that he could get dirt on those nice pants. "Are you okay?"

"Yeah," the boy said softly, pulling the ice pack from his eye. The man turned an angry glare on the other boy, and Addie saw Nick actually shrink away. The man didn't say anything, which had Addie breathing a sigh of relief. The last thing she needed was an outraged parent taking matters into his own hands.

She walked to the door and stood waiting for a

gap in the softly spoken conversation. "Mr. Skylar," she finally said. "Won't you come in?"

"I DON'T UNDERSTAND." The tall, dark-haired man paced in front of Addie's desk. "Ryan has never been a problem. He's never gotten into trouble."

Addie watched Marcus Skylar shove his fingers through his thick hair again.

"He's never gotten into a fight."

Addie made herself focus. "From what he's told me, he has been through a lot." Her heart still ached for the boy. "He's had a lot to adjust to."

"I guess." Marcus suddenly sat on one of the chairs facing her. "It's been one hell of a year," he whispered. "I'm not making excuses."

"I think we need to give Ryan a break." She leaned forward, trying to look like she was in charge here. She knew what she was doing, but this man set her on edge and she didn't know why. "Have you considered counseling?"

She expected him to get angry. Half-expected the man who was very near the edge himself to rise up and rail at her. Instead, he silently looked at her, then leaned forward, putting his elbows on his knees, and stared at the carpeting. "I have. And we did. For a bit."

He wasn't like anyone she'd ever met. Nothing like her brothers, who would have already blasted her about psychobabble and being able to take care of themselves. She waited while he sat there, staring, seeing something he wasn't sharing with her.

"Mr. Skylar, our school has a no-tolerance policy. I have to give Ryan, both boys actually, a week's detention for fighting.

Marcus sat silent for a long moment. When he finally looked up at her again, his gaze was clear. "I understand. He'll be there." He waited a moment before shooting to his feet. "Guess, I'll…" His voice faded, and he turned toward the door. Now he looked more like she expected. "Sorry to have taken up so much of your time."

Pausing in the doorway, he curled his fingers around the knob until his knuckles showed white against his tanned skin. "Have a good afternoon, Ms. Hawkins." He pulled the door open and, through the opening, she saw Ryan look up at his dad. "Come on, Ry," she heard him say. "Let's get you home and cleaned up."

She stared after him. He wasn't angry. He wasn't yelling at his son, like so many other fathers would be doing. He actually looked…she tried to find the right description…beaten?

What battle was he waging? Against his son? Against himself, and his own grief? He'd lost his wife the same time Ryan had lost his mother. "Mr. Skylar?" She hurried around the desk, stopping in the open doorway just as he turned to look at her. "Yes?"

"Is…" What was she thinking? What was she even doing? "Is there anything I can do to help? You…or…" She looked at Ryan. "You, Ryan?"

"Thank you." Marcus straightened his already impressive shoulders. "But we'll be fine. Come on, Ryan."

With his hand on Ryan's shoulder, he headed out the door, and she heard their footsteps echo down the empty hall. It was a lonely, nearly painful sound. She'd have to keep an eye on them. On Ryan, she reminded herself. She was a principal. The father was not her concern, unless his actions affected the boy.

Then all bets were off.

MARCUS DIDN'T LET go of Ryan's shoulder until they reached the car. The boy was silent as he threw his backpack in the rear and slammed his backside into the passenger seat. He pouted, crossing his thin arms over his equally thin chest. Only once he was settled behind the wheel did Marcus speak.

"You want to explain what happened?"

He didn't yell at Ryan, though he wanted to. His own father would have already blistered his ears with accusations and curses, but Marcus knew how it felt to be the boy who'd made a mistake he couldn't take back.

"No."

"Well, here's the deal." Marcus started the car

and steered out of the parking lot. "You can either tell me what happened, and I'll figure out what your punishment will be from that. Or you can remain silent, and I'll go with what the principal and the other boy say."

"That's not fair."

"Fair?" Marcus clenched his jaw. He would not lose his patience. "That's not the issue, son. The issue is whether you're going to be the one in control, or if you're going to let someone else have that honor."

The silence in the car was thick with the hot afternoon air and a teenage boy's simmering anger. "I didn't start it," he finally said, quietly staring out the side window.

"I didn't think you did. Tell me what happened." He tried to use the voice that had worked so well for Carolyn in coaxing their son into opening up. Times like this he really missed her. Missed the mother she'd become the day they'd adopted Ryan.

"We were having a discussion in lit class." Silence grew.

Lit class? What book was he reading in that class? Marcus shook his head. It didn't matter. Ryan did.

"Nick said—" Ryan's voice cracked. "Nick said my real mom didn't like me and that's why she gave me away." His broken voice faded to a whisper before he finished.

CHAPTER THREE

WHEN MARCUS HAD been Ryan's age, his father had come home on one of his infrequent leaves from who knew where. James Skylar had offered to help a buddy fix his deck and had subsequently volunteered Marcus to join them. Somewhere in the process, something went wrong. Marcus couldn't remember much since he'd gotten a concussion from a wooden beam that fell on his head.

He felt like that now, sitting next to Ryan at the stoplight.

"Care—" He cleared his throat. "Care to explain?" They'd never hidden Ryan's adoption, but they'd gotten him when he was three days old. It had been a closed adoption. His birth mother had wanted it that way, and they'd respected her wishes. The reality of the situation seldom crossed his mind anymore. Apparently, it did Ryan's.

With Carolyn's death, he probably should have expected this. But he hadn't even thought about it.

"We're reading some short stories for lit class," Ryan said, breaking into Marcus's thoughts. "Mr. Hudson has us discuss them. One is about a bunch of kids in an orphanage." Ryan shrugged and turned his gaze from the passenger window to stare out the windshield. "Nick made a crack about kids whose birth parents gave them away— said their mom and dad didn't like them."

Marcus took a deep breath. "You know that's ridiculous, right? We've talked about this before, remember?"

"I remember. I know it's not true. It's just—" Ryan went silent for a couple of blocks, and Marcus didn't push him. "It's just that…" He shifted in his seat. "I wasn't mad for me so much…"

Ryan turned to look at Marcus. They pulled into the drive, and Marcus killed the engine.

"I was mad for…for my birth mother," Ryan said. "He had no right. He doesn't know why she gave me up." His indignation came across loud and clear.

Marcus took another deep breath before saying anything. "I'm proud of you for wanting to stick up for her, for caring, but it's not something to fight about."

"I know." Ryan reached for the door handle and pushed it open. "But what he said was so wrong." He slammed the door closed with a bit too much force.

Marcus followed him, grabbing his own backpack from the rear. He watched Ryan walk inside. His son was growing up so fast, and their conversation brought back memories of when they'd first brought Ryan home. Good memories.

Had that really been thirteen years ago?

Inside the kitchen, both backpacks hit the kitchen table with a loud thud, and Marcus watched Ryan head to the fridge. It was a routine Carolyn never would have allowed, but one they'd fallen into since moving here.

Carolyn. He thought of his wife, and, while his heart still hitched at her loss, it wasn't nearly as bad as it used to be. He thought about his conversation with Principal Hawkins—

—who wasn't anything like he'd expected from a school principal. She was young and pretty—the first woman to pique his interest in a long time. And while she hadn't smiled much during their meeting, he got the impression she normally did.

He'd told her that they'd gone to counseling, and they had. Not just after Carolyn's death, but for months before. Hospice had been a godsend as he'd tried to deal with her impending death, as well as Ryan and his reactions.

"Can I have the rest of the lasagna?" Ryan's muffled voice came from inside the fridge.

"For dinner?"

"No, now. For a snack." He turned around, the take-out container in his hands, his expression hopeful.

"Uh, no. I'll make dinner in a bit." Another skill he'd picked up after losing Carolyn.

"I've got an idea."

Marcus nearly groaned. Those words always meant that Ryan was up to something. He smiled. How had he managed to raise a son who was a con artist at heart? Marcus leaned back against the edge of the counter and crossed his arms over his chest, waiting. "What?"

"I can eat the lasagna now and get started right away on my homework."

"And?"

"And I'll be done in time to play in a *Castle Battle* tournament tonight at seven."

"Ryan, it's a school night." Video games were normally off-limits except on the weekends.

"It's *the* tournament of the year. Come on, Dad. I'm really good at it. I could win."

Marcus looked at his son. The bruise around his eye was going to be dark by morning. "Put ice on that eye tonight." Principal Hawkins's words came to him. Did Ryan deserve a break in this? As it was, he'd be spending the next week in detention after school. Was that punishment enough? It wasn't as if Ryan regularly got into trouble.

Ryan's earlier explanation almost made Marcus proud of his son. Proud of his convictions, anyway.

But Marcus also knew Ryan. He'd learned

over the past few months how to deal with Ryan's "ideas." He could "outdeal" him, or accept the proposition. Carolyn had been so much better at this than he was.

He didn't have the energy for dealing tonight. "I want you off the computer by ten. Lights out by eleven."

Ryan did a fist pump and shoved the plastic container into the microwave.

"But—" Marcus knew better than to let Ryan think he was totally off the hook.

Ryan slowly pivoted on his heel. "But what?"

"Tonight you get the tournament. Tomorrow we'll discuss your punishment."

The boy's smile melted. "I'm sorry you got called, Dad."

"But you're not sorry for the fight?"

Ryan had to think a minute. "Not really." The microwave's timer sounded, and Ryan grabbed the hot dish. "Gotta go. Got homework to do."

"We *will* discuss this," Marcus yelled over the sound of Ryan's footsteps on the stairs.

"Sure, Dad," Ryan yelled back, his footsteps crossing the ceiling overhead.

Marcus sighed. To be young and so resilient. "Sorry, Carolyn," he whispered, "I'm trying." But the life she'd tried to help him build, the one with the family that came home and had dinner together every night, just wasn't meant to be.

Marcus glanced at the kitchen table. It was covered with his backpack, books and laptop. They wouldn't be eating there anytime soon.

Besides, it wasn't as if he had a lot of extra time. Today was the deadline for the midterm essays. It could be an awfully long night.

EVERYONE ON THE teaching staff took a turn monitoring detention. While it wasn't the norm for Addie to take a rotation, she was happy to step in since Lindy was out of the rotation right now. It was swim season, and between coaches and club sponsors, options were few.

Today there were four kids seated in the desks where, normally, Mr. Hudson taught English lit. Addie knew all four of them. She'd been the one to assign them detention.

Ryan was already seated in the back, his work out in front of him. Two other boys were here for fighting as well, and a girl, Melissa Hopper, had cut history class one time too many. Nick was nowhere to be found. Why wasn't she surprised?

"Afternoon, everyone." Addie put her own stack of work on the teacher's desk. The irony that she was in detention, something she'd never gotten in school the first time around, wasn't lost on her.

There were a few mumbled responses. The door slammed open then, and Nick came stomping in. He slumped into the first seat he came to, dropped his backpack and propped his feet on the chair in front of him.

"Good of you to join us, Mr. Holden." She stood and walked over to him. "You can work on your homework for the next hour."

"I don't got none."

"You do know I can call your teachers and check, right?" She really tried to give him the benefit of the doubt.

"They already went home." Defiance came across loud and clear.

She debated arguing with him. Part of her was tempted to let him sit there and be bored for the next hour. It would serve him right. She owed it to her staff to encourage him to get his work done.

"You ain't my mother, you know."

Thank God. "No, I'm not. I'm your principal. Almost the same thing." As a teacher, she'd often spent more time with some of the kids than their parents did.

He glared at her and, with a heavy sigh, reached for the backpack. The rasp of the bag's zipper was loud in the quiet room.

"Thank you," she said and returned to the desk. The other kids were watching, a fact she didn't acknowledge. Ryan's eyes were wide, though, when Nick pulled out his phone. "You know the rules, Nick. No phones. Put it away. Now, or it's mine."

"But I don't have anything else to do."

"Sorry, that's the way it is. Kindly, put it away."

Ryan watched closely as Nick sullenly shoved the phone into a side pocket. She could see Ryan wanted to get up and help her out. Thankfully, he didn't. That protective streak. She wondered if he'd gotten that from his father.

Marcus Skylar's face came to mind, and she found herself curious about him.

He'd done a good job with Ryan. The boy was a good kid. She'd done some investigating after they'd left her office. Paul Hudson had been more than happy to fill her in on what he knew. He'd defended Ryan, but didn't know the complete details. She'd get them, she knew. She just had to find the right person to tell her. If it wasn't for the school's no-tolerance policy on fighting, she wasn't sure Ryan would be here right now.

The hour dragged by. Even Ryan ran out of work to do and started fidgeting in his seat before it was time to leave.

"It looks like most of you finished your work," Addie finally said. The looks she got were almost comical. She could tell they were hoping she'd let them go early. Not a chance, but they didn't have to know that. She looked at the expectant faces. With the exception of Nick, these were all pretty good kids.

"Let's talk about a couple of things." She walked around to perch on the front of the desk.

"How many of you are looking for summer jobs?"
Eighth grade—the year before high school—was
usually the year kids started to seriously think
about jobs, about spending money and getting out
of the house to hang out with their friends.

Three of the five students shot their hands up.
Nick ignored her, and Ryan shrugged. "Ryan?"

"I don't know. We just moved here."

She nodded. "That can be a challenge. Does
anyone have any ideas to help Ryan get to know
the area?"

"What part of town do you live in?" Melissa
asked.

"In Sommerfield. Over by the baseball fields."

That wasn't far from where Addie lived, and
where she'd grown up. "You could see if the parks
department is hiring," one of the other boys offered. "They take care of the ball fields. Use kids
to do it sometimes."

"That'd be cool." Ryan grinned and nodded.
"I'm hoping to play baseball this year."

Nick paid attention to the conversation for the
first time. "Yeah, like you could throw a ball."

Addie speared him with a glance. "You like
being in detention, Nick?" she asked him. "That
wasn't polite." She looked over at Ryan, half expecting to see either anger or hurt in his eyes. The
boy was standing, hard determination on his face.
"Sit down, Ryan. Nick, apologize."

"Sorry," Nick mumbled.

"As an apology, that could use some work." It had been a whole lot easier when she'd had to deal with her three brothers. At least then she'd had the final weapon—Mom.

Sighing, she chose to take the win with the other kids and ignore Nick's behavior. "Back to our conversation. Anyone have other ideas to help Ryan? Each other?"

"There's a strip mall east of there that has lots of shops," the other boy offered. Everyone, except Nick again, nodded.

"Lots of good ideas," Addie said. "Here's what I'd like you all to think about. As the principal, I get people contacting me who are looking to hire students. I hear about opportunities. I'm more than happy to share that information with anyone who shows potential."

Four heads nodded. "But…" She looked at each kid, holding their gazes for a long moment. "Detention doesn't show potential." Nearly every gaze fell. "So, think about your actions, about what you do through to the end of the year. You stay out of here for the rest of the year, and I'll seriously consider sharing any job information with you."

"Thanks, Ms. Hawkins." Melissa smiled. Like the others, she wasn't a bad kid—she just needed to engage and want to work at school.

Addie made the same offer to any of the kids

who were in detention. Sometimes it worked, sometimes it didn't. Sometimes they just needed a little nudge in the right direction. Other times, nothing worked. She glanced at Nick.

"Okay, everyone. The hour's up. You can leave, but remember what I said." The noise of everyone gathering their belongings filled the room. "See you all here tomorrow."

She or one of the teachers would, anyway.

Ryan stopped at the door and looked back. "Ms. Hawkins?"

"Yes?"

"Can I ask you a sorta personal question?"

"Uh, yes. Not sure I'll answer." She'd learned to hedge her bets a long time ago.

"How long have you lived in Austin?"

"Most of my life. Why?"

He shrugged. "Just curious. We lived in Chicago before we came here. It's different."

"I'd expect it to be. Do you miss Chicago?"

He thought about it for a minute. "I miss some of my friends, but my dad's happier here. I like that. Have you ever been to Chicago?"

Her answer seemed to be important to him. He must have a strong sense of pride for his hometown. "No. But I'd like to."

"Are you sure?" he asked urgently.

"I think I'd have noticed."

"Oh." He looked a little crestfallen.

Addie frowned. This seemed a bit more than hometown pride. Her answer seemed to confuse him. "But I promise, if I ever go, I'll be sure and check with you to see about what I need to see."

"There's a lot of cool stuff." He nodded, though his smile didn't return. "You gotta try the pizza."

"I'll remember that. You'd better hustle so you don't miss the bus."

"I walk home. It's close enough."

She nodded. "Healthier, too."

"Yeah. See you tomorrow." And when he was gone, the silence of the room suddenly seemed heavy. Addie gathered her things, her mind already three steps ahead. She still had way too much to do before she headed home. But she had to admit, she'd enjoyed chatting with the students. Damn Lindy for being right.

ADDIE TAPPED HER pen on the desk. Another Monday was nearly over—for the kids anyway. Surprisingly, after a week of supervising detention, she missed it. She'd managed to get something done while the kids worked on their homework.

And she'd gotten to know them all a little bit. They'd ended each session with a few minutes of discussion. And every day Ryan had stayed behind to ask a question or two.

He now knew that her favorite color was blue. He'd learned that while she hadn't been to Chicago, she had gone to college at the University of Illinois in Urbana. That answer had made his eyes light up with his smile. He'd been extremely interested in hearing about her siblings, especially Wyatt's ranch and the horses.

She missed their interactions. Glancing at the clock, she figured it'd be another couple of hours, at least, before she finished with the pile of paperwork. She had finally figured out the budget, though. She wanted to pat herself on the back for getting that done. Now the employee files perched on her desk taunted her. She sighed.

Time to look at year-end reviews. What exactly did this have to do with education?

"I'm heading over to the admin office with this," Gina said from the doorway, a box in her arms. "Do you need anything before I take off?"

"A million dollars?" Addie mumbled to herself. "No. Thanks." She stared out the window. The bus stop was just outside, and she watched as kids waited and the big yellow buses arrived.

Maybe a cup of tea would help her concentration. She stood, intending to head to the teachers' lounge. That's when she saw them.

Ryan was with another boy, leaning against the wall at the corner of the gym building. This was his first day out of detention.

She couldn't quite identify who the other boy was. Their heads were bent over the screen of one of their phones. She was almost afraid to wonder what had grabbed their attention. Whatever it was, it was apparently quite enthralling.

She liked seeing the smiles on both their faces, though she didn't really want to know what was going on inside the heads of two thirteen-year-old boys. Still—

She moved closer to the window. From here, she could see them more clearly. The other boy was Dex Silvano. Dex was one of those kids everyone loved, but who she was convinced would grow up to be something great—like a jewel thief or used-car salesman.

He and his family lived only a couple of blocks from her, and Addie frequently ran into his mother at the grocery store. Addie knew more about Dex than she did any of the other kids at the school. That wasn't necessarily a good thing.

Maybe some fresh air would help more than tea. She headed to the door and outside. "Hey, Principal Hawkins," rang out several times. She smiled, stopping to talk to several kids who'd been her students last year. It helped fill up that little hole that grew inside when she spent too much time alone.

She wondered why Ryan and Dex were still here. They both lived within walking distance. Addie herself sometimes walked to work on nice days. Like today.

"Hello, boys."

Ryan looked up, and, while his smile didn't go away, it faded some. She felt a little guilty. He thumbed the screen of his phone dark.

"Hello, Ms. Hawkins." He shoved the phone into his pocket. "Am I in trouble?"

Addie laughed. "No. I'm just taking a break. Thought I'd enjoy the sunshine." She lifted her hands toward the sky. "Nice day, huh?"

"Yeah."

She looked over at the other boy. "Hi, Dex."

"Hello." The boy nodded.

"You heading home?" she hinted with a glance toward Ryan.

"Yeah. My dad's picking me up today." Ryan gathered up his backpack and hitched it over his shoulder. Dex didn't have his backpack with him. She almost asked him where it was, but didn't. His mother would be checking on him, making sure he got his homework done.

"Baseball tryouts start tomorrow," she reminded Ryan. He'd mentioned it the first day of detention, but not otherwise. Nick's presence hadn't helped.

He looked up, seemingly surprised she remembered. "Yeah."

"Are you going to try out?"

He shrugged. "I dunno."

She looked closer. "What happened to the boy who couldn't wait for practice to start last week?"

Ryan glanced over at Dex. Was he worried about what his friend would think of his wanting to play baseball? Dex didn't let her down, though.

"You didn't tell me you were playin' ball. Cool. What position?"

"I dunno yet. I might not make the team."

"Did something happen? Why the doubts?" she asked.

"No doubts." Ryan glanced sideways at Dex again. She inwardly smiled. Oh, yeah, even thirteen-year-old boys had to uphold their macho image. He reminded her of her brother DJ. At about the same age, he'd wanted so badly to be just like their brother Wyatt.

"I think you can do whatever you set your mind to." She repeated the words she'd heard her mom tell DJ back then. "But make sure it's you you're trying to be, not someone else. *You*—" she emphasized the word "—like baseball don't you?"

"Yeah."

"You should go for it, man. Show that dumbass Nick—" As if suddenly recognizing what he'd said, and to whom, Dex colored. "Uh—"

"I'll let you off the hook for your language, Dex." She didn't want it to interfere with her conversation. "But I expect you—both of you—to let me, or one of your teachers, know if there are problems with other kids."

"Everything's fine," Ryan answered too quickly.

And there it was. The lie he'd nearly told her last week in her office, and in detention. It hurt that he did so now.

"Well, have a good afternoon, gentlemen." She turned away, then paused and turned back. "Remember, my door is always open."

"Yes, ma'am," Ryan whispered.

Had she missed something? Why was he distant all of a sudden? She took a few steps backward. "Maybe I'll stop in at practice tomorrow. See what coach is planning this year."

That got a smile out of him, and she was shocked at how it transformed his features. She couldn't look away.

Memories of another boy, another time—an equally devastating smile—overwhelmed her. Before the ache became too much, she shook her head. Reality, and the school grounds, thankfully returned.

Marcus Skylar was going to have his hands full with this one. Someday, some girl was going to fall head over heels for that smile. Addie just prayed Ryan didn't break that girl's heart like Cal had hers.

As if summoned by her thoughts, a late-model Jeep pulled up to the curb near the boys. Ryan's father sat behind the wheel. He glanced at Addie and their gazes locked. For just an instant. He smiled, not the way his son had, but gentle and warm, inviting.

Addie looked away first, turning to go inside. What was wrong with her? Twice, in a few minutes, she'd lost complete track of her thoughts.

She needed caffeine more than she'd thought.

CHAPTER FOUR

IT WAS LATE when Marcus walked into the coffee shop. Only a few people sat at the scattered tables. The scents of coffee, vanilla and rich aromas from around the world wafted around him. He took a deep breath—and savored it.

Ryan had gone to a weekend baseball camp this morning, leaving the house far too empty for Marcus. Ryan's joining the baseball team last month had been one of the best things that had happened to Ryan since they'd moved here. He was a happier kid than he'd been in a long while, and he'd made friends with his teammates. For once, Marcus wasn't worried.

At least as far as his son was concerned. He'd have to remember to thank Principal Hawkins for encouraging Ryan. It had made a difference.

After Ryan left, Marcus had rattled around in the house until he couldn't stand it anymore. He wondered for the millionth time why he'd let his thirteen-year-old son talk him into buying the place.

Still, it was starting to feel like his, and in reality, Marcus didn't really care where he lived. Home was an abstract concept for him.

He did like the fact that the coffee shop, as well as several other stores and services, were within walking distance. He'd gotten into the habit of walking to the shop a couple of nights a week, even a couple of mornings. It was a nice change.

As he waited for the barista to make his drink, his phone rang. He thumbed the screen to see who was calling. Not Ryan, please. He wanted his son to be having fun, not checking in with his dad.

His sister Anne's number filled the display. "Hey, sis." He was always cautious when his sister called. He loved her, but she wasn't the type to call and chat. She always had news, was always on a mission.

"Hey, yourself. Thought I'd check and see if you've heard from the folks," she said.

Yep, that was Anne, and there was the pre-planned topic of discussion. "When you say, *heard from them*, what exactly do you mean?"

"Did they tell you what they have in mind?" She was impatient, which was also normal. He was used to being treated like a younger, less competent brother.

"No. Last I heard, Dad was still overseas, and Mom was heading to another fundraiser." The story of his parents' life.

"Then consider yourself warned. They're heading your way."

"What do you mean, my way?"

"Dad's home. Has been for a couple weeks. Last night at dinner, he announced that he was taking Mom to Texas to check on you two. They already bought airline tickets."

Marcus groaned. "I don't have time for this."

"Well, you'd better make time. At least I saved you from one of their surprise visits."

Marcus closed his eyes, trying to gather his patience. James Skylar did whatever he damned well pleased. He'd show up on some relative's doorstep and announce he was there to visit for a few days. How many times had they done that when Marcus was a kid? And the big intimidating man that James was—he wasn't someone people could ignore. They sure as heck didn't close a door in his face. He'd probably break it down.

Not that that had ever happened. Most of the relatives had actually seemed happy to see him.

Marcus wasn't like his relatives. "When are they getting here?" he asked, resignation in his voice.

"Not sure. Soon, I'd guess. You know Dad. He found the cheapest, most inconvenient-for-you flight." She laughed.

"Thanks for the heads-up." There was a long silence. "How's life with you?"

Anne was silent, as well. Marcus knew better than to read anything into it. Anne wasn't a big talker, and she thought out what she was going to say. "Good. Busy, just like you. I'm actually looking forward to their being gone for a bit, sorry."

Marcus smiled. "You're not sorry."

"No, you're right. Since Dad's been home, he's—"

"Difficult?"

"That about covers it. He's talking retirement. Seriously. Mom might shove him out of the plane somewhere over Kansas if he isn't careful."

"How did their marriage ever survive this long?" Marcus recalled the angry words that were frequent in his childhood.

"Dad being gone so much is probably the only thing that saved them. All bets are off now."

"Yeah." He looked around, realizing the barista had set his drink on the counter. He grabbed it and headed to find an empty table. "Will *you* survive? What about Lance?" His brother-in-law usually did fairly well with their parents. Mom loved him.

Anne sighed on the other end of the line. "Even his patience is thin."

That wasn't good. Lance was the most laid-back, tolerant person Marcus had ever met.

"And you sent them to me?"

Anne laughed. "Hey, I didn't send them. This was all Dad's idea. I didn't do much to dissuade them." She went silent again. "Mom's worried about you, you know."

Not like he hadn't given her cause in the past. "I know. I'm doing fine. Really."

"Would you even tell us if you weren't okay?" Anne whispered.

"I don't know."

"That's okay. Ryan'll tell me."

"Smug doesn't become you." He liked it, though. This persona he recognized. "Anne?"

"Yeah."

"Don't go all big sister, okay? I love you anyway."

Emotion wasn't something his family had ever been comfortable with, and he felt that discomfort come through the phone now. He didn't care. He'd learned its value.

"Gotta go. Keep me posted. Love you, too." The last came out in a hasty whisper as she disconnected the call.

Marcus pocketed his phone. Pleased with himself for setting his sister on edge in a good way, he set his backpack on a small table in the corner. The knot of pressure between his shoulder blades intensified. If his parents were coming to visit, he couldn't waste any time tonight.

Turning to sit, he noticed a woman seated near the window. She looked vaguely familiar. He frowned, watching her as he absently opened his backpack. She was reading a hardcover book that was most definitely fiction. Her long golden hair kept tumbling down, and every so often, she'd fling it back over her shoulder.

Was that—? Just as he sat, she looked up. Their eyes met. Recognition dawned in her eyes. She smiled.

"Marcus, right?" she asked.

"Uh, yeah. You're—"

"Addie Hawkins. Ryan's principal."

"I thought I recognized you." It was nice to satisfy that nagging itch of not being able to identify someone.

"That's okay if you didn't." She laughed. "I'm out of my natural habitat. Even the students who see me every day do a double take in public."

He didn't think the double take was from recognition. She really was lovely. He halted that train of thought. "Sorry to interrupt your reading." He nodded toward her book, and she turned the page to continue.

The fact that there was no ring on her left hand didn't escape his notice. The fact that he noticed shocked him. He hadn't noticed that on anyone else in ages. He shook his head. That wasn't why he was here.

He set his own book on the table. Not fiction, though. This book was also part of the reason he'd come here. He didn't want to read it at home.

Alone. In a big lonely house. This was an old book, the spine thin, worn. Not from many hands touching it in a library or bookstore. No, this was a hand-created work, done as a labor of love—a memoir by a man who'd served in Vietnam at the same time his father had. There was a big difference, though.

This man had been a foot soldier, a private on the ground. His father had been high above, watching from the cockpit of a surveillance plane.

Marcus stared at the book's cover. Odd that Anne had called tonight. Knowing his father would be here soon, Marcus questioned if he really wanted to read it now. Did he truly want to know what was inside? There was no turning back once he started to read.

How would it affect his interaction with his father? Would it confirm his suspicions that his father was hiding something he'd been involved in back then? Or would it alleviate Marcus's long-held suspicions? What would his next meeting with his father be like?

Marcus had gotten this book from the author's son. Sam Tilton had died last year from cancer that was most likely the result of Agent Orange. No one could prove it, though, and Sam hadn't cared.

Marcus had met him once, early in his diagnosis when he'd been sure he'd beat the monster.

Marcus had meant to see him again, but Carolyn's illness—the rest of life—had gotten in the way. This was the first time since he and Ryan had moved that he'd pulled the book out.

Now he second-guessed his decision.

"I tell my students that osmosis doesn't really work." Addie's voice gave him an excuse to break out of his troubled thoughts. He tried to laugh, but he wasn't very good at it anymore.

She moved—a smooth motion, standing, then walking to his side. "It's a beautiful book." She stood close. Warmth from her arm touched his as she caressed the hand-tooled leather cover. "Almost too pretty to open," she whispered.

"Yeah. What's inside isn't nearly as pretty."

"Have you read it before?"

Marcus shook his head. "No. I know the author. I know what it's about."

She moved to tug on the chair across from him. "May I?" At his nod, she pulled the chair out and sat. "I don't mean to interrupt…but can I help? You look troubled."

Addie was obviously a caring person. He'd known a few—very few—people like that in his life. Carolyn had been like that. He swallowed the pain in his throat.

He tapped the book cover, breaking the hold of his memories. "This is a memoir. One of the men who was with my father in Vietnam wrote it."

Her eyebrows lifted. He regretted surprising her like that. "I'm sorry," he said softly. "It's going to be a tough read. But I need to read it."

"Why?" Her shock faded, curiosity replacing it in her eyes.

Marcus shrugged. "To find answers. I—"

She waited. Not filling in the blanks, but waiting for him, listening.

"My father doesn't talk about his experiences. He keeps it all locked up inside." Letting loose only when he couldn't hold back anymore—usually with a well-aimed fist or a mouthful of filthy language. "He's got issues."

"He's still around, then?"

"Yeah. We don't see each other often." Though apparently, that was going to change soon. "Never did. He didn't take his family on any of his assignments."

"I'm sorry." Her gaze grew distant. "My father died when I was—" She swallowed, then frowned. "About Ryan's age actually."

"I'm sorry," he said.

The silence grew between them, but it wasn't uncomfortable. If anything, he found it oddly comforting that she was here, willing to listen as he waded into the murky waters of his father's past.

"My dad was a great guy." She seemed to shake herself out of the memories. "There were six of us kids. Mom had her hands full. So, when he died, we picked ourselves up and got the job done."

"Wow. Sounds rough."

"Not really. Everyone's grown now. All out in the world, with families and kids. We…we lost Mom last year." She stumbled over her words for a second, then once again recovered. "She was ready to join him," she whispered.

He envied her. His mother wouldn't be interested in joining his dad—anywhere, here or in the afterlife. She'd stayed married to him, just like she'd stayed behind when he'd deployed. She'd earned the military pension just like he had. She'd said it so many times, he could hear her saying it now.

Addie looked at him, then slowly rose. He had to tilt his chin up only slightly to meet her gaze. She couldn't be much over five feet.

"I'm sorry." She moved to her table and gathered her things. "I didn't mean to ruin your evening. This got a little maudlin."

"No. I interrupted you," he said. She turned to leave, and he reached out to stop her. "Wait." She looked back at him. "How about we start over? I'm Marcus." He stood and put his hand out in greeting.

Their eyes met. She smiled and took his hand. "I'm Addie. Nice to meet you."

He liked this friendly woman. "Can I get you

something?" He gestured to the bakery case and the counter.

"No, thanks. I already have a cup of tea that's probably half-cold by now." She took another step, then paused and glanced over her shoulder at him. "But if you'd like some conversation—"

"I would." He pulled the chair out that she'd been sitting on. Not sure if it was because of how she moved, or the closeness of where he stood to her, but a soft whisper of perfume pleasantly startled him. The long hair that had tumbled over Addie's shoulder while she read brushed his arm.

So soft. He shivered.

For the first time since he'd moved here, since Carolyn's death, he didn't feel quite so alone.

ADDIE USED TO come to the coffee shop when the hours of taking care of Mom had been too long. Now she used it as a transition. The full day of kids and constant activity at school was too drastically different from her quiet home. She came here and read—then she could face the silence.

Growing up in a houseful of kids hadn't prepared her for being alone very well.

"You live near here, right?" she asked Marcus as she moved her book bag and purse to his table. The table was small, and while he wasn't as tall or as muscular as her brothers, he managed to take up more than enough space in the room.

"A few blocks. You?"

"Yeah, it's just a short walk over that way. Do you come here often?"

He smiled, and she realized he'd caught her unintended use of a pickup line. Her cheeks warmed, and she ducked her head, hoping he didn't notice.

He must have taken pity on her. "Sometimes. It's a nice break."

"From?"

"A thirteen-year-old boy." He took a sip of his coffee before saying anymore. "I often wonder if I was like him at that age."

"You could ask your mother." She took a sip of her now-cooled drink. Lovely.

"Uh, no." His smile dimmed. "Mom's not exactly the reminiscing kind."

Addie tilted her head just a bit, wondering about him. "She's not?"

"No. She'll gladly tell you how much money they raised for diabetes research in 1989, but she couldn't tell you what I did for my birthday that year."

"Sounds like a woman who believes in helping people."

He frowned. "I'd say she's more interested in the disease of the week and who's the keynote speaker at the fundraiser." He shook his head. "I'm sorry. That didn't sound very charitable. She found her way to cope with being alone so much."

She couldn't help but wonder what he meant by all that. She wanted to ask, but if she'd learned anything being a teacher, it was patience.

"Every family has its issues."

"Issues. That's a nice way to put it."

"Hey, I'm not pointing any fingers. I have five siblings and there're plenty of stories, believe me."

"Five. That's…incredible. Your parents must have been saints or crazy. Ryan is enough challenge for me."

She laughed. "A bit of both, I think." She stared into her tea. Her voice broke. "I keep thinking I should be over the grief by now."

The silence stretched. "I don't know if it ever goes away."

The pain in his eyes reminded her of his wife. What had she been thinking? What was wrong with her? She needed to shake this funk. "I'm sorry." She put her hand on his. "I didn't mean to remind you—"

"It's okay. I'm used to it."

"You get used to it, really?" His skin was warm under her palm. It felt good to touch him, too good. She pulled her hand away and he let her, though he watched her movements.

Their gazes met. His eyes were a bright, rich blue, a contrast to his dark hair. What was he thinking? About his wife? About his son? About the book that he'd yet to open? About her?

"I really should get home." She stood and hastily gathered her things. "Tomorrow's an early day."

"Yeah. I should get going, too. Early class, as well."

"Class?"

He shoved the still-unopened book into the backpack. "I teach at the university."

"I didn't realize I was with a fellow educator." She liked knowing she had that connection with him. "What subject?"

"History. Military history, specifically."

"Really?" Why did that surprise her? Then she remembered the book he'd been reading. "So, the book—" she tilted her head toward the backpack "—that's for class?"

He shouldered the pack. "I don't know yet. Maybe later. Right now, it's…personal."

They headed toward the door, and she expected him to turn in the opposite direction. Instead, he fell into step beside her. "Do you live this way?"

"Uh, yeah." He stopped and, with a self-deprecating smile, gestured for her to precede him down the walk. "I guess we're headed the same way. You don't mind, do you?"

"No. I—" What were the odds? It was a small community, one of the carefully planned midcentury communities. Both from small towns, her parents had specifically chosen to live and raise their family here for that reason.

"What made you decide to move here?" she asked before she had time to think and stop herself.

"Actually, it was Ryan's idea." He walked on the outside of the sidewalk and didn't speak again until they'd reached the corner. "After Carolyn's death, both of us needed a change. We wanted out of Chicago."

"Is that where you were raised?"

"Yeah." This time he tilted his head and looked at her, smiling. "You ask a lot of questions."

"Occupational hazard. Sorry." She felt her cheeks warm again. "You don't have to answer."

"No, it's no problem. Yeah, I grew up in Chicago. We lived in an apartment on Lake Shore Drive."

"Not in a house?" Why did that seem so strange to her? She thought of the big house where she'd lived with her family, and the big ranch where Wyatt now lived that had belonged to her grandparents. An apartment would have been so strange.

"Dad was gone most of the time." He said that through clenched teeth. "So, Mom was a single parent in reality. It was just me and my sister. An apartment made more sense." He shrugged again, and his eyes grew distant.

What was he seeing inside his mind? She

wanted to ask, but refrained from uttering another question.

The sun was setting, and the shadows reached out. At the next corner, they both turned left. "Go ahead. I know you want to ask."

This time she laughed. "Am I that easy to read?"

"Yes, and no. Remember, I'm a teacher, too. It's in our nature to see the ones who want to ask but won't."

"True. Okay, so why was your dad gone so much? What did he do?"

"I'm not totally sure." He kept walking for a good half a block. "He was career military, and even after his official retirement, he still contracts with them."

"That must have been rough."

"We weren't used to him being around." He shrugged. "When he came home, it was worse than when he was gone." Again, he looked at the horizon—watching the clouds? Or his memories?

"I'd have loved to have more time with my dad," she whispered.

"I'm sorry. Tonight wasn't very upbeat." Marcus rubbed the back of his neck in a nervous gesture. He lifted the shoulder that had the backpack on it. "I think this book is influencing my mood."

They'd reached her house, and she paused at the end of her walk, just outside the white picket fence that had attracted her to the house in the first place. "This is it." She waved at the house, then faced him. "It was a lovely evening. Really." She meant it. He seemed honest and sincere. She liked that. She hadn't found those qualities in many of the men she'd met in the past few years. "Thank you for sharing with me." She paused, then grinned at him. "And for walking me home. I don't think anyone's done that since I was, like, fourteen."

He laughed, a deep, heavy sound that warmed her from the inside out. "And I'll bet your dad, or one of those brothers, stood at the door making sure nothing went on, too."

"Yeah." She smiled at him. "My brother Wyatt."

"You're welcome." He stood there, not moving for a long minute. Finally, he stepped back. "I'm just a couple blocks over. Have a great night, Addie."

"You, too." She wanted to say more. Wanted to know a whole lot more about him. The silence stretched out, awkward all of a sudden, full of expectation, until he resumed walking.

She watched until he reached the corner. He turned to wave before making that last turn. He was heading toward the street Mom used to live on. She couldn't remember which of the houses, other than Mom's, had been for sale recently. Of course, she hadn't gone over there much.

Maybe that needed to change.

His house was dark when Marcus finally reached it. He'd have rather gone into Addie's house, where he saw a light, inviting and warm, just inside that big front window. He made a mental note to leave a light on next time.

Next time? Next time he went to the coffee shop in the evening, he told himself. Nothing more than that.

Her house was similar to this one—the hazards of a planned development. Somehow, though, he liked it. For an instant, he pictured her. Moving around, locking the doors, checking the windows, closing everything up for the night.

Did she have a dog or a cat that'd run to greet her? Or was her house silent, like this one?

Shaking his head, he tried to cast thoughts of Addie out of his mind, but it wasn't easy. Her comments, gestures and expressions were too strong. Despite his attraction to her, he couldn't be interested in a relationship with anyone. Not now. Maybe never.

He had enough to worry about. Walking through the big house, he headed to the kitchen. He'd thought to grab a sandwich at the coffee shop, but hadn't felt hungry. Nothing had looked good, so he'd settled for just the coffee. Now, surprisingly, he *was* hungry.

Tossing his backpack onto the kitchen table— covered with dozens of books—he headed to the counter. He hadn't expected this room to become his makeshift office, but something about it drew him, made him feel comfortable.

A jar of peanut butter sat on the counter, right next to the bread—where Ryan always left it. Smiling, Marcus made himself a sandwich. Biting into the thick peanut-buttery goo, he grinned. Ryan had no clue what he was talking about. Peanut butter did not taste like crap without jelly.

It tasted just right.

CHAPTER FIVE

WHEN RYAN VOLUNTEERED him to chaperone the eighth-grade, year-end dance, Marcus knew exactly what his son was up to. Ryan had noticed—and commented on—the wave he'd sent Principal Hawkins that day he'd picked the boys up after school. Ryan had read way too much into a simple gesture.

Now he was determined to put Marcus in close proximity to his pretty school principal.

Which was why Marcus hadn't mentioned meeting her at the coffee shop the other night. Though he had to admit, Addie was definitely eye-catching, and talking with her had been challenging and interesting.

But mostly, she'd made him laugh. Something he couldn't remember doing in ages. She'd popped into his thoughts so many times since then.

But he'd found, and lost, the love of his life. He wasn't going to find anyone else like Carolyn, and he'd worked hard the past couple years to reconcile himself to that.

The problem wasn't his. It was Ryan's. The boy

was determined that Marcus would not spend his life alone, and put considerable effort into finding someone to replace his mother.

Somehow, that made Marcus sad.

Carolyn might not have been Ryan's biological mother, but she'd loved him, wanted him and created a life that had been everything they could hope for. It wasn't anyone's fault that it hadn't lasted.

Marcus forced himself to focus on the room around him instead of on the world that had been. If his son was any example, a room full of thirteen-year-olds could get into plenty of trouble.

Even with half a dozen chaperones around.

"So, how did he con you into doing this?" The woman's voice came from behind him. Since the music wasn't nearly as loud as at the dances when he was a kid, he could actually hear her. Marcus looked over his shoulder to find Addie standing there, a plastic cup of punch in one hand, the other hand shoving the riot of blond curls behind one ear.

Maybe she was the one controlling the volume of the music. He heard the half-dozen metal bracelets clatter as they fell along the length of her forearm.

"He said it was mandatory."

She laughed. "We do push for each parent to do their turn, but we don't use that word."

"Apparently, my son does." He stared into his own cup of overly sweet punch.

"We'll work on that." She moved beside him. "Look at the positive side. You've done your turn once this is over." She smiled, and her face transformed, softened, sweetened.

He smiled back, unable to resist her infectious optimism. "How do you do this every day?"

"Do what? We only have two dances a year."

He laughed. "No. Do this." He pointed at the room. "Survive all this teenage energy. Just being around Ryan wears me out. You deal with it most of your day."

"I guess I'm used to it. Being the principal gives me less student contact than when I was a teacher."

"Do you miss it?"

"Sometimes." She glanced toward the center of the gym floor. A grand total of two couples were dancing. "This is my first year as a principal, so it's all new. I'm learning."

New challenges. He understood that. He tried to find his son's familiar blond head in the crowd. He'd been over by the basketball backboard with Dex, the neighbor kid who'd become Ryan's new best friend. And while Ryan thought Dex was the next best thing, Marcus wasn't convinced.

His concern must have shown on his face. "Don't worry." She leaned toward him. "We have a dozen parents here tonight. They can't get into too much trouble."

"Have you met my son?" Marcus looked at her askance. "He doesn't need five seconds to find trouble."

She laughed. "I'd say that's pretty normal for his age. He's a very inquisitive kid."

"That's for sure. From the minute he could talk he was asking questions." He saw Ryan and Dex appear out of the crowd, chasing each other and laughing.

The silence between Marcus and Addie wasn't quiet, but it was comfortable. They stood there through the length of a couple of songs, listening, watching, waiting. For what, he didn't have a clue.

"Did you ever get around to reading your book?" she asked.

"Book?" Then he remembered the coffee shop. "No, I haven't had time." Nor the inclination. He was still waiting for his parents to appear on his doorstep as his sister had predicted.

A man came over shortly after the song ended, his smile too wide. "Hello, Addie." The man stepped in too close to her. "How are you?"

"Hello, Mr. Wilson. How's Bethany doing tonight?" Addie leaned around the man to observe the kids, despite the man's attempts to dominate her attention.

"She's having a good time. So glad you still

have these types of activities for the kids. Keeps them off the streets and out of trouble."

"We do what we can."

Marcus watched, noting her forced smile and the way she leaned away from the guy. She didn't like him, but she did a fairly good job of hiding that fact. The man stepped closer, and if it weren't for the table directly behind them, she'd have probably stepped away. She was trapped, and the realization flashed in her eyes.

"Hello, I'm Marcus Skylar." Marcus moved closer as well, sticking his hand out as a barrier between her and the other man. He actually looked surprised to see Marcus there. Addie looked relieved, and Marcus pushed Wilson to interact with him.

"And you are?"

The stranger looked perturbed, but shook Marcus's hand. "Jack Wilson." He stepped back, and Addie seemed to breathe a sigh of relief.

"Excuse me." She stepped away, granting Marcus a faint, thankful smile before she headed toward a couple of boys who seemed to be heading toward the door.

"Which kid is yours?" Marcus asked.

"My daughter's over there." Jack pointed toward a group of girls huddled along the bleachers, ignoring everyone around them. "The pretty one on the end."

Marcus wasn't sure which girl he meant. There were half a dozen of them, and all of them were dolled up. A sense of dread hit him. Thankfully, Ryan was still oblivious to girls. A reprieve…for a while at least.

But someday, and probably soon, Ryan was going to notice.

ADDIE ROAMED THROUGH the gym. The boys were mostly on one side, the girls on the other. She liked this age. They weren't yet single-minded. The operative word being *yet*. She smiled and took another trip around the room.

A girl's voice came from around the corner of the bleachers. "Boys are just stupid."

"Oh, you're just mad because Peter broke up with you right before the dance."

"Am not." She was definitely pouting.

"Are, too." The girl laughed. "Come on, Jill. There are lots of other guys here. Look around."

"I don't want to. Guys suck," she repeated.

"Did you see *him*?" The second girl's excited, breathy voice perked up Addie's ears.

"Who?" the first girl asked.

"The dark-haired guy," she whispered.

There was a bit of shuffling. "The old guy?"

"He's not old. He's gorgeous."

"You're crazy, Malory."

That narrowed it down to just a few girls in the

school. Addie leaned against the bleachers, following what was obviously the girls' gazes. Marcus stood there, chatting with Jack Wilson.

She didn't like Jack much, though, as the principal, she wasn't supposed to like or dislike parents. Specific parents anyway. But Jack was one of those guys who just—how did she describe it? He was oily. Like a salesman who didn't know when to take no for an answer. In her case, he was always selling himself.

He was divorced, and if the tales his daughter shared were true, not amicably. The idea of actually taking him up on any of his offers made Addie's skin crawl.

Marcus Skylar, on the other hand... She thought about that night at the coffee shop. She'd found herself thinking about their chat, about the book he wasn't reading and the enjoyable walk home several times since.

Just then, Jack said something that made Marcus smile. He had a nice smile, though he didn't often use it. She'd managed to coax a few smiles from him so far. She recalled the girls' comments and was pretty sure her voice would sound as breathy as the girls had if she were to say anything.

"I heard he's the dad of the new kid." The girls were speculating again.

"What new kid?"

"The computer whiz. Didn't you see him in class last week?"

"I'm not sure."

"He's blond. Talked about the computer camp he went to last summer. He was bragging about how he met some famous hacker who could break into anything."

"Oh, him. He's kinda cute."

"For a nerd."

"Hey, that's not very nice."

"I'm going to go talk to him," the girl said, and Addie almost reached out to stop her. Then realized that would let them know she'd been eavesdropping. She was the adult in charge, so, while eavesdropping was expected, it wasn't how Addie liked to deal with the kids. Even though it sometimes was the only way she knew what was going on.

"The nerd?" The girls continued their conversation.

"No, his dad, silly."

"Why would you want to do that?"

"Mike said he's a widower. He looks lonely, right?" There were a chorus of giggles, and Addie decided to come out of hiding.

"Okay, ladies. Let's get out and join the party."

Several of the girls shared uncertain glances as they hustled away from Addie. She smiled, only slightly enjoying the power she had over a bunch of teenage girls who thought they ruled the world.

"Well, well, well." Lindy stepped out of her own set of shadows. "Wasn't that fun to watch?" She laughed, and Addie realized she was looking farther down than normal. She was wearing heels and Lindy had hers in her hand.

"What was fun?" Addie kept her same pace, moving around the room, watching and checking on everyone.

"Why, seeing this side of you."

"What side of me?"

"The woman who's interested in someone, who doesn't want anyone—especially the person who she's interested in—to know she's interested."

"Thank God you don't teach English."

"Yeah, not my best subject." Lindy fell into step with her. "But you got my point."

Addie huffed. "Yeah, I got your point." There wasn't much reason to hide anything from Lindy. They knew each other too well.

Lindy also knew why Addie would never act on her attraction.

"You know I'm right." Lindy was always right— or so she believed.

"Maybe." Addie wasn't giving her the credit that easily.

"Okay, must I sacrifice myself for our friendship?" Lindy sighed and stopped to slip her feet into her shoes. She put a hand on Addie's shoulder for balance. "You, my friend, need a nudge. You'll thank me. And I expect wine with that thank-you, thank you very much."

Addie cringed, glad that gym class seldom required papers that Lindy had to grade. "Where are you going?"

"Watch and learn, sister. Watch and learn. Follow my lead."

With a swagger that did all womankind proud, Lindy headed straight toward Jack Wilson. The man was talking loudly, with his hands flying in the air, explaining something to Marcus. The instant he caught sight of Lindy heading toward them, he froze. Hands in midair. For an instant, he actually looked shocked, maybe even frightened.

Then Lindy must have smiled—Addie couldn't see Lindy's face from here. But the man—both men—smiled. Marcus's looked a bit more like relief than joy, but Addie wasn't sure. She didn't know him that well yet. *Whoa. Wait. Reverse that thought. Delete* yet *from that statement.*

Addie couldn't hear what Lindy was saying, but the way she looked at Jack, and the way she curled her hand around his arm, said plenty.

They started to stroll away, Lindy guiding him through the crowd of kids. She turned and winked at Addie as they left, as if to say, "Go for it."

Marcus stayed where he was, watching Addie.

Their gazes met, and something flipped in her stomach. She continued slowly the rest of the way around the gym until she was once again at the punch table.

"Your friend seems to have distracted your, uh, admirer," Marcus said, leaning close. The music had gotten a bit louder. She'd given specific instructions on how loud the music could be, as much to protect everyone's hearing as the ancient walls that had been built well before the advent of rock and roll. She didn't have the budget for repairs.

The guys in the sound booth were definitely pushing it right now.

"Yeah, she's a good friend."

He laughed, and she wished the music wasn't so loud. She wanted to hear him.

"Hope she doesn't have to be very often."

Addie shook her head. It wasn't as if they had too many of these functions throughout the year. Thank God her path crossed with Jack's only a couple of times a year. His ex took care of most of their daughter's school interactions. Addie and Marcus stood there for several long minutes, not saying anything, watching the strobe lights match the beat of the music. Again, the silence between them seemed comfortable and neither seemed inclined to break it.

Soon, the evening started winding down and

Marcus turned to find his son to leave. "Bye, Addie." He stepped closer, and while his breath brushed her ear, his body heat brushed the rest of her. "See you around. Maybe at the coffee shop sometime."

"Yeah, maybe."

His grin was quick, and he moved away before she could confirm or deny anything.

Oh, for heaven's sake, what was she thinking? They weren't teenagers anymore. She was over thirty—not seventeen—and she was supposed to be supervising wayward kids. Not becoming one.

What was wrong with her? Hadn't she learned her lesson? The last time she'd let herself fall for someone, she'd ended up heartbroken and alone. She'd sworn to never let that happen again.

ADDIE DIDN'T GO to the coffee shop the next night. Nor the one after that. She didn't go for a week. She kept telling herself that she was too busy, that she had misunderstood his intentions. She'd been doing a pretty good job of fooling herself until Mandy called.

Her younger sister was in town for a training class. She helped on some of her fiancé's fire crews, and was intent on learning all she could. Mandy called after the day's training was done. "Meet me for coffee before I head home. I'll need some caffeine for the road. Is that little coffee shop still there by the mall? I love their tea cakes."

"Yeah," Addie agreed. Mandy didn't often get time for herself. Having a one-year-old did that. "I can be there by five." She couldn't deny her sister much of anything, and she craved some sister time herself.

"Perfect. I'm on my way."

Addie was anxious to talk to Mandy, who'd recently acquired that beautiful engagement ring. It had been too noisy, and too hectic, at the diner's reopening to get the details of Lane's long-awaited proposal.

For her sister's sake, she'd chance going to the coffee shop. Really, that was the only reason she was going. Yet, still she walked down the hall to the teachers' lounge and ducked into the ladies' room to fix her hair and makeup.

She stared at her reflection. "You're being stupid," she told the woman in the mirror. She gave her hair one last fluff and left the scent of hairspray behind.

When Addie arrived, Mandy was already there, parked at a corner table by the big glass window. A large cup sat in front of her, and a plate of teacakes was in the center of the table.

"No fair," Addie said, mimicking their childhood taunts. "I planned to treat you as congratulations."

Mandy grinned at her. "I'll let you treat yourself, then. Wasn't sure what you wanted."

Addie went to the counter with a smile. She wasn't like her siblings, who all drank coffee—some by the gallon. Mandy was a creature of habit, and ordered the same drink no matter where they went. Addie much preferred tea, and with so many to choose from, it was always fun to go to the counter. If they were advertising a deal, she'd try that.

Today, however, she hesitated. The drink on the sign was blue. Bright neon blue. She liked being around her students, but she wasn't quite ready to completely join their world. Blue was *not* something she could drink.

"Chai tea." She was celebrating, after all, and ready for a long gab session with her sister.

Mandy laughed when Addie finally reached the table with her steaming cup. "I thought you'd order the blue thing."

"Yeah, right. You know better."

"Yeah. That's more Tara's speed." Their youngest sister was even more adventurous than Addie. In everything. "It would be fun if she was here. We need a girls' night."

"You need a girls' night. I need a nap." Addie sat, enjoying the chance to just sit. "This job is a lot of work."

"You still like it?"

"Mostly." Addie looked out the window in the direction of the school. She couldn't see the building, but she saw it in her mind's eye. It had been a long day. The Haldons, now that they'd decided to come back from their various travels, had been in today. Amazing how upset they'd been regarding yet another slugfest that their son had gotten into. She'd expected Nick to be suspended before the end of the year.

She'd been right.

"Oh, my." Mandy's eyes widened at the just-opening door. "That's an intense stare."

Addie followed her gaze. Marcus had just walked in, and was looking right at her. His backpack was slung over his broad shoulder, and the way he stopped told her he was surprised to see her.

Her stomach did an irritating summersault, and she tore her gaze back to the contents of her cup. She swallowed and focused on her drink.

Mandy looked at her with a quizzical frown. She leaned back in her seat. "So, what's up with you…and him?"

"Me? Nothing." Addie hadn't come here to discuss herself. "I want to know about the proposal."

"Ooh, there's something there." At Addie's frown, Mandy didn't push anymore, focusing instead on choosing just the right cake from the plate sitting between them. "These are yummy."

She bit into one, unable to quiet her sigh of plea-sure. "Though not as good as your cookies. You sure you don't have anything to share?"

"I'm sure," Addie said, focusing on selecting her own sweet cake. And there wasn't anything to share. They'd had drinks and he was the par-ent of a student. End of story.

Mandy quietly drank, and Addie pretended to ignore the looks her sister was giving her. She was not explaining. Heck, she didn't even understand what she was thinking and feeling anymore.

Marcus didn't come over. Instead, he headed to the counter to order. She tried not to watch him. He looked tired, and she wondered if he'd brought the book.

He looked so... Her thoughts slid away as he reached into the backpack and pulled out a worn leather wallet to pay the barista. He looked all business. But she saw the tiny details that belied his facade.

The way his hair curled a bit too long beyond the collar of his white shirt. The five o'clock shadow that framed his wide jaw. The loose tie, the knot lopsided.

She wondered what his students thought of him. What kind of teacher was he? So many of the pro-fessors were much more casual these days. She'd like to see him teach. She was curious about his style—that was all, she told herself.

"Yoo-hoo!" Mandy pulled Addie's mind to their conversation.

"Want to hear about Lane's proposal? Or tell me about where your mind just went?" Mandy's eyes sparkled with younger-sister mischief.

Addie laughed. "The proposal." She forced herself to not look at Marcus. "Tell me everything." She loved Mandy's ability to tell a story. She picked up her mug and sat back, waiting to be entertained. This was going to be good.

SHE WAS HERE. But she wasn't alone. The other woman was doing most of the talking, while Addie smiled and laughed.

He didn't even have to work hard to look for her, like he had nearly every night in the past week. She lit up the room with her riot of blond curls that caught the fading sunlight. Her laughter reached out and tugged him toward her.

He should go home. He glanced at his watch. Ryan was at baseball practice for another hour. Or he could grab a cup and take it to the ballpark and watch.

Instead, he decided to stay. And what, wait? He found a table and opened his backpack. This place was small with few patrons tonight. He could hear their entire conversation without even trying.

"Lane was out in the field with his crew when he ran into that guy he worked for on the fire here.

Guess he gave Lane a hard time about letting me go." The smugness in the other woman's voice was unmistakable.

"But he didn't let you go," Addie said.

"He pointed out that Lane wasn't wearing a ring, so I must be a free woman." The woman's laughter filled the small room. "Lane went and got a ring that night. Once the fire was out, he came home and got down on a knee before he'd even showered all the smoke off."

Marcus knew he should leave. Eavesdropping was rude. But he had to wait for his drink. He shoved his hands into the pockets of his jeans and paced to the counter, hoping they'd hurry.

"Something must have scared him." Addie's voice was soft.

The two women were silent for a moment. "It was a rough fire. One of the guys was hurt." The other woman took her time taking a drink, but quickly recovered. "Actually, now that he's over the asking, he's all gung-ho to get the whole thing going. He wants to get married soon."

"How soon?" Addie's voice was hesitant.

"As soon as I can buy a dress, he said. But I told him we were only going to do this once, and we are going to do it right. I'll let *him* know when I'm ready."

"Don't make the poor guy suffer too long," Addie admonished.

"Oh, I won't. I just need to figure out how to do it all." There was a note of panic in the woman's voice.

"We'll help."

"I hoped you would." The relief was strong in the other woman's voice.

They laughed again, the sound filling the air around him. Both Addie and the other woman stood then.

"It's so good to see you, sis." The redhead gave Addie a hug.

Ah, her sister.

"You, too."

The already quiet coffee shop fell silent. He would not turn around. He shouldn't look over his shoulder. Damn. Her perfume reached out to him.

Then he realized they had to walk past him to get to the door.

"Hello, Marcus." Her voice was soft, and yet rough at the same time. Tinged with surprise? Pleasure? He couldn't ignore her. That would be rude—and impossible.

He turned. She took his breath away. The evening sunlight fell in the window and over her hair. Her eyes were bright and crystal blue. She took a step back as if she was as surprised as he was that she'd said anything.

"Hello, Addie." He tried to keep it informal and yet—what?—professional? Whom was he kidding? For a long minute, they stared at each other, neither of them speaking. Did they need to?

"Ahem."

Addie visibly shook herself. And stepped back. "I—uh." She swallowed, and he missed the intensity of her gaze on him. She glanced at the woman, her cheeks turning a warm shade of pink. "Marcus, this is my sister, Mandy. Mandy, this is Marcus Skylar. His son goes to my school."

The woman grinned at him, then turned to her sister, and that grin widened. "Nice to meet you."

She nudged Addie and the look Addie threw her made Marcus actually laugh out loud. His sister, Anne, had a similar dagger-throwing glare. One that inspired the phrase "if looks could kill."

"I'll be taking off now, Ad." Mandy shouldered her purse and turned toward the door. "You guys have a nice time. Both of you."

Then she was gone and he stood there next to Addie.

What the hell was he supposed to do now?

CHAPTER SIX

"I HOPE THAT wasn't your ride," Marcus said, watching the bright blue car pull away.

Addie laughed. "No, she knows I normally walk home from here." She shouldered her purse. "She has to get going—she's got a one-year-old and a wedding to plan."

"Sounds…hectic."

"Yeah. My family never does anything the normal way." The silence stretched out. "Well, guess I'll be heading home. Good to see you again."

"I'll walk with you." He wasn't quite ready to be alone again.

"Uh—sure." Together, they headed toward the sidewalk.

"So, tell me more about this family of yours," he said, falling into step with her. He'd always wondered what it would be like to have a brother, or a bunch of siblings growing up.

"It's definitely interesting." She walked at a leisurely pace. "Wyatt's the oldest, but only by a couple years. He owns our granddad's ranch west of here. My younger brother DJ helps him. He was in

Afghanistan and came home wounded, so while Wyatt's all cowboy, DJ is a begrudging one."

Marcus laughed. "How is one a begrudging cowboy?"

"Begrudgingly?"

Her laughter echoed over the evening air, and Marcus found himself enthralled with the sweet sound. "I'll bet your teachers just loved you."

"Why yes, they did in fact." Again, her laughter wrapped around him. This time, he couldn't resist joining her.

"Okay, who else?"

"My other brother, Jason, is married to Lauren Ramsey...the world-famous ballerina. You've heard of her?"

"I have, though don't tell the guys. I have a reputation to uphold." He winked. "Actually, my sister, Anne, is a huge patron of the ballet. She'll be green with envy when I tell her."

"You sound like a typical brother. Let me guess, she's older than you?"

"Good guess, considering you had a fifty-fifty chance. Tell me more."

"Let's see. Wyatt and DJ are both married. DJ's wife, Tammie, is expecting their second child any day now. They got married last year. Their son, Tyler, was the best man."

His double take must have surprised her.

"Told you, we do things a bit differently in my family."

"You did warn me." They walked for a bit longer before he nudged her again. "Next?"

"You met Mandy. Her fiancé is a hotshot firefighter. Like I said, they have a one-year-old son, Lucas. It's about time Lane finally proposed."

"Yeah. About time." Marcus savored her obvious enjoyment at sharing the stories of her family.

"And last?"

"My baby sister, Tara, is a chef. She just opened a diner in Haskins Corners. It's a small town near the ranch."

"And I suppose she has a husband, too?"

"Not yet. But I'm guessing her boyfriend, Morgan, will pop the question soon. I certainly hope so."

"Sounds like quite the family. A happy bunch." Marcus was enthralled and a bit jealous, he had to admit. "You helped raise them all?" He recalled her comment the other night about losing her father.

"I helped Mom and Wyatt." Her footsteps slowed. "Sometimes I think I know how to be a parent without ever really being one."

"What about you? Ever been in love? Married? Almost married?" Why was he asking that? He told himself to stop.

Something changed with that question, and as

soon as he looked in her eyes, he regretted asking. She'd been happy sharing her family life with him. Not now. Now there were shutters in her eyes that fell just as he got a glimpse of the pain. "Once upon a time," she whispered. "I believed in the fairy tale for me." She fell silent. He didn't ask anything more—he didn't want to twist the knife that she obviously felt.

They'd reached the white picket fence surrounding her yard. He almost asked how a girl who lived in a house with a white picket fence could live in it alone, but he didn't.

"Thanks for walking with me," she hastily said, then pushed the gate open, and just as hastily closed it between them. "Enjoy the rest of your evening." She rushed into the house, not looking back, not even to wave goodbye.

Why did he feel so disappointed?

SLEEP DIDN'T COME EASY. Addie tossed and turned until well past midnight. At this rate, she would be exhausted in the morning. She knew she was in trouble when she started counting the few hours she'd get if she fell asleep right now. Four was not a lucky number.

Marcus's simple question had no simple answer. Too many memories flooded her mind. Of that last, fateful summer. The summer of fun and love and sunshine—and Cal. His image came to mind, and even now, his smile had the power to lift her spirits. She'd been so head over heels, she'd barely known which way was up.

And she hadn't much cared. She'd just wanted to be with him all the time. Thought they'd have forever. The life she'd planned back then, at the grand old age of eighteen, was drastically different from the one she lived now. Not that it was bad. It was good—just, she admitted to herself, lonely sometimes.

Especially now that her siblings had moved on with their lives. And they didn't need her anymore.

Punching her pillow, she forced her eyes to stay closed. She'd keep them closed until she fell asleep. How hard could it be? She was tired, after all.

When the bright light woke her, she swore she'd just finally fallen asleep. Something was wrong. Very wrong. The light was too bright. What time was it? Was she late? What day was it?

The house had been cool, thanks to the air-conditioning when she'd fallen asleep.

Now, she was soaked in sweat and the air was hot and thick.

She glanced at the alarm clock, but her eyes refused to focus. It took a minute to blink her gaze clear. Ten fifteen. She flung back the covers and swung her legs over the edge of the bed. The room spun. She sat there for several long minutes trying to regain her sense of equilibrium.

Texas was famous for the thick heat of summer, the heavy, humid air that came in from the gulf. But it was too early in the season for the worst of the heat. Still, this was unbearable.

Slowly, she stood, using the edge of the nightstand to balance, then the dresser to make her way to the vent. No cool air rushed from the metal grate. Something must be wrong with the air-conditioning unit. She'd have to call someone. Her mind grasped the problem but struggled to hold onto it.

Was it cooler outside? Surely, it had to be. She made her way to the window. The frame was stubborn. She didn't open it often. It took her several tries, but she finally got it open. Only a slight breeze came in. It was enough for now, she thought. She hoped.

Her head hurt. Pain stabbed behind her eyes, sharp and blinding. Somewhere in the back of her mind, she knew she should do something. But what? Call someone? Who?

The men on the ranch were very careful when they were out in the sun all day. Why did that thought pop into her head now? They drank lots of water. Where was there water? Bathroom. Her thoughts were disjointed, but she knew she could get to the bathroom.

Furniture walking, she finally reached the door frame. Stepping inside, she was thankful to lean against the counter. The tile floor under her bare feet was blessedly cool, and she nearly sank down to it. Was it just the heat? Did she have a fever? Was she sick?

Nothing made sense. She looked around, trying to make her mind focus on something specific. Why was she in here? What was she doing?

She needed to get ready to go to work, didn't she? Yes. Work.

She stripped out of her nightgown and stepped toward the shower. That would make her feel better. Reaching into the stall, she twisted the knobs, cringing when warm water cascaded over her hand. She turned it to the right. All the way. Ah, yes. Coolness. Aching to feel a chill again, she stepped underneath the spray.

She leaned against the tiled wall, her cheek resting on the smooth surface. Cool.

She half expected the water to steam around her she felt so hot. And then something shifted. She started to shiver. Hard. Body-shaking hard. Her stomach churned, and she flailed around to find the faucet. What had felt so good moments ago was too cold, like needles of ice beating against her skin. She slammed the water off and nearly fell to her knees.

Her stomach protested the movement. What

was wrong with her? What was happening to her? She was alone. No one was here to help her. No one knew she wasn't okay. No one was worrying about her.

Her teeth chattered despite the warm air of the room washing over her. She shook. She took a step away from the wall, but even that small movement made the pain in her head intensify. Made her whole body quake.

Slowly, she made herself take the two steps out of the shower stall. She struggled to keep her stomach from churning itself empty. She couldn't afford to be sick. Her full calendar leaped into her mind. She had too much to do.

She cursed and knew she couldn't move anymore. Not now. Not by herself. Her legs gave out, and she let herself slip to the floor. Better than falling face-first into the tile. Her knees took most of the impact. The tile was solid as the rock it had once been.

And still cold. She shivered. Where was her towel? Had she grabbed one? Her robe? It still hung on the back of the door.

Tears burned her eyes. What was she supposed to do? Defeat slipped over her.

What was that sound? Addie tried to get her brain to focus, to wake up. Her stomach churned, and she tried to focus on the sound, to take her body's attention off the misery.

That was her phone. Where was it? She pushed up, slowly, her arms trembling from the effort. Who was calling? Why were they calling?

Her robe was on the back of the door. She managed to lift her arms up enough to pull it down and slip it on. She cringed. The fabric scraped her sensitive skin. One more discomfort.

The sound stopped, only to start up again. Where was it? She stumbled out of the bathroom, toward the bed. The ringing came from the nightstand. Oh, there it was.

"H—hello?"

"Addie, where are you?" Lindy's voice came through the phone, loud and painful.

"I—" She looked around. "At home." She moaned and fell into bed. It was so soft after sitting on the floor. So, inviting. "I'm sick," she managed to get out. "Just wanna sleep."

"Oh, poor baby. Do you need me to do anything?"

"Just let me die in peace." Not the best joke she'd ever made.

Lindy managed to chuckle anyway. "Get some rest. I'll let Gina, and the rest of the team, know. I'll check on you later. Okay?"

"Mmm…hmm." Addie moaned and rolled over, thumbing off the phone and tossing it aside. She just wanted to sleep and prayed her stomach would cooperate. She'd never make it to the bathroom in time.

Tears burned her eyes. She missed her mom. Addie remembered taking care of her siblings when they were sick, but Mom had always taken care of her. What was she supposed to do, now? Defeat slipped over her along with the dark silence.

"DAD!" RYAN SCREAMED AT the top of his lungs. Marcus saw him come through the rear gate, his backpack smacking the latch with a solid crack. "Dad!" he screamed again. "We gotta help her!"

The kitchen door flew open, hitting the counter nearly as hard as the gate. "Whoa. What's the matter?"

Fear filled Ryan's eyes, fear that Marcus had thought they'd chased away. He gulped in air from his run. "Why aren't you at practice?"

"She's sick." Ryan dropped his backpack, not even bothering to notice where it landed. "She wasn't at school. And I went by her house. I saw her in the window, lying on the couch. But she didn't wake up when I knocked. Dad, help her." A sob broke from his son's throat, and Marcus's heart hurt.

He knew who "she"—Addie—was, and his own fear ratcheted up. Watching Carolyn's slow death had left a permanent scar on them both.

The idea of losing Addie, either of them losing her, was painful to even think about.

Yet it could happen. Life had no guarantees. "Why didn't you call me?" He followed his son to the door.

Ryan still tried to catch his breath as he headed to the door. "Dex and I were using it too much." They both headed to the door. "Battery's dead. Come on. We gotta check on her!" The urgency in Ryan's voice hurt Marcus to hear.

His heart pounded in his chest as they sprinted across the yard to the driveway. The open sides of the Jeep made it easy to climb in, and it started right up. Why did it feel like hours before they pulled up in front of Addie's house?

He swung into the driveway, nearly kissing the garage door with his bumper as he slammed on the brakes. Ryan was out of the Jeep before he'd even come to a complete halt.

"The front door's locked," Ryan said, heading for the back door. "Maybe this one's open."

"Ryan, hold on. You don't live here." The drive had calmed him a bit. Ryan was probably overreacting. For all he knew, Addie could be the world's soundest sleeper. Last thing they needed was to scare her into calling the cops.

ADDIE STARED AT the wide window. Had someone been out there? Were they still out there? The nagging sense of helplessness irritated her. She'd lived on her own long enough to have a healthy sense of caution. Glancing at the door, she confirmed it was locked and secure.

The air moved, the breeze came in the open kitchen windows, clanged the pots on the rack over the cooktop together. Her head was still fuzzy and ached. All day she'd been here alone, her head full of fog and pain. Even now, she wondered if she'd be able to make it to the couch. She certainly wasn't going to make it up the stairs to her bedroom. She'd probably fall if she even tried.

Turning, she aimed herself toward the living room, but stopped at the end of the counter. Exhaustion tugged at her. She needed to lie down. Her head spun again. She grasped the edge of the counter, trying to catch her balance. Still, the world spun.

She couldn't begin to think. Her head felt like a knife hacked against it. She sank onto the kitchen chair, the smooth, modern chair she'd bought with the rest of the set, not the familiar chair that still sat in the corner, safe and apart.

Like her, she realized.

Unable to think or move, she laid her head on the tabletop and let her entire body relax. The wood felt cool against her cheek.

What was that sound? Pounding? Was there someone at the door? Why? Why did she care?

She coughed, the sound loud as it bounced off the hard surface where her head rested.

"Addie?" A male voice came out of the darkness somewhere. A familiar voice, but not too familiar. "Addie?" the man called again. She tried to sift through the repertoire of voices in her memory. Not Wyatt. Besides, he had a key. Not either of her other brothers. DJ and Jason had deep, warm voices, but even they didn't speak in that mellow baritone.

Not Lane, or Morgan. "Who—" She tried to focus, tried to open her eyes and see.

She couldn't move, realizing she could barely even breathe.

"Is she…?" A young, familiar, pain-filled voice cut through her agony, and she wanted so badly to comfort Ryan. But she could barely breathe, or move.

"No. But we need to get her to a doctor," the deep voice said, the timbre sliding over her skin, soothing, smoothing, comfortable. Marcus.

Something warm, solid, slid around her. Arms. His arms. She wanted to open her eyes, wanted to protest the touch she hadn't invited, wanted to take in the comfortable sense of belonging it gave her.

"Get the door, Ryan," he commanded in his deep voice, making her shiver. Then she couldn't seem to stop the shivering. The arms, strong and solid, tightened around her, pulling her close to a warm, solid body that should have stopped her trembling.

"Why is she shaking, Dad?" The boy's voice broke, full of fear. Addie ached to comfort him. He sounded so frightened.

"She's got a fever." She felt movement, heard the familiar squeal of the back door's hinges, then the brush of the air on her skin. She should be afraid of being out of control, should be fighting his touch and the fact that he was taking her away from her home, away from her safety. But she couldn't move. She could barely stay awake.

And then his arms were gone, or were they? She was floating through the breeze. She wasn't walking. He must still be holding her. Something was. Shouldn't she open her eyes? She suddenly wanted to so badly, but her eyelids were so heavy, so weak.

Light snuck under her slitted lids after a minute, stabbing at her brain. She moaned in pain.

"Hang in there," Marcus said softly, smooth against her ear. "We're almost to the car."

Car? What car? His? Hers? Something else?

Something smooth and soft cocooned her, and she leaned her head back and thought she smiled. The warm, comfortable arms slid away, leaving a cold shiver in their place.

"No," she managed to say. But that was all she

was able to say, or even think as the warmth vanished and the darkness took her away from him.

MARCUS SAT ON the hard vinyl seat in the hospital's waiting room. His gut clenched, and he closed his eyes. He was heartily sick of hospitals and waiting rooms—the antiseptic smell they tried to cover with sweet scents. The sound of rushing feet and rubber wheels from gurneys and wheelchairs on the vinyl floor. They could make it look like wood, but it was still a hospital underneath all the fake decor.

Ryan sat staring at his phone as if the mysteries of the universe were buried in the screen. Maybe they were. Marcus hadn't gotten sucked into the social media craze; he was too busy burying himself in grading papers and the books that went with his research.

"How did you know where Ms. Hawkins lived?" Marcus asked carefully. He didn't want to upset his son, but something seemed out of sync.

"Dex's mom knows her. He told me."

"But you'd never go there uninvited, right?" Marcus knew that Ryan missed his mother. Since the funeral, he'd been drawn to teachers and to Marcus's sister, Anne.

"Uh-huh."

Marcus looked at his boy now, not sure why he'd started to gravitate to other women. Before she'd gotten sick, Ryan hadn't been overly close to Carolyn—no more so than was normal for a boy and his mom. Carolyn would know. But she couldn't tell him now, and Ryan wasn't volunteering any information.

Now wasn't the time to push the point, but he needed to remember later. Just then, a nurse in bright blue scrubs approached. "Mr. Skylar?"

"Yes?" He stood.

"We need some information, and the patient isn't able to provide it. Can you help with that?"

He stared wide-eyed at the woman. "Uh, no."

She frowned.

"She's the principal at my son's school and our neighbor." He shrugged.

"Are you her family?" The woman seemed to just realize they had minimal connection to her patient.

"We don't know her family. I just knew she was really sick."

"She is." The woman tapped her pen on the clipboard, looking frustrated. "Do you know anything?" She looked between him and Ryan. "Did you bring her purse, or her ID with you?" She tried to sound hopeful.

"Uh, no." For someone who prided himself on his organizational skills, he was sure blowing that now. He racked his brain for the information she'd shared about her siblings. "She has several siblings in the area." But he couldn't remember any of their names.

"Her brother owns a ranch outside of town," Ryan offered. The phone made an obnoxious noise, and Ryan hit the button to darken the screen. "Bet he'd know stuff."

"Where'd you learn that?"

Ryan shrugged. "We talked when I was in detention."

"Do you know his name?" the nurse asked.

Ryan shook his head. "Nope. But the ranch is same as her last name. Hawkins."

"That's a little help." The woman turned toward the doors. "Let me see what I can find out."

She disappeared behind the doors and Marcus sat, this time staring at his son. "I guess we can head home. They'll take care of her."

"We can't go!" Ryan screeched. "We can't leave her all alone."

Marcus got the impression he needed to tread carefully. "She doesn't even know we're here."

"She knows we're here." Ryan mutinously glared at him. "I know she does. She knew we brought her here." He crossed his arms in a gesture Marcus remembered him making as early as a year of age. Stubbornness. "I'm not leaving."

Marcus sighed. The past couple of years had been so hard on Ryan. Not that it had been so good for Marcus, either. He'd refrained from punishment so many times since Carolyn's death.

The nurse came out, a small smile on her face. "We just got a hold of her brother Wyatt. He's on his way here." She put her hand on Ryan's shoulder. "You were a big help."

Ryan smiled, and Marcus knew they weren't going anywhere. The relief and something else—pride—on Ryan's face was the best thing he'd seen in months.

CHAPTER SEVEN

"WHAT THE HELL was Addie thinking?" A pair of tall, dusty cowboys strode into the emergency room through the sliding glass door nearly an hour later.

Marcus watched them move across the waiting area to the reception desk. They had to be Addie's brothers.

"She takes care of everyone else," the first man said to the one behind him. "Why doesn't she take care of herself?" Marcus heard the concern and fear in the man's voice.

"I'm Wyatt Hawkins," the cowboy told the woman behind the counter. "I received a call that my sister is here."

"Yes, thank you for coming." The woman looked relieved. "She's in back. If you'll wait here, I'll let the doctor know you've arrived."

As the woman disappeared through a door, he stepped back and paced between the rows of vinyl chairs. The other man leaned against the wall.

"Are you Ms. Hawkins's brother?" Ryan hopped up from his seat and approached the cowboy. Marcus shot to his feet. He might be Addie's brother, but he was still a stranger.

"I am. We are. I'm Wyatt. This is DJ. And who are you?"

Ryan stood in front of Wyatt. He had to tilt his head way back to look at the much taller man. "I'm Ryan Skylar. Ms. Hawkins is my principal. My dad and I brought her here."

Wyatt looked around. "You did?" He pinned Marcus with a stare. "Are you his dad?"

"I am. Marcus Skylar." They shook hands. "Can you tell me what happened?"

Marcus frowned. "Not really. Ryan was worried since she wasn't at school today. She was nearly unconscious when we went to her place to check on her."

"You went to her house?"

"Yeah, we're neighbors of a sort."

"I appreciate your helping her."

"Glad to. Ryan, now that Mr. Hawkins is here, we can head home."

"But, Dad—"

"Mr. Hawkins?" the nurse called from the doorway.

Wyatt paused, looking at Marcus. "If you don't mind, can you hang out for a bit? I'd like to know what's going on."

Marcus nodded. "For a bit. But I really do need to get back to work." He'd already canceled one class. He couldn't afford to miss getting ready for tomorrow.

"Thanks." The two men disappeared behind the steel fire door that the nurse held open for them. Marcus could see half a dozen curtained-off cubicles. His gut twisted. He really hated being here.

Thankfully, the door closed, and he couldn't see any more. He just wanted out of here, away from this place. But he'd promised the men he'd stay. He sat on the hard seat to wait. Again.

ADDIE HEARD THE curtain swish, the metal hooks overhead rattled against the track. She was on a gurney, an IV in her arm, and a warm, heavy blanket wrapped around her.

The medicine they'd told her was in the IV bag had calmed her stomach, and the blanket had eased her shivering. She knew her hair was a tangled mess on the white pillow, but she didn't have the energy to ask for a brush. She kept her eyes closed.

Marcus had seen her at her worst now. She groaned in humiliation.

"Addie?" a voice, whispered.

Her eyes flew open. "Wyatt? What are you doing here?"

"Well, when a hospital calls and says my sister's there, what do you think I do?"

She frowned, and the curtain shifted again. DJ

walked in. "You, too? Please tell me everyone isn't here with you." The idea of her whole family here made her cringe.

"No. Just us two. So far." DJ frowned. He was always intense, and she could tell his frown was from worrying about her.

"Oh, Wyatt. Why did they call you guys? How long have I been here?" she whispered, knowing it took over an hour to get here from the ranch.

"A while, I'd guess." He sat on the stiff chair the nurse had pulled up beside the bed, while DJ stood with his arms crossed over his chest. "We just got here. What happened?"

"I woke up feeling sick this morning. I—I don't know. Ryan? Marcus? I remember..." She put a hand to her forehead, frowning, not really remembering anything. "I don't know."

"Don't worry about it, Ad. Not right now."

"Are you her brother?" Another man, wearing dark-blue scrubs, came through the curtain then, a tablet in his hand and a stethoscope around his neck.

"I am." Wyatt stood. "Can you tell me what's going on?"

"Some. Some you'll have to get from Ms. Hawkins when she's a bit more coherent." He pulled a pair of glasses from atop his head and turned to Addie. "You're overheated. Heatstroke can be a serious problem." He went on to explain how one got it, which Wyatt wasn't really interested in. He was interested in how Addie had.

"I took a cold shower." She remembered how awful that had made her feel.

The doctor shook his head. "That's probably what sent you into shock. If this ever happens again, you need to cool down slowly." He scribbled on the tablet's screen. "Drink cool liquids. Put ice packs on your neck, your feet. Don't jump into a cold shower. It's too abrupt and will send you into shock."

"My air-conditioning," she whispered. "I think I need a repairman." She looked at Wyatt.

He glared at her. "You should have called us." She glared back. He smiled. "You must be getting better."

"The IV is to stop the vomiting," the doctor said, interrupting them. "We can't get her hydrated if we can't keep the fluids in her system. She's doing fine now. Should be able to go home in a couple hours."

"Good," Addie said, though there wasn't much enthusiasm or energy in her answer.

"We'll take you back to the ranch—"

"No, you won't. I've got to go to work tomorrow."

"I'd advise against that," the doctor said as he wrote on the tablet. "You should take at least a day to get your strength back. Maybe two."

"Tomorrow is Friday." She cringed at the sound of her whining voice. "There's a big assembly at school. I can't miss it."

"We'll see." Wyatt didn't argue with her right now, but that look told her he would. Too bad. She was going to that assembly.

"I'd like her to have another bag of the solution before we release her." The doctor pointed at the IV bag. "Should take another hour, or less."

"Thanks." Wyatt shook the doctor's hand as he left. The nurse came in with a new IV seconds later. Addie didn't move, and she closed her eyes again. So tired.

"You'll be okay," Wyatt reassured her and put his hand over hers.

"Thanks," she whispered, barely able to stay awake.

"We'll be right back. You get some rest." Wyatt didn't wait for an answer. Good thing, because he wasn't going to get one.

"Is she okay?" Ryan looked up, concern on his face when the two cowboys emerged from the doors. Marcus stood, trying not to pace.

"She will be," Wyatt said. "They're giving her another IV, but will release her after that's finished."

"Thank goodness." Marcus sank back in his seat, relief taking away the anxiety that had been prodding him upright. He hadn't realized how worried he'd been.

Everyone was silent for a long moment. "The doc says she's got heatstroke. She mumbled something about her air conditioner? Do you know what happened?"

Marcus shook his head. "No. Ryan? Did anyone say anything about that at school?"

Ryan looked up, a concerned frown on his face. "She wasn't there all day today, and everyone in the office seemed surprised. Ms. Hanson said she's never sick. That's why we went over to her house."

"Did you notice if the air conditioner was running?"

Ryan frowned again, thinking. "It was kinda warm, but I didn't go check." He shrugged.

"Was she in the kitchen? Making cookies?" Wyatt asked, as if he expected her to be doing that. Marcus frowned. That seemed odd. He was grasping at straws, and he knew it. But what else could he do? He was clearly worried.

"Uh—maybe? We found her in the kitchen."

Wyatt looked at Marcus. "Did *you* notice if the oven was on?"

"I don't really remember. Damn." He started thinking. Was the stove still on? Had it been on? He'd been focused on her.

"We need to go check. I'll stay here with her.

DJ, you got your keys to her place?" He pulled them out of his pocket.

"I'll go check," the younger cowboy said. "It's supposed to get into the nineties tomorrow."

"Letting her go back home if the same situation still exists seems stupid. If the AC isn't fixed, she's not staying."

"I can look at it, but I don't know that I can do much with it," Marcus offered.

"That's okay. DJ, maybe get a window unit, if nothing else. If I know my stubborn sister, she won't go to a hotel. She sure as heck won't go to my place. Already tried that."

"She can stay at our place, right, Dad?" Ryan piped up, his hopes written all over his face.

Marcus gulped. He couldn't tell them no. It would break Ryan's heart. Besides, it seemed the right thing to do. "Of—of course, she's welcome," Marcus responded, though there wasn't near the excitement in his voice as in his son's.

Marcus knew the men were curious, wondering about how well they knew Addie. He wouldn't let his sister stay with just anyone, either.

THIS TIME WHEN Addie opened her eyes, she was convinced she'd lost her mind. The curve of the window frame. The pale mauve on the walls. The way the morning light reflected off the wood floor. It was all intimately familiar.

She was in her old bedroom. Except—that wasn't possible. That room was gone. There weren't any dolls scattered on the floor, no clothes prompting Mom to yell for them to be picked up, no unmade beds. Just the single bed frame, a dresser, a chair and—she glanced over at the wall—a family photo. Marcus, Ryan, and a woman. A petite, blond woman with a smile for them both.

It had to be Marcus's wife, Carolyn.

No. This wasn't Addie's room anymore.

Though it had been—a long time ago.

She sat up, her head barely spinning, but still light. She felt much better now. Thank goodness.

Slowly, Addie stood, an accomplishment considering how she'd felt the last time she'd woken up. Slowly, she walked over to the photo. Ryan was much younger. His front tooth was missing. She leaned closer. Or two? He was adorable. Marcus looked younger, too. There were fewer lines on his face. His smile was more open. Genuine. She reached out and touched the cool glass over their faces.

Addie's reserves were low. She couldn't dodge the bolt of envy that shot through her when she looked at the other woman's happy smile. Stepping back from the picture, she nearly stumbled. She reprimanded herself, reminding herself that Carolyn was gone. She'd lost her battle with whatever disease she'd had. Carolyn could never again be with the people she loved. A love that clearly shone in the pretty blonde's photographed eyes.

Addie wondered what was wrong with her. How could she envy someone who'd lost everything?

She shouldn't...but she did.

Looking at Ryan's cute baby face, a familiar ache grew in Addie's chest, and she returned to sit on the side of the bed. If things had been different... But they weren't. Like always, she tried to shut down the hurt. She took deep, slow breaths, trying to ease the tightness. In with the good. Out with the bad. Inhale. Exhale. And again.

Addie's eyes burned, but the sound of footsteps in the hall gave her the impetus to hastily blink the moisture away.

A knock came at the door. "Addie?" Marcus asked softly. "Are you awake?"

"Yes." She tried to make her voice sound normal. Despite the fact she was wearing pajamas—that she only vaguely remembered putting on—she hastily pulled up the covers.

Marcus pushed the door open. He made his way to the bed with a tray in his hands. "Doctor says you need to stay hydrated." There were two glasses of juice and one of water on the tray. "I wasn't sure what you liked."

"Thanks." She watched him settle the tray on

the nightstand before moving to the wing-backed chair in the corner.

"How are you feeling?" he asked.

"Better." She took a slow sip. It tasted like heaven. She drank a bit more, her eyes involuntarily returning to the photo.

Marcus saw the path of her gaze but didn't say anything.

"You bought my mother's house." She chose a different topic.

"I didn't realize that until last night. Wyatt was a bit surprised that you didn't know."

She shrugged. "I thought a trust bought it."

"Yeah." He nodded. "After Carolyn's death, I put everything in a trust. That way, if something happens to me, Ryan doesn't ever have to worry. He'll always have a home."

She nodded, her eyes again drawn to the photo. She hastily looked around at everything but the warm family scene. "This used to be my room. Though it looks different."

"Yeah, Wyatt said something about that last night, too."

"He was here? I don't remember."

"Yeah. He and your other brother DJ." At her nod, he continued. "They helped us get you settled and brought you an overnight bag. It's over there. Don't you remember?"

She frowned at the now-empty juice glass. She

didn't remember drinking all of it, either. "Vague snatches, but not really. Sorry. Still a little foggy."

"Don't be sorry. You've had a lot to deal with."

"Uh, yes." The silence stretched between them.

Finally, Marcus stood. "I'll head down and make some breakfast if you're up to it. Feel free to take a shower." He walked to the door carrying the tray. "I'd tell you where it is, but guess you know that. After breakfast, I'll gladly take you home." He smiled, but she couldn't smile back.

"I'll be right down," was all she said.

Half an hour later, showered and changed, Addie headed downstairs. It was strange being here, especially with someone else's belongings in the house.

Stepping into the kitchen, she could only stare. Laid out similar to hers, it was definitely not Mom's anymore. A few items sat on the counter, but what drew her attention was the big dining table that they'd left with the house. It was stacked with an assortment of…stuff. She saw a laptop, books and so much more.

She had to keep reminding herself that Mom was gone and that the house had sold several months ago. It wasn't her responsibility or her home any longer. Still…

"There you are." Marcus's deep voice came through the back door from the shadows of the patio. A few seconds later, he stepped inside.

"Oh, hello." She felt her cheeks warm at being caught gawking. "It's…different."

"I'll bet. I'm not much of a housekeeper. Sorry." He hastily grabbed a few things and shoved them into cupboards. A loaf of bread and jar of peanut butter were all that was still out. It looked better—marginally. "There's no point in putting it away." He pointed at the peanut butter. "Ryan eats it by the gallon."

She smiled. "Healthy for him."

"Yeah." He stepped to the back door and indicated she precede him. "I set breakfast out on the patio. We eat out here, mostly."

Stepping out onto the small patio, she frowned. The grass was just waking up from being winter dormant. Hopefully, when Marcus turned on the sprinklers, it would green up. The trees looked good, but the vines. Oh, the beautiful vines were nearly bare, their leaves withered and dry on the wall of Dad's workshop.

Those had been Mom's pride and joy. Would they even bloom this year?

"You look better today." Marcus interrupted her thoughts. "I almost wouldn't recognize you. Sorry." He looked a bit sheepish.

"You mean without the pallor of sickness?" He had seen her at her worst. But this man had carried her into the emergency room and gotten her the necessary help. When she'd woken up after the second IV bag, he and Ryan had been long gone. Wyatt had brought her here, apparently. She hadn't had the chance to thank either of them properly.

She'd have to figure out something more, but the words would have to do for now. "Thank you."

"It's nice to have company for a real breakfast."

"Yes, for that. But also for getting me to the hospital. I'm sure it totally messed up your day." She sat on the nearest chair, realizing she really was hungry. The pastries and juice looked delicious.

"I only had one class yesterday, so no problem. I didn't think you'd want anything too heavy." He sat beside her, and they both looked out over the yard. It was a while before Marcus finally spoke. "Uh, you are up to eating something, aren't you? I guess I should have asked."

"Don't worry. I'm famished," she replied almost too quickly. She did appreciate his caring and, without thinking, reached out to put her hand on his. His skin was warm and solid beneath hers. She froze and looked at him. He returned her gaze. Time stopped.

Hastily, Addie pulled her hand back and focused on taking a pastry. She didn't look at him again until she'd eaten nearly half of it. He ate slowly, focusing on his plate.

"That used to be my father's workshop," she

said, trying to think of something to say to break the awkwardness between them.

"I wondered. What kind of workshop?"

"Woodworking." She smiled, thankful for the safe topic. "He wanted to learn to make furniture. I think he thought if we kids were going to keep breaking it, he should learn to fix it."

Marcus laughed. "Sounds like a logical man."

"He was. He had advice for everything."

"There are a bunch of boxes in the rafters I was going to look through."

"Oh, I'm sorry. We didn't mean to leave anything. I thought the guys got it all."

"It's not a problem, Addie." Marcus smiled at her. "Really. I can't imagine how much stuff was here if you all grew up in this house."

"Tons. Mom got rid of a lot when she got sick. But Dad's stuff was hard for her to part with."

The silence stretched out again. "I can understand that." His eyes grew distant, and she wondered what he was thinking about. The picture from her old bedroom came to mind.

He shook his head, though, and refocused on her. "I'll take a look at it and let you know what it is."

They continued eating in silence. Finally finished, she stood. "I'll grab my stuff. I can walk home. The assembly is this afternoon, and I'd really like to be there."

"I said I'd take you. I'm heading to the campus, as well." He stood and gathered the dishes as she headed upstairs.

Everything was put away when she returned. "I don't want to be a bother—"

"Addie, stop." Marcus stood in front of her. "Wyatt warned me about you, you know."

"Warned you?" She frowned at him, which made him laugh. It really was a wonderful sound.

"He said you're terrible at taking care of yourself."

"I do fine most of the time." She lifted a defensive chin.

"It's okay to need help, you know. Besides, it wasn't that big of a deal. But you're welcome. Ryan was really worried about you."

"I'm sorry I scared him." The quiet surrounded them, slowly filling with the sounds of nature and the neighborhood that filtered in. "I didn't mean to."

They stood there, then he canted his head just a bit to the side. "Carolyn's illness was hard on him. On us both. He's getting attached to you. I'm not sure why."

"I don't know." She took a step back, the concern in his eyes more intense than she'd expected. "I only missed school yesterday. I think I talked with Lindy. You met her at the dance. But that's foggy, too." She shrugged and moved toward the door. "I'll talk to him—"

"No. He'll have to learn to deal with these types of emotions. Let's see how it goes."

Addie nodded. She was the one who took care of her family. It was easy taking on concern for Ryan. What she didn't have much experience doing was taking care of herself. "I only vaguely remember hearing your voices. I don't think I even answered the door when you got there, did I?" She rubbed her forehead, wishing the memories were clearer, less fever damaged.

He shook his head. "It's a good thing we knew where you lived, I guess." He reached past her to pull open the door. "Ryan came home pretty upset."

"I didn't mean to—"

"It's okay." For a long minute, he looked at her. "He was worried." He took a deep breath. "Me, too."

"Thank you," she whispered. Rising on her tiptoes, she gently kissed him.

It was a light kiss, on the cheek, and yet…she froze. Marcus turned his head, his gaze finding hers. So blue, so intense. So close, then gone as her eyelids drifted shut and her lips parted.

CHAPTER EIGHT

MARCUS'S LIPS WERE warm against hers. Addie hadn't expected this when she'd initiated the simple thank-you kiss. But now? A part of her had wanted it. Wanted it badly.

She reached out. His forearms were hard and strong beneath her hands. She curled her fingers around his arms, feeling his muscles flex beneath her touch. He shifted, and those warm, solid hands settled at her waist, pulling her close.

Marcus's touch was gentle, yet firm as he wrapped his arms around her. This was a man she could lean on, who would comfort and warm her, who would give as good as he got. It felt right being with him. She gave herself up to his kiss, returning it with her own soft sigh.

Then he was gone. He took a deep, harsh breath. "I—" He took another breath, his hands clenched at his side as he stepped away. "I haven't kissed anyone besides—" He stared at her.

"Your wife?"

He shoved a hand through his thick hair, and

Addie curled her own hand into a fist, resisting the urge to do the same.

"No one else since I was eighteen."

Addie's heart ached as much from the cool air now brushing her lips asfrom the envy of the other woman. Addie would love to have someone love her like that.

But she didn't. Would she ever?

"I'm sorry. I didn't mean—" She backed away, not wanting to make him feel any worse than he did. She remembered that first kiss after losing Cal. It had been nearly a year later, but it had still hurt. Badly.

"I'll be on my way." She turned and hurried out the door, not bothering to close it behind her.

The familiar whack of the old screen door sounded so final. Even though it was a warm day, she hurried away, intent on burning off her frustration and mortification.

WAS SHE EVEN HOME? Was she feeling okay? Marcus walked slowly along the sidewalk across the street from Addie's house. Ryan had texted him that she'd been at the assembly earlier. He'd even sent a picture that Marcus had saved to his phone.

He'd thought about her, about that kiss, dozens of times today. He'd wondered what would have happened if he'd followed her like he should have. If nothing else, to make sure she really was better.

Now, it was a beautiful evening, the night falling gently over him and the neighborhood.

And he still hadn't stopped thinking about her. Using the excuse that she'd left without taking the overnight case her brothers had packed for her, he'd decided to bring it over to her.

As he'd walked, he looked around, still a bit overwhelmed at this great place where he'd landed.

Ryan had actually been the one who'd found the house on the market. He'd liked the big yard, the huge attic room and the fact that it was near both a middle school and high school. "I can live there forever, Dad." Marcus remembered his son's passionate pitch about the place.

Marcus hadn't argued. It was a great house, and if they were moving to Austin anyway, why not let his son have what he wanted? Marcus hadn't gotten overly attached to any place he'd ever lived, anyway.

Marcus thought about his own upbringing. So different from what he and Carolyn had tried to give Ryan. So different from Addie's.

Marcus's father had been career army, a colonel who hadn't been home much. He'd preferred to be in the middle of the world's troubles. There wasn't a conflict his father hadn't been smack in the center of in the past twenty years.

Marcus wondered how his father was dealing

with his imminent retirement. He wasn't sure what his father would do without a war to follow.

Not that Marcus would actually know. He and his father didn't speak often. His parents still lived on Lake Shore Drive in Chicago. His dad still left for some remote places. So like all the time and places they'd lived when he and his sister were growing up. No yard, no house, no streets to run with his buddies well past the sunset. New neighbors every few weeks. Nothing lasting.

Marcus couldn't remember the last time he and his father had spent more than a few minutes on the phone as a conversation.

The porch light came on at Addie's, startling Marcus. He stared across the street, past the picket fence, over the wide, green lawn, to the front door of the Craftsman-style home.

The house was similar to his. The roofline was slightly different, and where he had a brick fireplace in the living room, she had a bay window.

The wide panes would show him most of the room—if there was a light on inside.

Then there was one. A little flame. She leaned over the soft glow, a long match in her hand as she lit several thick candles. The light from the wicks danced on her skin, bouncing off the bright gold curls, and wavering as if beckoning him to cross the street and knock on the door.

She pursed her lips and blew on the match. The

flame on the wooden stick went out, doing little to diminish the glow in the candlelit room. It looked so enticing and she looked—he swallowed—breathtakingly beautiful.

As quickly as she'd appeared, she vanished, and something akin to disappointment settled over him. Maybe that was a good thing. It wouldn't be good if she caught him staring in her windows like some sick peeping tom.

The door opened then, and she stood in the shadowed opening, staring across the street. At him, a smile flirting with her lips. "Hi," she called, her voice floating to him on the evening's faint breeze.

He'd screwed up. No woman wanted to be reminded of someone else in the middle of a kiss. Marcus wanted to kick himself for being stupid. He owed Addie an apology.

He was glad for the approaching darkness. She couldn't see the discomfort on his face from there, could she? He lifted a hand. A casual wave that he gave purpose to when he lifted the small bag she'd left behind.

"Want to come in?" she asked.

"I—I should be heading home."

Did her smile actually dim, or was he imagining it?

But when she'd opened the door, all coherent thought flew out of his head. The flickering candlelight outlined her, glinting off her curls and showing him her sweet curves. Relief washed over him as she smiled. He couldn't have screwed up too badly—could he?

He strode slowly across the street, opening the gate and heading up her walk. He stopped at the steps that led to the front door. He had to look up to meet her smile.

ADDIE LEANED AGAINST the door frame, hoping Marcus couldn't see her uncertainty. "Nice evening for a walk."

"It is." He looked around, for a hiding place? An escape? Witnesses? "We need to talk," he finally said instead.

She held her breath, waiting for Marcus to look at her. It took him a beat. Finally, that deep-blue gaze found hers. She didn't know how to tell him that she wasn't the one-night-stand type, that she was a long-term kind of gal. She didn't want to wake up tomorrow to have regret steal all the joy.

"Won't you come in?" she whispered. He took the first step, and her breath caught at the intensity in his eyes. "Is something wrong?"

"No." He took the next step, and she curled her hands into fists to keep herself from reaching out to him. He set the small case on the floor just inside before he said anything. "Are you okay? You feeling okay?"

Why did she get the sense there was more behind those questions than yesterday's illness? "Are *you* okay?" she asked him instead of responding.

His smile was slow but intense. "Yeah. I'll be honest when I say this is strange for me."

"You have to be sure."

He didn't even hesitate. "I'm sure. I want this," he whispered, leaning close.

"Come in." Addie extended her hand in invitation toward the living room. He took it, his hand warm against hers, and followed her inside.

MARCUS STEPPED THROUGH Addie's front door, more than a little curious about what he'd see inside. There was no cat. No dog, big or small. Just a quiet, warm home.

"Nice place," he said as she closed the door and led the way into the living room.

"I like it. I know it's similar to Mom's, er, your place. But it's different enough."

He nodded. Then realized how stupid all this was. Why were they awkward with each other? They'd enjoyed conversations, knew each other well enough to understand each other, but still there were no words making complete sentences in his head.

"Feels like your air-conditioning's fixed."

"Yeah. Comes in handy to have a brother who's a former marine. The poor repairman probably thought he was in boot camp." She settled in an overstuffed chair and curled her legs under her skirt. She looked dainty and sweet sitting there. He wished she'd sat on the couch. "Won't you have a seat?" She waved to the sofa in front of the picture window.

"Sure." He sat on the end of the couch nearest her, telling himself it was better to hear and see her expressions. In reality, he hoped she'd move closer. "Looks like you're feeling better."

"Yeah."

The silence stretched out. There was no more small talk, and nothing important to discuss. The sound of crickets outside almost made him laugh at the absurdity of the whole situation.

She must have thought so, too. "Why *did* you come over tonight, Marcus? Other than the suitcase, of course." They both knew there wasn't anything urgent inside. Her question was a breathy whisper. Her eyes were wide as she looked at him.

"I—" Why had he come over? When Ryan had left for the movies, Marcus had found the house empty and lonely. He couldn't stop thinking about her, about that kiss.

Put the two together, and there wasn't anything else he could do. Slowly, he stood and stepped over to stand in front of her. He extended his hand. She didn't say anything, neither did he, but she put her hand in his and let him guide her to her feet.

Other than their hands, they weren't touching, but he felt every single inch of her over the brief space between them.

"I couldn't stay away," he said, slipping his arm loosely around her waist, pulling her slowly against him. He bit back the satisfied sigh as her curves settled close.

Addie flattened her palms against the front of his shirt, toying with the open collar. His heart beat hard against her touch. Slowly, she inched her hands up and hesitantly slipped her fingers into the hair at the nape of his neck. "I'm glad."

Was that a blush on her cheeks? "Where do we go from here?" He didn't move. He had no idea how to take the next step with a woman. He hadn't had to do that in over a decade. He certainly hoped she knew what to do.

"I'm not sure. I—" She looked up then, her gaze meeting his.

He knew he was lost. Gently, slowly, he cupped her chin. She leaned into his palm, and he slid the pad of his thumb over her lips. "So beautiful," he said before he realized what he meant to say. Her skin was soft against his touch, and her hair slid over the back of his hand in a sweet caress.

"Marcus…" She swallowed hard. "Kiss me, please," she whispered, her breath fanning his wrist, hot and soft.

His heart pounded, and her lips parted, inviting him to taste. He'd already sampled, but this would be more. So much more.

He didn't have to lean far. Bending his head, Marcus gently put his lips on hers, not intending to do more than kiss her.

All his good intentions vanished as Addie slid her arms up around his neck. She held him to her, and returned his kiss with a heated one of her own.

Her lips parted, tasting him and inviting him inside. Every inch of him ached to take all of her, hard and fast and completely, but he held back. He wanted that, but he wanted this sweet joining to last.

And apparently, so did she.

ADDIE DIDN'T REMEMBER the last time, if ever, that she'd felt this wanted. Marcus's touch was gentle and yet strong. His arms tight around her waist held her to him, but his kiss was slow and easy, letting her set the pace.

She held on tight, not wanting him to let go anytime soon, if ever.

His lips were firm and warm, and the scent of his subtle cologne wrapped in and around her. He tasted and smelled like a man whose touch could slip past every barrier she'd ever erected around her heart.

Oh, Marcus. She leaned into him, and he

supported her with his strength. She couldn't get close enough.

Her blood rushed through her veins, and the temperature rose nearly ten degrees. His body heat combined with hers. She fought to pull in air as her lungs forgot to breathe. Her entire body forgot it had anything else to do but taste and feel him.

Finally, he pulled back, but only far enough to sever the kiss and move his lips to the edge of her jaw and down the length of her neck. Wanting, needing, to give him better access, she tilted her head, hoping and praying he wanted to move lower.

Her breasts tingled in anticipation, aching to feel his touch. But he seemed content to taste the skin of her neck, his tongue darting out where her pulse beat against her skin. Her moan seemed loud in the silent room, reminding her how alone they were.

No one would interrupt them. No one except the two of them would have a part in this moment. Her heart soared at the thought of sharing him with no one.

"Addie," he said, the heat of his breath fanning over her skin. "I need you."

Her knees grew weak, and the only thing keeping her standing was his hold. "Marcus," she whispered, not even sure what she intended to say next. Her mind scrambled, and all she could do was feel. And ache.

"I—" Marcus's voice came out in a harsh whisper. Then he slowly pulled her arms away from around his neck. "I need to go."

Her heart sank, and the blood that had sung in her veins turned to a burning blush of mortification in her cheeks. She looked down, hoping he wouldn't see her embarrassment.

"No, wait." He tilted her chin up with a gentle finger. "Don't misunderstand," he croaked. "I want you. My god, I want you so bad." He cleared his throat and stepped back. "But Ryan's going to be home soon. When I make love to you, I don't want any interruptions. I don't want to sneak out of here. I sure as hell won't want to stop."

She gasped. Words failed her. The soft little sigh that escaped her lips felt like a plea.

Marcus growled and, despite his intention to leave, pulled her against him again. This time his lips were hungry and hot, and he took everything he could get. She let him, curling her fingers into the muscles of his back as if she could hold him here.

"You're driving me crazy," he finally said as he set her away from him again. This time he put several inches between them. "I *will* be back." He opened the door and left without another word or touch.

Addie stood there for several long minutes not sure what had happened, but wishing he'd hurry back.

THE NEXT DAY, her phone rang. That might not have been a problem if she weren't standing on a ladder trying to replace the lightbulbs in the ceiling fan. She caught herself before she hurried to answer. She'd promised both Wyatt and DJ that she'd take better care of her house, and better care of herself.

She understood their concerns. Really, she did. She just—well, she wasn't used to thinking about herself. The kids at school, her siblings and now her nieces and nephews were infinitely more important.

"If it's important, they'll call back," she spoke out loud. Maybe she'd get used to thinking that way if she said it often enough.

She'd just climbed down when it rang again. "See?" she told her reflection in the hall mirror. "I was right. Hello?" she said on the fourth ring, just before it went to voice mail.

"Addie?" Marcus asked. "Are you okay?"

"Yeah. Why?" She looked out the window to see if he might be standing across the street like last night. He wasn't, and she tried to ignore her disappointment. Her cheeks burned as she remembered their kiss.

"You sound out of breath. I called a bit ago, but you didn't answer. Everything okay?"

"I'm fine!" She bit the words out. One little episode of nearly dying and everyone was her keeper. "Wyatt has called already. Both my sisters and DJ, as well."

He was silent for a long time. "Everyone is worried about you. They care."

The words to ask if he was in that camp were on the tip of her tongue. She didn't utter them. If he said no, she wasn't sure if she could take it.

"What are you doing this afternoon?" he asked.

"Apparently rolling myself up in cotton and not moving," she mumbled.

"What?"

"Nothing." She contemplated if she could fold up the ladder and not drop the phone. Probably not. She sat on the bottom step. She'd take care of it when they hung up.

"Want to come over? A couple of those boxes in the garage I think you should look at. I'll grill."

"Uh—" She tamped down her surprise and pleasure. "Now, how is a girl supposed to turn that kind of offer down? Dirty garage-cleaning work followed by a man who cooks. Sure." She couldn't help smiling when his laughter rang out through the phone. She closed her eyes, picturing his face. His smile lit up his eyes and brightened up everything.

"How do you like your steak?"

"Steak? That garage must be really dirty."

He laughed again. "About five? That'll give us plenty of time before dark to go through things."

"Sounds good. What can I bring?"

"Nothing. I'm cooking. You're a guest."

"Guests bring a dish."

"That's not necessary. I've got everything covered." He sighed. "Just bring your lovely self. See you later, Addie." He ended the call, his laughter still hanging in the air.

A long few minutes passed as she sat on that step. She couldn't show up empty-handed. That went against everything her mother had taught her. And the fact that she was going over to Mom's old house—yeah Mom's spirit would probably smack her. No, she smiled. She wasn't taking that chance.

Her smile grew as she realized what she *had* to take. She always kept cookie ingredients around. And there were several bottles of wine in the garage from the last girls' night. Perfect.

She forgot about the ladder until the second batch of cookies was in the oven. She reminded herself to do it once everything was done.

She hoped Marcus and Ryan liked her cookies. The jar of peanut butter on the counter was a good indication.

Out of habit, she'd pulled her recipe box from

the cupboard and found the old, battered card. She'd given Mom's old recipes to Tara, who used them in her diner, but Addie had kept copies for herself. This one, however, was just hers. She leaned the card against the flour canister. She didn't have to look at it, the recipe so well memorized, but she always got it out.

The first time she'd made these cookies, she'd been with Cal. He'd loved these sweet treats. It had been his mother's recipe. She had made them just for him, and had shared the recipe with Addie, hoping she'd make them for him after they got married.

It had been a happy day. They'd watched his mother make the cookies, laughing and eating them as soon as she scooped them off the baking sheet.

Now, Addie watched the gooey delights through the oven window. She loved this part of baking. The sweet dough rose and bubbled, the chocolate chunks melted and slid into the dough.

Addie glanced once more at the recipe card leaning against the flour canister.

That night had also been the first time they'd made love. Later, down at the river…the moonlight washed down over the blanket on the sand.

No! She shut off that train of thought, yanking open the oven door to pull out the hot pan. She focused on the calming, even rhythm of the spatula scooping the cookies onto the cooling rack.

When Cal died, Elizabeth had tried to destroy the wonderful recipe. The old-fashioned card had been ripped into a dozen pieces. When Addie's family had gone to the house to pay their respects, Addie had seen the pieces and pulled them out of the trash. She'd meticulously taped them together.

She'd needed something—anything—of Cal's to hold on to. She'd had no clue she was pregnant until weeks later.

Straightening now, Addie picked up the card, running her finger over one of the lines of yellowed tape. It didn't hurt so much today—that flash of memory that always came with looking at this card.

CHAPTER NINE

ADDIE HEARD FOOTSTEPS running down the stairs when she rang the doorbell at Marcus's house. Somehow, she didn't think it was him.

"I got it, Dad."

She smiled. Ryan. He opened the door and grinned at her. "Hi! Dad said you were coming over."

"And here I am." She stepped inside, a weird wave of memories flashing through her. It was still the same house, but different. Ryan headed to the kitchen and she followed.

"Dad, she's here," he called.

Marcus sat at the table, his laptop open and papers scattered all over the surface. Mom would have cringed at the mess, but Addie remembered doing plenty of homework at that table.

The table had been too big for any of her siblings to take, and the real estate agent had suggested they leave it with the house. The buyer—apparently Marcus—had been happy to have it. It still looked right at home.

Marcus stood. "I see that." He smiled.

"I brought these." She handed Ryan the box of cookies, and he took a deep inhale. "Yum! Peanut butter?"

"And this." She extended the bottle of wine to Marcus. Silence greeted her. Father and son shared a glance, and Ryan seemed to hold his breath.

Marcus gave a slight nod, and Ryan turned to put the cookies on the counter. "Thank you, but I don't drink," Marcus finally said.

The relief that poured off Ryan was so thick Addie felt it fill the room. He smiled over his shoulder at his dad, his eyes full of something she couldn't quite grasp. What was going on?

"Can I have one now?" the boy asked, lifting the lid on the cookie container.

Marcus laughed. "If it's okay with Addie. We're going to the garage, so it might be a while before I start dinner."

"Cool." At her nod, Ryan grabbed one of the cookies and shoved it into his mouth as he left the room. "I'll finish my homework while you do that."

Marcus stepped closer to Addie, stopping just inches from her. "He's afraid I'll make him clean the garage. Homework's the lesser of the two evils." Marcus placed a soft kiss on her cheek before he took the wine bottle and set it on the counter.

He must have seen the questions in her eyes.

He leaned against the counter, crossing his arms over his chest. "After Carolyn's funeral I—" She watched the muscles of his throat constrict as he swallowed. "I spent about six months barely functioning. I drank. A lot. All the time, actually."

"You don't have to tell me." Addie's chest hurt, seeing the regret and anguish on his face.

"Yes, I do." He straightened and took her hand in his. "I'm not a fan of keeping secrets." He took a deep breath. "I nearly lost everything. I did lose my job. Lost nearly six months of my son's life. Thank God, my sister stepped in and smacked me upside the head one day, literally." His laughter held no humor. "I promised Ryan I'd never do that to him again."

Addie couldn't picture what Marcus was telling her. She couldn't imagine him so out of control. She tilted her head, trying, and failing, to put the two together.

He laughed. "Is there anything you don't try to figure out?"

"Nope." She smiled at him. "Thank you for sharing. I'll take the bottle home. The cookies are all yours."

"Thank you."

That awkwardness was back, and she didn't know why. She couldn't tear her gaze from him. The blue polo shirt he wore drew her eyes to his broad chest. Her gaze wandered to take in the worn jeans that fit snug.

He pushed away from the counter. "Like what you see?" he whispered.

Nodding was all she could manage. She caught herself biting her lip.

"Me, too." He stepped closer, and she felt a tug on a curl that fell over her shoulder. "But my earlier promise stands. No interruptions." His gaze shifted upward. Ryan.

Her face flamed. "Wouldn't—wouldn't that make for an interesting day at school on Monday?"

"Yeah." He took her hand and tugged. "Let's go look at the garage."

Dust coated the old-fashioned window, letting very little light into the garage.

"I probably should have brought some window cleaner." Marcus used his hand to brush off what dirt he could.

"There's a light somewhere." She moved deeper inside, where Dad's workshop had been. The overhead light came on as she reached it.

Someone, probably Wyatt and DJ, had straightened up the place once upon a time. All the tools, the lathe, the awls and all the other items she'd never been able to identify were gone.

The faint smell of cut wood still hung around in

the shop, and a few stray curls of pine lay in the corner. Time had faded them gray, but she could see them, bright golden as they'd slid from the sharp blade of the plane or the hand lathe.

Dad's vise was still bolted to the bench, and absently Addie spun the handle with a finger. It moved as smoothly as ever. An image came to mind—the clamp holding a narrow piece of oak as Dad used hand tools to create a curved line along the edge.

She frowned, trying to remember what he'd been making. Had he ever finished it? She shook her head and banished the image. It was too real, too tempting. She missed him too much.

"It was never this clean when I was a kid," she said. It had been a mess. Or at least to her it seemed messy. Yet, Dad always knew where every single tool, every single piece of a project was put. He could pull it out in an instant.

"Don't touch anything," he'd frequently admonished. "Or I'll get mixed up." She hadn't believed him, but as a kid, there had been just enough doubt that she kept her hands clasped behind her back whenever she was in Dad's shop.

"These are the boxes I mentioned." Marcus lifted two cardboard boxes up onto the workbench. Neither was sealed.

"Wonder how my brothers missed these."

"They were up there in the corner." He pointed

up to a spot on the rafters. "I didn't even see them in the dim light until I climbed up there."

She nodded and moved closer. She stood on tip-toe to peer inside. The first box was full of scrap pieces of wood. Most had been cut at angles, or jagged. Small pieces. Dad had never been one to throw out something he might be able to find a use for later.

The second box had only a couple things in it. She frowned. "Is that—?" She reached in.

"That's what I thought you might want to see." Marcus stood close as she set the package on the workbench.

A thick coat of dust covered the wrapped rect-angle. With a swipe of her hand, she cleared off the bright blue wrapping paper. "What the heck is it?" She leaned over it, noticing the paper was crumpled on one end and a battered, dust-covered tag was tied around it.

She turned the tag over and saw her name in her father's familiar scrawl. She gasped, then gri-maced when she felt her dust-coated hand touch her face.

Marcus chuckled and reached for a rag. He dusted off her hands, then reached out and care-fully removed the marks from her cheek. "There."

She stared at the narrow package for a long time. The dim sunlight barely reached into the room, but she felt as if the package glowed with light. "Wonder what it is," she whispered.

"Looks like a gift."

"But what for?" She frowned, trying to remember. "The accident was in February. My birthday was a month later."

She stared then slowly picked it up.

"Open it," Marcus encouraged.

Carefully, reverently, she pulled the old tape loose. It didn't take much. The paper crinkled. Inside, she found a narrow wooden box with tiny hinges on one side. A lid. She set the paper aside and put the box next to it.

Slowly, she lifted the lid, looking first at Marcus, then at the box. The box was lined with tan velvet, and a narrow piece of carved, smooth wood lay on top of the fabric. She picked up the piece of wood. So smooth and dainty.

Then she remembered.

"Dad laughed at me when I wished for a magic wand. Course, I was mad at some sibling and wanted to turn them into a toad," she whispered to herself as much as Marcus.

"How old were you?" he asked.

"Twelve." Just a couple of years from losing him, though she'd had no idea what lay ahead. "He found a design in one of his woodworking books and showed it to me." She remembered squealing in twelve-year-old delight that it was perfect.

"He promised he'd make me one." Someday. A promise that had gotten lost over the hectic years of running a business, supporting a family and just getting through the days, she knew.

A promise, she realized now, that he had tried to keep. She clutched the piece of wood tight in her hand, and close to her chest. "Thank you, Daddy," she whispered, feeling some of the anger and grief she'd never really dealt with loosen its hold.

Her eyes blurred, and she closed her eyes to hold in the tears. She didn't want Marcus to think she was upset, or sad. These were happy tears, sweet, happy tears.

He'd obviously been watching her closely. His arms closed around her, pulling her tight. The comfort rolled off him, and she couldn't resist taking just a bit of it. It felt so right.

He let her tears fall, not shushing her or pushing her to stop.

"He remembered," she whispered, treasuring the belated gift. "He remembered," she repeated.

THE SCENT OF steaks on the gas grill wafted around the neighborhood. Addie inhaled, enjoying the spicy-sweet scent.

"I'm serious," Marcus had said when they came out of the garage. "You're my guest. You get to sit, relax and watch me dazzle you with my cooking." He winked at her as he lit the grill.

"You do know my sister is a chef, right?" She took the glass of lemonade he handed her.

"Oh, sure. Add pressure. I see how you are." He was working hard to distract her from the tears. It was working. Determined to not let the past interfere with tonight, she slipped inside and put the wooden box on the counter next to the wine.

When she returned to the patio, Marcus uncovered three juicy sirloins. The sizzle of them was loud and enticing.

"Yep. Gotta keep you on your toes. So, I saw the book you weren't reading on the table. Have you read it yet?"

He shook his head, turning away from her and focusing on the grill. "I've tried several times. It's not going anywhere, so—" He shrugged and didn't say anymore.

Addie watched him for a while, enjoying the view, the fire, the yard beyond. She tried not to feel like she was back home. This wasn't her home anymore, but it did feel good to sit out here and soak up the beauty.

He'd kicked on the sprinklers since her last visit, and the yard was a bright, thick green. The vines she'd been worried about a few days ago were lush and thick. The sounds of summer and the warmth that would arrive soon hinted in the air.

Footsteps announced Ryan's arrival. "What do you need me to do?" he asked from the doorway.

"Grab the plates and let's set the table." Ryan nodded and ducked inside. He returned a bit later, his arms full.

"You could take more than one trip."

"I got it." He nearly dropped the loaf of bread he had stacked on top.

Addie laughed.

"Don't encourage him," Marcus teasingly admonished.

After a few minutes of Ryan's working diligently to put everything on the table, the steaks were done, and the whole meal was arranged perfectly on the table. "You're a good pair," she said.

"We've been working on it." Ryan filled his plate. "Dad's teaching me to cook, too. So I can help."

"Yeah, after I learn. Grilling, I got."

Addie savored the food and the company. It was quiet, though not silent. As if by some unspoken agreement, they didn't discuss school. Baseball seemed to be the biggest topic on Ryan's agenda.

"Thanks for encouraging him to go out for the team, by the way," Marcus said.

She looked up and their eyes met. "You're welcome, both of you." She couldn't look away. "According to the coach, he's got talent." Her words came out slow, distracted. The intensity in Marcus's eyes told her he was feeling it, too.

"Speaking of baseball. Dex wanted me to give

him some pointers tonight. I told him I'd try to come over after dinner. Is that okay?"

"Uh, yeah." Marcus tore his gaze away from hers, looking at his son. "Got all your homework done?"

"Yep." Ryan grinned.

"I'll help clean up," Addie offered. When Marcus went to argue, she held up her hand like she did for silence during the assemblies. "You two cooked. I can help clean up. Besides—" she glanced at Marcus "—Ryan doesn't want to run out of daylight helping Dex, now, do you?"

"Thanks." Ryan jumped up. "Can I take a cookie to go?"

"Grab one and leave the rest for us," Marcus teased.

The silence descended. They could hear Ryan running upstairs to grab his gear, then running back down. "See you later," he yelled as the front door slammed closed.

Then he was gone. And they were alone. Blessedly alone.

Finally, Marcus cleared his throat. "It won't take long to clean this up." He waved at the table.

"It will take half as long if we both do it." Addie stood and gathered dishes. Marcus did the same. It took only a few minutes, and soon everything was put away with the soft hum of the dishwasher in the background.

"Do you want a cookie?" she asked, trying to find something else to do.

"I'd definitely like something sweet," he whispered in her ear. She started, not realizing he'd come up behind her. "Sorry, didn't mean to scare you."

Addie smiled as he slipped his arms around her waist. He gently pulled her back, and she leaned against him. The warm length of his body against her felt so good. She swallowed a groan of pleasure.

Closing her eyes, she took a deep breath. Marcus leaned his head against hers. Softly, he pushed aside her thick curls, and his lips found the sensitive skin of her neck. The warm tip of his tongue drew a path down to her shoulder where the wide neck of her dress gave him access. She shivered.

Slowly, Marcus moved around her until they stood face-to-face. This time his finger traced the path his lips had just found. She tilted her head and looked at him. "Ryan's not going to interrupt us."

He nodded, stepping in even closer. This time, she was the one slipping her arms around his waist. The fabric of his shirt was soft against her skin, but his body beneath was solid and firm, muscles defined against her fingers. She vaguely wondered if he worked out.

But that thought, and every other thought she

might have had, vanished as Marcus's lips found hers. She leaned into him and he pulled her tight.

He'd kissed her before, but this was different. Very different. This was the hot, hard kiss of a man who had much more on his mind.

And her body responded. She curled her fingers into the fabric of his shirt, pulling and holding him tight. He couldn't get close enough. Her breasts ached, anticipating his touch. The juncture between her legs tightened, and flushed, knowing she wanted him there.

She fought to catch her breath, and the hard rush of his breath against her told her he felt the same.

He pushed her against the counter, the hard evidence of his desire pressing against her, right where she ached to have him, but where there were too many layers of clothing.

"Marcus," she whispered when his lips finally moved from hers and returned again to tease the soft skin of her shoulder. She burrowed her fingers into his hair, holding him there, pushing ever so gently as she impatiently waited for him to deepen his touch.

"Mmm." He didn't speak, but that moan told her way more than she'd expected.

His hand settled in the center of her back, gently, insistently pulling her closer, her breasts pressing hard into his chest. She threw her head back, wanting, needing, begging him to touch her, to take more.

He wasn't turning down the invitation. When his long, hard fingers closed around her breast, she gasped. Even through the fabric, he found her nipple, the pad of his thumb circling the sensitive skin, setting her on fire. Her breath came in quick pants as the sparks of desire moved from where he touched her to scatter throughout her entire body.

It felt wonderful. But it wasn't enough. She wanted more. So, so much more.

"Addie, you're driving me crazy," he whispered, then pulled back just an inch to gaze at her face. "I want you."

Her smile grew. "I want you, too." He returned her smile, then took her lips with his again. Gentle and sweet at first, it didn't take long for the fire to return.

ADDIE SET HIM on fire, and in about two seconds he was going to sweep her up in his arms and carry her to the nearest horizontal surface.

Then a sound filtered in. A door somewhere opening. The same instant it registered with him, Addie must have heard it. She pulled back and looked around, startled.

"Who's that?" A familiar, gruff voice cut through every last drop of passion in the room.

"That's my principal," Ryan supplied.

"Oh, my." His mother's voice joined the others.

Marcus whispered a curse, but he didn't let go of her. "Sorry," he whispered, giving her and himself a moment to recover.

Finally, certain she was ready to face them, and there wasn't any piece of clothing out of place, Marcus stepped back. He looked at her, noting the bright blush in her cheeks, waiting for her to give him a sign that she was okay. She simply nodded.

His parents, and his son, stood in the doorway. Ryan's eyes were wide. His grin even wider.

"Addie." Marcus cleared his throat. "These are my parents. James and Donna."

"H-hello." She stepped forward, offering her hand like they were at a school function instead of his kitchen after a hot-and-heavy make-out session.

"Nice to meet you," his father said.

"Yes," was all his mother managed to say. She looked at Addie, then at Marcus. He couldn't tell what was stronger in her eyes—shock or concern.

"Well, I was just—uh—leaving." Awkwardly, Addie grabbed the wooden box she'd set on the counter earlier.

"You don't have to." Marcus reached out for her hand. She froze, then briefly leaned over to give him a kiss on the cheek. Soft as a butterfly kiss, it had him hot all over again.

Rather than pass their audience to get to the

front door, Addie opened the back door, hurrying across the yard and around the house. The only thing left was the echo of her heels against the sidewalk as she headed home.

MEMORIES HAD ASSAULTED her all day. She was exhausted. Grief had threatened to creep in so many times. Recalling Cal as she'd made the cookies. Seeing her father's things again. Talking to Marcus about his past. The wand.

She'd shed a few tears each time. And laughed all through dinner. Her emotions had bounced about like a tennis ball at Wimbledon.

She refused to think about that kiss, or Marcus—or his parents.

So why wouldn't her mind turn off now? Why couldn't she just close her eyes and go to sleep? Her body was exhausted, and her brain was glitchy—hopping from thought to thought.

With a groan of frustration, Addie turned on the light. She still hadn't finished the book she'd started over a month ago, the one she'd been reading the night she'd met Marcus at the coffee shop.

As she opened to where she'd left off, she wondered again about the book he hadn't read yet. Somehow, she didn't think he really wanted to read it. He'd given her the impression it was not a happy book.

She remembered seeing that book on the table

in the kitchen. The kitchen where he'd kissed her. What would have happened if his parents hadn't arrived, if Ryan had spent the evening at Dex's house?

"Enough," she told herself. She needed to get the man out of her head! Rolling over, she propped herself up on her elbow and focused on the book. The heroine was running through the woods, hiding behind a fallen log, when a loud shrill sound broke through the gloom and doom.

She nearly jumped out of bed as her phone rang. She cursed. "I'm gonna kill whichever one of you scared me half to death," she spoke to the nameless, faceless sibling who had to be on the other end. Those were the only people who would call this late.

"Uh—" Marcus's voice slipped in her ear, and she shivered. "Addie?"

"Oh. Uh. Yeah. Hi!" She sat up, trying to still her heart. "I was reading. I lost track of things. Sorry."

"Okay." He laughed softly. "I was wondering if there was a problem. There's a ladder in your living room and the lights are on."

She climbed out of bed and ran to the window. She parted the curtains and peered out. His Jeep was parked at the curb, the headlights shooting down the street. Then she dragged her gaze back and saw the golden squares of light falling from the front window onto the front lawn. "Oh." She waved. She couldn't see him through the dark, but knew he could see her. She glanced down, then yanked the curtains back. Her nightgown wasn't meant for public display.

"You scramble my brain," she said before she thought clearly. How much could he see? Her cheeks flamed. "I was fixing the light earlier and forgot." She'd been too focused on getting ready for dinner, then that lovely dinner—and that kiss.

"Want me to come in and help put the ladder away?"

"I—" She'd grabbed her robe and was halfway to the door before she realized how late it was. "Why are you out so late?"

He was silent for a minute, and she heard the silence grow as he turned off the Jeep's engine. "I couldn't sleep," he whispered. "My parents are already driving me crazy, and I couldn't sleep thinking about—" He cleared his throat as if to stop his words. "I thought maybe a drive would relax me."

"And you drove by here?" She headed down the stairs.

He laughed. "I told you, driving by here is on my way to about everywhere."

"We probably need to find you some different routes." He was new to the neighborhood, she rationalized. She'd reached the front door, and heard footsteps on the other side. She took a deep breath before pulling the door open. "Hi!" she said entirely too brightly. Dear God, she felt seventeen again. And seventeen was the age of stupid.

"Hi, yourself." He stood there, his hands in his pockets, a grin on his face. They stood looking at each other for a long minute. She finally remembered to hang up the phone, and shoved it into her robe pocket.

"Would you like to come in?" She shook her head, trying to clear it and stepped back.

"Might be the easiest way to take care of that ladder."

"Uh, yeah. There is that." She pulled the door open wider. He stepped through, and somehow the sound of the door latching closed seemed loud. Her house might be full of light, but the only sound she heard was her heartbeat, loud in her ears.

"Where does it go?" he asked, walking over to the ladder that sat exactly where she'd left it.

"In the garage." She headed toward the door in the kitchen as she heard the metal-on-metal clang as he folded the ladder. It rattled a bit as he walked through the kitchen behind her. He made short work of hanging it on the hooks on the long wall.

"Thanks. I probably would have noticed it in the morning." She closed the garage door after he'd come back in, and the kitchen settled quietly around them. Their gazes locked.

No one would interrupt them if they finished what they'd started earlier. It was late enough that even her siblings wouldn't call. Ryan wasn't here. The neighbors were all asleep, as well.

"Yeah, probably. This saves you the effort—and the cost of the lights on all night." He shoved his hands into his pockets, leaning back against the counter as if he had no intention of going anywhere anytime soon. Relaxed. Comfortable. Gorgeous.

She swallowed, unable to look away.

"Where is everyone?" She made a show of looking around, mocking his promise to not be interrupted.

"Ryan was asleep when I last checked. My parents are at my house, hopefully asleep, as well."

"So, you snuck out of your own house?"

"Yeah. Pretty much."

CHAPTER TEN

MARCUS COULDN'T HELP but laugh at the absurdity of the whole situation. When Addie's sweet laughter joined his, it made him laugh even harder.

"Okay." She wiped her eyes and took a deep breath. "It's too late to offer you coffee. And I know better than to offer you a drink." She met his gaze, and his heart hammered against his ribs.

Even rumpled, without makeup, in a robe that covered too much, she was pretty.

He wanted nothing more than to pick up where they had left off this afternoon. He'd gladly haul her into the bedroom and spend a couple of hours making sweet love to her.

But Addie Hawkins wasn't a one-night-stand kind of girl. She was the all-or-nothing type, and while he'd love every minute of having her, he'd have to leave. And sneak back into his own house.

That scenario left a bitter taste in his mouth.

It was what he'd had in mind when he'd driven here, though. And every inch of him ached to continue with the plan. Everything but that minuscule piece of his brain that held logic.

"I don't need anything, thanks." What he needed was to leave before he changed his mind.

He looked around, hoping to distract himself from the indecision. The footprint of her kitchen was nearly the same as his. Instead of the giant dining room table, though, she had a smaller one, with matching chairs. It looked polished and new.

A solitary chair sat in the corner. It looked older and vaguely familiar, yet he knew he'd never seen it before. Maybe something similar? "That chair? It looks...familiar."

She noticed where he was looking. "It's one that used to go with the table in your kitchen." At his frown, she moved over and sat on it. "Mom and Dad got the original set when they first married. Over the years, we kids broke most, if not all, of the chairs. They replaced them one at a time. A bit mismatched, but when Mom died, we each took our chair as a reminder." She lovingly ran a hand over the curved back, lightly caressing the spindles. "The table was too big, and since it worked for you..." She shrugged.

"It—" He glanced around, frowning when he didn't see the box from this afternoon. "Where's your magic wand?"

"Somehow that just sounded weird. I wish it really was magical." She left the room, then returned carrying the box. She handed it to him.

He pulled out the polished piece of wood and held it up. "Look." He extended it to her.

With a frown, Addie took it, then looked at the chair. "It matches." She moved closer. "It used to be one of the spindles. This must have been one of the original chairs." Her excitement and pleasure filled the room.

Slowly, she knelt, holding the wand up against the chair. The handle perfectly matched the ridges of the spindle design. A few inches down, the wood had been straightened, the ridges from the other end trimmed away to create the narrow point. She smiled. "How clever." She stood, turning the wand back and forth, examining and studying it.

"The other box in your garage." She spoke slowly, thoughtfully. "It had other pieces. Now I wonder what else was in it."

"It's still there. You can come back and look through it again."

"I will. Thank you." She turned and reached out to hug him.

Instinctively, his arms went around her, aligning her sweet curves with his body. They both froze. He looked into her face. She was staring back, her eyes wide with awareness.

"Addie," he whispered, trying to remember the promise he'd made to himself earlier. "I can't stay." And she was someone you stayed with.

"I know," she whispered back. "I'm not asking for promises. I understand."

But did she? Did she really? He wanted to ask her what she thought she understood, but her parted lips and the warmth of her arms around him was too much. He stopped thinking and leaned down to kiss her.

Her robe was little barrier between them. He'd caught a glimpse of the sheer nightgown underneath when she'd first looked out the window. Seeing it again in his thoughts did not help with his promise to himself to keep his distance.

The robe fell open, and his hands found the silky-soft material. He knew there was nothing else beneath. That realization was too much.

He growled and lifted her, settling her on the counter. She automatically wrapped her legs around his waist as he stepped between her thighs. She pulled him in tight.

Slowly, Marcus broke the kiss, letting his gaze travel down to where her robe parted. He pushed it farther apart, then down off her shoulders.

The nightgown's tiny straps were barely attached to a row of lace. Through the sheer lace, he could see the outline of her breast and the darker shape of her nipple. His groan seemed loud in the silent kitchen.

Addie's soft, small hands went to the back of his shirt, giving it a tug until it came loose from his jeans. Slowly, torturously slowly, she slipped her hands beneath the fabric, her fingers hot against his back. She urged him closer.

"Ah, Addie." He leaned his forehead on hers. "I want to continue this. So bad."

"Then do." She leaned her head back and smiled at him.

He laughed. "It sounds so simple." If only it were. Resisting her was far from simple. Slowly, reverently, he reached up and pushed her scattered curls behind her ear. The smooth outline of her jaw fit perfectly in his palm, and she nuzzled against him, placing a simple kiss in the center of his palm.

"Addie." He breathed, then pulled her close again, unable to resist her any longer.

Slipping the robe off to pool around her waist, he carefully slid a finger beneath the narrow strap of her gown. Inch by sensual inch, he pushed it down, exposing the firm contour of her breast. Her nipple puckered as the cool air and, he hoped, desire hit.

There was no turning back now. He cupped her breast. Dipping his head, he tasted her. His moan of pleasure elicited an answering one from her.

ADDIE COULDN'T REMEMBER how long it had been since she'd been touched so intimately, caressed so boldly and held—just plain held—against another body. This felt so wonderful. She didn't want him to ever stop.

She returned Marcus's kiss and slowly moved her fingers over his body. Exploring. Discovering. Feeling. Hard muscles. Rough calluses. Soft kisses. Every inch of him was new to her.

She finished pulling the gown off, then reached up and nudged him to take off his shirt. He fisted the collar at his back and pulled, giving her a full view of his bare chest an instant later. She couldn't look away.

At first, she wanted to touch. Feeling him, touching the taut skin and light hair. Just as he'd touched her. Impatient, he pulled her against him, and the friction of his skin against her nipples sent her desire through the roof.

Even skin to skin, they weren't close enough. She reached for the closure of his jeans, popping the button only an instant before his hand took hers.

"Easy," he whispered, his lips against her shoulder. "We've got plenty of time."

Her moan of frustration made him laugh. "Plenty of time," he repeated as his big, rough hand moved lower, finding the heat at the juncture of her thighs. He easily found her most sensitive spot.

"Marcus!"

"Hmm?" He slid a finger along the damp curls, pushing her closer and closer to the edge.

"I need you," she whispered, struggling to move off the counter. His frown as she pulled the robe back over her shoulders made her laugh. When they were both standing again, she took his hand and, with a gentle tug, headed toward the bedroom.

They were halfway down the hall when he stopped and cursed. She turned back, not letting go of his hand. "What?"

A scowl marred his beautiful, previously aroused features. "Tell me you're on birth control."

"Uh…" A bucket of ice water couldn't have been more effective. "No." Why would she be? She hadn't been with anyone in ages. Hadn't needed to.

Marcus cursed again. "I don't have anything." Regret—painful regret—was written all over his face.

"I'm not used to—" As a responsible school principal she had to give them both points for using their heads. As Addie, standing in the hallway with a man she was taking to her bedroom, she wanted to kick herself.

Marcus let go of her hand and stepped back. He shoved his fingers through his hair, making more of a mess of it than she'd done. Making him look even better. She bit back a groan of disappointment.

"Being married, we never had to—" Another frustrated shove of his fingers. "Carolyn couldn't—" He took a deep breath. "That's why we adopted Ryan."

Addie pulled the robe tight around her, knotting the belt. Did she take a step backward? Had he? He seemed farther away.

"I—I probably should go." Marcus turned to the door.

"I'm sorry," she said, not even sure what she was sorry for. Not having any protection handy? Not following through with their desires?

"Don't apologize. This is on me." He walked into the kitchen, then quickly returned, his discarded shirt in hand. He went straight to the front door, his big hand making the door handle look small. "Don't take this wrong, Addie," he whispered. "I still want you. Dear God, I want you. But I won't put either of us at risk."

"I appreciate that." She stood there in the hall, shivering. "I—" What else was she going to say? She had no idea. Her brain stopped functioning.

Marcus pulled the door open and stepped out into the night. Neither of them said anything. He closed the door, and she knew he was headed to his Jeep. She waited until she heard the engine roar to life before she turned the dead bolt into place.

ADDIE AIMLESSLY WANDERED through the house, turning off lights. Finally, she sank hard onto the old kitchen chair. The wood groaned just a little at the impact. *I'm an idiot.* Hadn't she learned the lesson of unprotected sex, the hard way, years ago? The fact that it had never crossed her mind, and that Marcus had to bring it up, made her entire body blush. As if to belabor the point, memories taunted her.

Cal had been her first love, and for a long time now, her only love. She'd shied away from any serious relationships, as much because she hadn't met anyone who measured up as because of fear.

Cal had been one of those shining lights who blasted into the world. One of the most popular kids at his school, and in the county, he'd blown her away when she went to spend time at her grandfather's ranch.

Wyatt had been living there then, Grandpa grooming him to take over someday. She'd missed him and gone to visit.

She hadn't planned on meeting anyone. Hadn't been looking to find a relationship. The summer between her junior and senior year of high school, though, had been an eye-opening time. To all the things the world had ahead. To all the opportunities. To all the possibilities.

Love had been on that list.

She'd come home to Austin after meeting Cal and finished her senior year. She'd made plans to go to college. She'd always dreamed of being a teacher, and that's what she focused on.

And Cal called her nearly every night. He'd even driven into Austin, in his dad's king-cab pickup truck, and taken her to her senior prom.

The world had been the brightest place, aglow with opportunity and joy. The only dark side was the distance between them—which she'd remedied after graduation.

Grandpa had turned ninety that year, and needed more help. Wyatt and the ranch foreman took over most of the ranch operations. She'd volunteered to go help, and had even gotten a part-time job at a small boutique in Haskins Corners. Mom was working and still had the four younger siblings to take care of. Mandy had been around to help with them that summer, Addie recalled.

She'd gotten to see Cal nearly every day. He was going to college in the fall as well, so they wanted to make the most of the time they had.

The day they'd made the cookies was the first time. They'd been fumbling, bumbling teens thinking they were grown-ups.

Fools. Her mind whispered the word. They'd been so anxious, so inexperienced, they'd never thought about protection or consequences. She remembered a fleeting thought of it not really mattering. They were going to get married anyway.

His mother's urgings to do just that when she'd shared the cookie recipe with Addie hadn't helped. Not that Elizabeth had been at fault, but Addie had latched on to the complicit approval.

She'd been on top of the world—in love, college ahead and then…the accident. Cal's death had been an end, but only the beginning of her pain. She still remembered the horror she'd felt when she'd figured out she was pregnant. Alone. Without him. So lost. Pain cut through her.

The darkness of the rest threatened to overwhelm her. *No.* She refused to think about the pain, the loss, the hurt that followed. She couldn't. It could easily destroy her.

The reliable coping mechanism she'd learned then worked now, too. She pictured a box, pictured herself pushing all the memories and emotions into it, then closing the lid—and forgetting.

Sitting there, in the chair that was so special to her, holding the wooden wand her father had made for her, brought his last words back to her. She let herself remember safer, less painful times.

He'd been working in his shop yet again, and she'd been mad at some sibling for something— she couldn't remember now.

"You're the oldest, Addie-girl. You have to be the responsible one." He'd kept sanding the piece of wood he was working on. "I'm counting on you to be a good girl and take care of them."

Had he been prophetic, or were those the words he'd have said to his oldest daughter anyway?

If only she could go back to that little girl, go back and change everything. Keep her dad with her so she could ask him. Be the good girl he'd expected of her.

She'd tried so hard. She'd taken care of them all. "Sorry, Daddy. I let you down," she whispered into the night.

MARCUS DROVE AROUND the streets for nearly an hour. Then sat in the parking lot of a twenty-four-hour pharmacy for another half hour, arguing with himself.

He drove home just as the sun was hinting that it would soon peek over the horizon. Driving by Addie's house again, he forced his foot to stay on the accelerator and not shift over to the brake. All the lights were off, her house closed up and dark.

She was probably sound asleep, though he gave the engine an extra shot of gas just to make sure he kept going.

He pulled into the drive as the first rays of sunshine reflected at him in the rearview mirror.

He leaned his head back on the seat and tried to force his eyes to stay open. It wasn't an easy task.

Slowly, he climbed out of the Jeep and headed

inside. The scent of fresh-brewed coffee greeted him. Dread followed on his tail. His dad had always been an early riser. He wasn't up to an argument this early in the day.

He was surprised when his mother was the one sitting at the kitchen table. This was the mom he liked best. She hadn't put on her makeup yet, her hair was down instead of wound up in some fancy do, and she was wearing a familiar, worn robe. She held a cup of coffee in her hand, and the damned book lay open in front of her.

"When did you get this?" she asked, spearing him with one of those Mom's-been-waiting-up-half-the-night looks.

He headed for the coffee. He wasn't going to get any sleep yet. He had a class in—he glanced at his watch—three and a half hours. Final projects were due. Today the presentations for those projects were also due. He almost groaned.

"I asked you a question."

"I know. Give me a minute to wake up." He drank the coffee black, hoping it sped into his veins.

"Are you sober?" She asked another question before he could even begin to answer the first.

"Yes, I'm sober," he snapped, then after another swallow of caffeine, he walked over to stand beside her. He put his hand on her shoulder. "I'm fine, Mom," he said softly. He gave her shoulder a squeeze, then slid into the chair beside her. "I don't drink anymore. I promised you all that. I'm actually getting on with my life."

"What does this have to do with either of those things?" She waved at the book.

"Not much, actually, which is why I haven't read it yet." He closed the cover and pushed it toward his computer. "I met Sam Tilton last year. He wrote it. When he passed away a few months ago, his son sent it to me."

She nodded, and some of the tension went out of her face. "I know you're a grown man. Heavens, you've been one for some time, but I can't stop being your mom." She tried to smile.

He liked that she smiled. Meant he wasn't in too much trouble. "Still, you can't help but want to know where I've been all night."

"Yeah. That." She was uncomfortable; he could see that. She rose and went to the coffeepot to refresh her cup. "You need any more?"

"Probably later. I need to get to the university soon." He drank another healthy swig, formulating his thoughts. "I went over to see Addie. I didn't want her—" Want her to what? "To be upset by earlier."

Donna smiled again, returning to her seat. She covered her hand with his. "I'm sorry for our timing. I'd have liked to visit with her a bit more."

"I hope you can." He'd like that, too. "She's—"

How did he describe this woman who'd suddenly come into his life when he wasn't even sure what his life was? "Different. Ryan thinks she's great. She actually grew up in this house with her five brothers and sisters."

"Oh, my." Donna looked around. "This house *is* made for a good-sized family. I can see that."

"Yeah. Unfortunately, I think that's what Ryan's hoping for."

"That you'll find someone for you, or find him a new mom?"

"I'm not sure. He misses Carolyn. I do, too, sometimes."

"Just sometimes?"

Guilt washed over him, but if there was one person he couldn't lie to, it was his mom. "I think I'm actually moving on, Mom. And Addie's a big part of that." He stared into the coffee, realizing he needed to eat something or his stomach would be burning. "When Carolyn died, I planned to spend the rest of my life alone. I couldn't imagine anyone else."

"Oh, Marcus, I don't want you alone for the rest of your life. Neither did Carolyn. You, and Ryan, are too young for that."

"I know." He smiled at her. "And Addie's shown me that was grief, not logic, thinking. I'll always love Carolyn, but—" He wasn't sure what he felt.

"But?" she prompted.

"But I know I can love someone else, and not be unfaithful to Carolyn. She told me to move on and find someone."

"But you were too stubborn to listen." At his laugh, she reached over and gave him a much-needed hug. "I know my boy. I raised you, you know."

"Yeah, you did." He hugged her back. "Thanks, Mom." He stood and put his cup in the sink. "Everything okay with you?"

"You mean with your dad home?" She hid behind the coffee cup.

"Yeah."

She hesitated. "It's an adjustment." She set her cup down and met his gaze straight on. "It'll take time. Give us that." Marcus nodded and moved away.

"Marcus?" she asked softly.

"Yeah?"

"After you've read that book—" she waved at the table in general "—let's finish this discussion, okay?"

He wasn't sure what she meant, but he knew his mother didn't say or ask for things that were frivolous. He'd respect her request. "Sounds like a plan. And now I've got to get a shower and head to class."

"Did you get any sleep?"

"Nope. And not because of what you think. I

was driving around most of the night." He headed to the stairs. "Those projects better be danged good today, or I'm going to suffer."

It sounded good to hear his mother's laughter follow him up the stairs.

CHAPTER ELEVEN

ADDIE OPENED HER eyes to the fading darkness and the glow of her phone screen. Curiosity wasn't going to let her roll over and go back to sleep. Neither would the memories of last night. Burying her face in the pillow, she groaned in frustration. Had Marcus managed to sleep any better than she had?

Her phone's ding signaled a text. She reached out and turned the phone toward her. DJ's text made her heart trip.

Headed to the hospital. It's baby time!

He'd sent it to them all, and just like her, her siblings were now awake. The responses came quick and predictable.

Drive careful.

From Wyatt.

Yippee!

From Tara.

No more sleep for you.

From Mandy. Jason was in LA, so Addie didn't expect a response from him yet. They would expect one from her.

Her mind was blank, and she tried to blame it on still being half-asleep. She stared at the phone. Memories of another long-ago night tried to crowd in. Memories she'd worked so hard to pack away.

Addie typed, Keep us posted.

She added one of those happy-face emoji symbols that represented something she didn't really feel. Was it easier to fake emotions or lie nowadays?

She'd just put her phone on the nightstand when another soft ding sounded. Jason had sent a whole string of smiley faces. That was all. It was enough.

DJ and Tammie had decided to come to Austin to have the baby. It was a smart decision. Haskins Corners had a small hospital, but if there were any complications, they'd send Tammie here. DJ wouldn't even consider taking any risks.

After a couple of more dings, Addie gave up. They'd be chatting all day now. Sunlight was peeping over the horizon, and sleep wouldn't return. She knew that.

The same had happened when Mandy had had Lucas. The phone calls and texts. The waiting. The baby plans.

The painful reminders.

Lack of sleep made the barriers she'd erected weak, brought the should-haves back.

Slowly, Addie padded over to the closet and pulled down the lone box on the top shelf. This was probably a bad idea. But she needed to face the sadness. Needed to remember for just a few minutes, so she could close it all up again.

She couldn't afford to be blindsided later.

This box wasn't make-believe. It was painfully real. The pale blue box was as pristine as the day she'd bought it. She'd touched it so few times. The old card shop in Haskins Corners where she'd bought it was long gone now, but the price sticker with their name was still on the bottom. She carefully lifted the lid.

Cal's face startled her, as it always did. She gasped. He stared at her, that broad smile and sparkling eyes so real in the picture. It captured exactly who he'd been.

She moved the picture and all the other memorabilia of their summers together. Movie tickets. Carnival trinkets. The memorial folder from his funeral was the worse for wear. Tear stained and crumpled from her sweaty hands.

Then, there on the bottom, were the two things

she'd been seeking. A folded piece of paper and the hospital band.

She touched the white plastic band she'd cut off her arm when she'd gotten home. The final thing she'd done that severed all the ties.

Then she reached for the paper. She wasn't supposed to have it, but it was only a copy. The original birth certificate was sealed in a court file somewhere.

The paper crackled loudly as she unfolded it. Baby Boy Hawkins. Date and time, weight and length. Below that in some stranger's precise handwriting—Mother: Addie Elaina Hawkins. Father: Calvin Michael Ferguson.

Time vanished as she read it over and over again. She blinked hard to chase away the hurt of losing Cal and of his never knowing, of the goodbyes she'd never really gotten to say.

For a brief instant, she let herself think about the what-ifs, the maybes, the should-haves. Finally, she whispered the word she'd never really said. "Goodbye."

Addie knew she'd done the right thing when she'd signed the final adoption papers. That part had never hurt. Too much else had.

Hadn't Marcus mentioned that Ryan was adopted? That Carolyn hadn't been able to conceive? The small comfort that came with knowing her baby had given something—to a couple like Carolyn and Marcus—to another couple somewhere helped. A little.

Suddenly, she missed Marcus. Missed the comfort his company gave her.

Carefully, Addie put everything away as it had been and slid the box into its spot on the shelf. She wiped the tears away and took a deep breath. It still hurt like hell, but it didn't destroy her anymore.

Something felt different this time. Instead of the image of Cal's face clinging to her thoughts, she saw Marcus's face smiling at her. Dare she look to a future?

Shaking her head to clear her thoughts, Addie squared her shoulders, and just like every other time before, she closed the closet door, and shut it all away.

People were counting on her, and she had to give them her best. DJ and Tammie were expecting the happy, doting aunt. And their new little one deserved that. The kids at school expected the principal to have her act together. The end of the school year was approaching. So much going on. They deserved a proper send-off to the rest of their lives.

And, damn it—that was what she was going to give them.

IT WAS NEARLY noon before Addie's phone rang. She'd just sat at the table in the teachers' lounge with a sandwich and a soda. "Hello?" she anxiously answered.

"Ad. She's here. She's perfect," her brother DJ, the former marine, and one of the toughest guys she'd ever known, whispered in awe over the phone.

She laughed despite the sharp pain in her chest. "Of course, she is." The thought of a little girl in the family made the pain not quite so sharp. "She's a Hawkins."

That made him laugh. "Rachel Ann Hawkins to be precise." His pride came loud and clear through the phone. "She's going to rule the world."

"I'll remind you that you said that when she's about fifteen. How's Tammie? And Tyler?" Everyone was fine, and the details he shared helped them both focus on the less emotional piece of a brand-new baby coming into the world.

"Are you coming to see her?" he asked.

"I— When are you heading home?"

"Tomorrow. Since we're so far out in the country, the doc wants to make sure everyone's perfect before we leave. Tara and Mandy are here. Wyatt's on his way in." Other than Jason and his wife, who were in Los Angeles, everyone was there. They expected her there, too.

She swallowed. She could do this. She had to do this. "I'll come after work, then. And DJ, congrats. You're a wonderful dad."

Last night's memories of their father came

back. She couldn't wait to share the wand with her siblings. She'd show them once everyone was settled, and Rachel Ann had finished with her time in the spotlight.

An hour later, her phone rang again, and Addie jumped. She wasn't expecting Marcus to call. Really, she wasn't. When it was Tara's number on the screen, she nearly panicked. Was something wrong?

"Nothing's wrong, Addie," Tara said before she could even ask. "But we've been sitting here talking."

"We?" She was obviously at the hospital. Addie could hear familiar voices in the background.

"Yeah. Since we've got everyone here, and Jason and Lauren are coming in this weekend—"

"They are?"

"Yeah. Don't you read your texts?"

"Not during school. Not exactly a good example for the principal to break the rules."

"Oh, yeah. I guess that makes sense." She paused to explain the delay in Addie's response to the others. "Well, we didn't get to the baby shower since little Miss Cute Britches here came nearly two weeks early. So, we thought we'd do a shower this weekend."

"Little miss what?"

"You heard me. We thought we'd kill several birds with one stone. The guys want to go to a horse auction on Saturday, and Mandy needs to start dress shopping. So, we thought we'd have the shower, too."

Suspicion crept into Addie's mind. "Okay..." She waited for the rest. There was definitely more. "What?"

"Well, we were thinking we could have it at your place."

Her place? What if Marcus came back? What if he wanted her and she had a house full of family? What if he didn't come back? He hadn't said he'd come back. Addie leaned her forehead on her palm. She was losing her mind.

"Addie, are you okay?" Tara's voice was filled with concern. "I should have thought. Have you recovered from being so sick? I didn't think—"

"No. No, I'm fine." Addie shook herself out of her own thoughts. "I was just distracted. Of course, you can have it at my place. Sounds like fun."

If Marcus came by, she'd just explain he was a neighbor. If he didn't? Well, this would distract her. Besides, she reminded herself, his parents were visiting. Weren't they from Chicago? They'd be here longer than a day or two. Wouldn't they? She knew so little about him, really. And yet, in her kitchen with her legs wrapped around his waist, she hadn't thought about any of that. She'd just wanted to—

"Addie? Did you hear anything I just said?"

"Sorry. Hey, I've got to go. I'll come by the hospital when I get out of here. We can talk then."

"Okay."

Her sister didn't sound convinced. She'd have to show her she was fine. "I've got to see my new niece, too." And she'd have to make sure Marcus stayed out of her head. The man was just too distracting.

The fact that her phone didn't ring the rest of the day was a plus. Wasn't it?

"YOU LOOK LIKE you pulled an all-nighter, Professor," Mitch, the thorn in Marcus's side, said from the third row.

"Still made it to class on time, though." The class laughed, and Marcus watched a couple of the boy's buddies nudge him. Mitch had been late for class again, and unfortunately, it was going to cost him a grade. Too bad. He was a smart student.

"Okay, let's get started. We've got a lot to get through today. Mitch, since you're so happy to be here, let's start with you."

The boy groaned, but managed to give his presentation. Marcus's head was already pounding, and the monotone voice nearly put him to sleep. And this was just the beginning.

Two hours later, the last presentation for the day was up. It was Natalie, the girl who'd asked to write about fashion. Mitch snickered, and Marcus already gave her points for having to put up with him. "Go ahead, Natalie. Mitch, unless you've got something to *add*?"

"No, sir." The boy sank down in his seat, not so much chastised as to show he wasn't interested. At this point, Marcus's head felt like it was going to split in two and he was struggling to stay awake. He wanted this finished, and the longer Mitch delayed her getting started, the worse it felt.

"My presentation is on the fashions of Vietnam, and America. I focused on one specific area, where the two collided. The black market and how clothing contributed to the atmosphere of protests, both here and in Vietnam."

Natalie surprised Marcus, and most of the class, all except Mitch, but he didn't really care anyway. Her presentation was fast-paced, interesting and unique. She showed slides of teens in Vietnam wearing American clothing that had been outlawed. She showed photos of the protests all over the United States, similar clothing worn for similar protests.

Her final slide was of a young girl on a motor scooter, also outlawed at the time. Youth. Protests. Fashion.

As he looked at the photo, something about it looked familiar. Just like in Addie's kitchen last night, when he'd noticed the chair spindles and recognized the similarity to the wand, this picture sparked something in his memory. He was too tired to put the pieces together.

"And that, people, is how you get an A in this class. You might take note, Mitch." Marcus walked to the front of the classroom. "The rest of you be ready to present next class. And those of you who've already presented, remember you owe your classmates an audience. Automatic point deduction for any absence."

They all groaned, which he ignored. The rules had been laid out early in the semester. This wasn't news to any of them.

"Natalie, can I have a minute of your time?"

"Uh…sure." She retraced her steps. "Is something wrong?"

"Not at all. You did a great job. I'm not kidding about the A. I'm curious about that last picture. I assume you credited your source in the paperwork you turned in?" Maybe if he looked at that, he'd figure out what the nagging in his brain was.

"I did. Just like the example you gave us. I sent it to your email."

"I got it, thanks. I just—" She was probably the last person he should talk to about this. "It just rang a bell, but I can't remember why it looks familiar."

"I checked the book out from the university library. Maybe you saw it before."

"Maybe that's it." He had read nearly every book on Vietnam that was out there. That was probably it. "Thanks, Natalie." He smiled at her, and she followed her classmates out the door. She stopped just before leaving, and waved at him.

Maybe she was right, and he'd simply seen the image in a book before. Why, then, didn't he think that was the case? Maybe he just needed to get some sleep.

WITHOUT KNOCKING, OR ASKING, Lindy came into Addie's office and plopped into one of the chairs. Addie didn't look up immediately. For one, the task she'd been trying to focus on for nearly an hour was not cooperating, and two, she wasn't sure she wanted to know why Lindy was here.

"You can't ignore me forever," Lindy said.

"Yes, I can." She finally looked up at her friend and sighed. "What's up?"

"I was going to ask you the same thing." Lindy had a grin on her face that made Addie think twice about telling her anything. "Is there anything you want to share with me?" She wiggled her eyebrows in an exaggerated gesture.

Addie wasn't falling for that trick. It worked only *after* she'd had a glass of wine—or two. "Uh, let me see? I have a new niece. Tammie and DJ had their baby yesterday."

"That's not what I meant, and you know it." Lindy actually looked disappointed.

"Then what do you mean?"

"Oh, I dunno." Lindy rolled her eyes. "There are some interesting rumors circulating out there." She tilted her head toward the halls. "Very interesting, indeed."

"Rumors about what?"

"About you." Lindy's grin widened. "And a certain new student's hunky dad."

Addie groaned and looked at the paperwork she'd been struggling with. She barely resisted the urge to cover her face with her hands. When she finally leaned back in her chair, and met Lindy's gaze, a shiver of panic shot through her. "How bad?" she whispered. Was she going to hear from the school board soon? Sweat filled her palms and snaked down her spine.

Lindy laughed. "Oh, nothing to panic over. Just enough to make me curious—and wonder why you aren't sharing details with your best friend. So, come on. Give."

"Shh…" Addie shot to her feet and quickly closed the door. "There's nothing to tell. Not…really." Memories of Marcus's late-night visit to her house, after his parents interrupted them, weren't that big of a deal. The heat in her cheeks made a liar out of her.

"Ha! There's something behind that blush.

Come on. I deserve details after I practically set you two up at the dance."

"You didn't set us up." Maybe she'd made it easier for Addie and Marcus to connect, but it wasn't a setup.

"So, my spending the rest of the evening with Jack Wilson didn't do you any good?" There wasn't a drop of regret in Lindy's voice, and Addie looked more closely at her friend.

"I didn't say that." She didn't want Lindy to think she didn't appreciate her effort.

"I knew it. You two did hook up!"

"We didn't…hook up." She hated that term. It sounded so…sordid. And what she and Marcus had wasn't sordid at all, it was sweet…and wonderful…and like nothing she'd ever felt before.

"Yoo-hoo." Lindy snapped her fingers in front of Addie's face. "Where'd you drift off to?"

Addie might have been irritated by Lindy's grin, if she didn't know she was right. "Stop it." She returned to looking at the scattered pages of what had been one of the teacher's end-of-year review. Right now she couldn't even remember whose. She pulled the papers together, hoping the action would distract Lindy—and herself.

Once she'd set the straightened stack, she looked up into Lindy's grin.

"Oh, you are in so much trouble."

"What do you mean?"

"You don't even know how far you've fallen." Lindy laughed. "Not a clue." She rubbed her hands together in mock glee. "This is going to be such fun."

"Cut it out." Addie gathered the file folders and continued straightening her already-organized desk. Whom was she trying to distract? Lindy or herself?

Lindy hopped to her feet, hopefully realizing she wasn't going to get any more information out of Addie. "Okay, but either you tell me, or I'll have to rely on the grapevine to get my gossip."

"There's nothing to tell."

"If you say so." Lindy stopped at the doorway. "Don't say I didn't warn you."

Was that laughter Addie heard coming back through the open door? She hated when Lindy was right.

BY SATURDAY AFTERNOON, Addie was exhausted. One night of little sleep had turned into two, then three. She kept waiting for the phone to ring. When it didn't, she debated about calling Marcus.

But his parents were still there, a fact she'd learned from Ryan when she'd seen him at school yesterday. She'd wait until they were gone.

When Saturday came, Girls' Night turned into Girls' Day. Mandy needed a wedding dress and bridesmaids' dresses—and a million other things.

And everyone wanted to play with little Rachel Ann and Lucas.

No baby shower had ever been done quite like this.

Addie stared at her not-as-big-as-she'd-like living room. Mandy was setting up chairs while Lucas snoozed on his favorite blanket in the spare bedroom. Tara was in the kitchen putting the final touches on enough food to feed the entire ranch, and Tammie snuggled in the big recliner with the baby in her arms.

Looking at Tammie, and the cozy mama-baby scene, Addie spun around and went to help Tara. She could take only so much. "Do we have enough?" She looked at her dining room table, her sarcasm strong as she feared it might buckle under the weight.

"Very funny," Tara said from the stove. "This was a brilliant idea."

"What? The party or the food?"

"Both. Combining everything. Today's been a blast."

"And waiting until after the kids are born to party, so we can all drink," Tammie said from the other room.

"Yes," Lauren signed before reaching for the Riesling and shoving the corkscrew into the cork. "Great idea." They were all learning sign language, but it was a slow process.

Thankfully, Lauren was patient, and a pro at reading lips. Her sense of humor fit right in with the rest of them.

The only one missing was Emily, who'd had a last-minute call from the court house. Being a judge in family court was a career she loved, but it occupied a lot of her time.

She'd called Mandy when they were leaving the dress shop, and swore she'd be here in time for the food. She'd just called to say she was on her way. It sounded like she'd be ready for a drink when she got here.

Finally, the food was all set, the wine poured and, other than Emily, everyone had a seat in the living room. No silly games at this shower. Tonight was about serious escape.

And opening presents. At least that part Addie looked forward to. Her siblings *loved* the noise-making toys she was famous for giving.

Emily came barreling in just then. "Sorry. I'd have been here sooner, but traffic sucked."

"I'll get you a glass of wine," Tara offered and headed to the kitchen.

"Uh, no thanks. I'll just take water or a soda, no caffeine, please."

Every woman in the room did a double take and stared at her. Frazzled Emily always needed a glass of wine.

She blushed. "I guess what you guys have is

contagious." She shrugged and beamed at them all. Though Emily slowly signed for Lauren, she didn't really need to. Lauren's expression showed she understood and was as happy as the rest of them that another baby was on the way.

Addie stared at the women of her family. The children of her brothers and sisters were all here, except for Tyler, who'd decided to go to the auction with the men, much to DJ's delight. He hadn't wanted anything to do with "girl or baby stuff."

Addie almost wished she had gone to the auction, too. Thankfully, the wine helped. She took a gulp, washing down the emotions she didn't dare acknowledge right now. In the kitchen a short while later, she couldn't stop her thoughts from turning to Marcus and the events of the other night.

The old chair from Mom's house was still in the corner. She still hadn't told anyone about the wooden wand. And now didn't seem the time— especially when she recalled what had almost happened between her and Marcus. She wasn't sure she could hide her emotions.

With the way the women in her family were procreating, there was no way the fates would have let her off the hook for not using protection.

"What are you thinking about?" Mandy asked, looking up from filling her plate.

Addie blushed and shook her head. She was

close to her sisters, but she wasn't sharing. "I'll tell you later," she said, deciding she'd share the information about the wand instead.

The sound of running footsteps startled her. She looked out the front picture window just in time to see Ryan racing up the steps. She almost beat the doorbell.

"Ryan, what's the matter?" He sucked in breath, and his face was flushed red from running.

"Dad. And Grandpa." He panted.

"Where's your grandmother?"

"She—" He tried to catch his breath. "Went to get her nails done." He panted some more. "I think they're gonna kill each other!"

CHAPTER TWELVE

MELODRAMA WAS THE weapon of choice for the thirteen-year-olds of Addie's everyday world. Right now, she was thankful she was used to it. "Okay, calm down. We'll take care of everything." Principal Hawkins came forward easily, even in a room full of her family. "Everyone?" She turned Ryan to face the room, as much to head off the questions as to give him another minute to catch his breath. "This is Ryan Skylar. He's, uh, one of the students at my school. Ryan, this is my family. My sisters. My sisters-in-law."

The women said hello, though Addie could clearly see their confusion. Why was a student coming to her house? She wasn't going to enlighten them. Her concern was with Marcus and if he was okay.

"You gotta help. I don't know what to do," Ryan pleaded.

"All right." He really was upset, and without someone to intervene, she wasn't sure what would happen. She didn't know Marcus's father, and she'd never seen Marcus angry. "I'll be back as soon as I can," she told the room and followed Ryan outside.

He'd obviously run over, but he was finally breathing normal again. "Why didn't you call?" she asked.

"I did. You didn't answer." He hurried, and she could tell he thought they should run. "I knew you were here."

"Sorry. I probably didn't hear my phone with everyone talking." She was disappointed in herself. She hated letting anyone down.

"No problem. You're here now."

Marcus's Jeep wasn't in the drive, like normal. For that matter, there weren't any cars parked at the house. Ryan didn't seem to notice, so she followed him inside.

The woman she'd been introduced to a couple of days ago, Donna Skylar, sat at the kitchen table looking a bit lost.

Ryan came to a skidding halt. "Where'd they go?" he asked.

"I got here just as they left," Donna said. "Your dad said he was going to his office. I'm not sure where your grandfather went." And it was almost like she didn't care. Almost. The shadows in her eyes told Addie she was as worried as Ryan.

"Oh." Ryan looked confused and his worry deflated. "Did they fight?"

Donna shook her head. "No, dear. They don't

usually get that far. One, or both of them, walks out. They'll be fine." She shook her head, and the sympathy for Ryan that reflected in her eyes was deep.

He turned and looked at Addie. "Guess I didn't need to come get you. Sorry. I messed up your party."

"No problem. You didn't mess up anything." She gave him a one-armed hug. "You know I'm always here for you."

He nodded and glanced at his grandmother. "They were really mad. I didn't know when you'd be back. So, I went to Addie's."

Donna sighed. "They usually are. You did the right thing," she reassured him.

Ryan's phone chimed, and he pulled it out of his pocket. "It's Dex. He's my best friend," he explained to his grandmother. "He wants to know if I can come over tonight." He stood there, indecisive. "Dad's not here to ask."

"You go ahead with your plans, dear. Don't let those two pigheaded fools ruin your fun."

Ryan's faint smile of relief showed how stressed he was with the adults in his life. "Thanks, Grandma."

Addie stood there for a minute after Ryan left, not sure what she should do. She had a house full of guests, but she felt guilty leaving the woman alone. Pulling one of the chairs out, she sat. She could afford a few minutes, at least, to be polite.

"I'm not trying to pry. Ryan was worried. He said they were arguing."

Donna sighed. "Unfortunately, that's probably true. They've never gotten along. Too much alike, I think."

"Oh." Addie wasn't sure about that. She had no idea what to say to the other woman. "I guess I'll be going, then." Addie stood.

Donna looked up, watching her. "So, how exactly did you meet my son?"

Donna didn't beat around the bush. Addie got the impression nothing short of the truth would satisfy her.

"Ryan got into a fight at school. It's standard procedure to call the parents into my office." Addie shrugged.

The older woman frowned. "That doesn't sound like Ryan."

"I didn't think so, either. But he had the black eye to prove it."

"Humpfh," was all Donna said. Just then, Ryan came into the kitchen, his backpack slung over one shoulder. "Ryan?" Donna called to him.

The boy already had the refrigerator door open. "Yeah?"

"Why did you get into a fight at school?"

Ryan froze. Addie watched, intrigued. She'd

managed to get the basics about the fight, but she'd never gotten the details about what Nick had done to instigate it. She did know it had been Nick, not Ryan, who'd started it.

"Uh, I don't, uh, remember." Ryan focused on the contents of the refrigerator.

"Oh, my dear." Donna shook her head. "I know you better than that."

For the first time in a while, Addie felt like the principal again instead of a neighbor, or even a friend. The way Ryan's gaze darted warily over his shoulder toward her didn't sit well. He looked afraid of getting into trouble again. She *was* still his principal, at least for a few more weeks.

Still, this was private and not her business. "I'll leave you two to chat."

"Oh, that won't be necessary, dear." The older woman put a light restraining hand on Addie's arm. "If Ryan's like the other men in my family, you have to stand your ground with them. Keep pushing or they'll avoid answering."

The poor kid looked trapped, and for a minute, Addie struggled with her own dilemma. Was she taking advantage of the situation? Did it really matter why Ryan and Nick had gotten into the fight? They'd managed to stay out of each other's way the past few weeks, and they'd both done their detention time.

"If you stick around long enough—" Donna

looked at Addie, completely ignoring Ryan, or so it seemed, although Addie got the impression the woman probably had eyes in the back of her head "—you'll learn about the Skylar men. They are stubborn, determined and, at times, unforgiving. It's what makes them so good at what they do—but not so great in relationships."

Was she talking about James or Marcus? If they weren't great at relationships, why had she and James stayed married?

"I see wheels turning in your head. You are an inquisitive one. Good, good. Marcus needs someone who challenges him."

"I—" Addie didn't want to bring up Ryan's mother. "I got the impression he was happily married. And you've been married quite a while." How did that translate into bad at relationships?

"Have you ever been married?"

"Uh, no."

"That explains it. Marriage is really just two very flawed people who decide they can put up with each other better than anyone else."

Addie frowned, thinking of the only long-term marriage she knew, her own parents. They'd been in love, and hadn't just been *putting up with* each other.

"Ah, I see you believe in the fairy tales." Donna shook her head and stood. The soft click of the front door closing didn't even seem to surprise her. "And just like the other two, he's snuck out. Well, he'll be back. They always come back." The sadness in the woman's voice surprised Addie.

She knew she was taking chances, but with a clear conscience, she couldn't leave the woman here alone. She looked sad and lost. "Would you like to go to a baby shower?"

THE HOUSE WAS ablaze with light and laughter when Addie walked in with Donna. The older woman didn't frown or look disapproving, as Addie had expected. She actually looked interested in everything that was going on.

After being introduced to everyone, she made a beeline for Rachel Ann, who was awake for the first time that Addie had seen her. Her big blue eyes stared at Donna with a one-week-old's fascination with the entire world.

"May I hold her?" she gently asked Tammie.

Tammie smiled. "I'm sure she'd be thrilled."

Carefully, Donna slipped her hands beneath the tiny girl, supporting her neck and snuggling her in the crook of her arm. In a long-remembered rhythm, she gently rocked back and forth. "Oh, I haven't done this in so long." She smiled and the features that Addie had previously thought reserved and stiff softened. "I used to love to rock Marcus when he was tiny."

She made cute faces at the little girl, then

looked up and caught Addie's gaze. "Carolyn was a bit of a paranoid mother. She didn't want anyone to expose poor Ryan to anything, so we were barely allowed to touch him." Her voice was distant. Her eyes even more so. "I didn't realize how much I missed it."

"Ryan seems pretty well-adjusted," Addie commented.

"That's because Marcus ignored all her demands." Donna laughed, seemingly proud of her son. "I told you, the Skylar men can be very single-minded." She cooed at the baby. "Makes for rough relationships, though." At her repeated admonishment, even Tammie gave the woman a frown before meeting Addie's stare.

Addie sipped the wine she'd poured herself, listening and pondering. "Would you like a glass, Donna?"

Donna looked at her, surprised. She paused a long minute before saying anything. "I—I believe I will. Something sweet?" She looked at Rachel Ann. "Sweet like this little bundle of joy?"

As Addie poured the wine, she remembered Marcus's revelation of how he'd coped with Carolyn's death. How had that affected Donna. She was curious when Donna agreed to the drink. She wondered if she should have resisted the offer.

"Who is she?" Tara came up behind Addie and whispered.

"She's Marcus's—" Then she remembered no one knew who Marcus was. "She's Ryan's grandmother. The boy who was here earlier."

Tara wasn't convinced. "So, who's Marcus?" She crossed her arms and waited, spearing Addie with an intense stare.

"Uh, Ryan's father."

"Uh-huh." She nodded slowly. "And how well do you know him? Them?"

Addie didn't say a word. What was she supposed to say? The images in her mind were not for public consumption. The blush she felt creeping up her cheeks, however, spoke loud and clear.

MARCUS STARED OUT the window of his office. Lights were coming on around the campus, and he could see the silhouettes of students against the setting sun as they moved about. Not in the hurried pace of the school week, but the relaxed weekend pace.

His office was quiet. The whole building was silent. He was pretty sure he was the only person in the whole place. Not like anyone normally came here on Saturday.

He shouldn't have gotten upset with his dad. But James had always known how to push his buttons. He didn't do it on purpose, Marcus knew. He just had a talent.

His mother's timing had been perfect. Ryan had

retreated to his room, and Marcus knew he had to get out of there. Driving by Addie's place, he'd seen the cars and guests filling her house.

His disappointment had multiplied, and he'd kept on driving.

The familiar ding of his phone had him digging through the clutter on his desk. It was Ryan.

Grandma said I could come over to Dex's. Gonna play games for a while.

That was probably a good idea. Marcus texted back.

What's your grandmother doing? Grandfather back?

He wasn't sure he wanted to know the last.

Don't know if he's back.Grandma's with Addie.

What? Did he really want to know how that happened?

Thanks. Go have fun.

He ended the session with his son and thumbed the screen to find a different number. Should he text her? Was Addie too busy? Was his mother telling stories? Was Addie?

He groaned and typed: Hi.

If she didn't answer he'd head home and make sure everything was okay.

She quickly answered.

Hi yourself.

She'd included a little smiley face. He couldn't help but smile back, then felt like a fool.

Everything okay? Ryan says Mom's with you.

She's having fun. Playing with my new niece.

Congratulations.

He didn't know what else to say. Addie didn't need to babysit his mother. She must have taken his mom back to her place. He should go pick her up and keep her entertained. The risk of running into his father was more than he was ready for right now, though.

Thanks. Busy here with all the family. Call me later?

His heart sped up. A phone call was not what he

wanted, but it was all he dared hope for. Memories of the other night rushed in, and he struggled to push them away.

Sure.

He hit Send, then typed some more.

Let me know and I'll come pick up Mom.

She sent a smiley face but that was all. He tried not to feel disappointed, and failed.

SCHOOL WAS DRAWING to a close. Addie was busy with end-of-year events, and Marcus was preparing for finals week. It was, to say the least, not a time for them to get together.

But her conversation with Ryan kept haunting her. She got the impression things were strained in their household. And she had something to do with it.

Addie hadn't been to the coffee shop in weeks. The summer crowd filled up most of the inside as they tried to find air-conditioning to drink their hot drinks. She laughed and ordered a tall iced tea. Soon, she was settled outside under a wide umbrella where a semi-cool breeze helped cut the threatening heat.

"You really think you can finish that book this time?" Marcus's voice came over her shoulder.

"Apparently not." She leaned her head back and was surprised when he planted a quick kiss on her lips.

He moved around the table and grabbed the other seat. "Mind if I join you?"

"Depends. Do you have work to get done?"

"Probably." He grinned at her and determinedly opened his backpack. "Finals are next week. I need to get everything else finished before that."

"Then you should probably sit over there. Way over there." She exaggerated the wave of her hand and smiled.

"Yeah, that ain't happening."

"I'm trying to be good here." She lifted her book and stared at the page. "Don't blame me when you have to pull an all-nighter." She glanced over the top of the book and noted the flush that swept up his rough cheeks. "What?"

His sheepish grin only made her more curious. He glanced at the others sitting around them, then leaned toward her. "You don't want me to explain."

"That's so unfair. Tease."

"Okay, but don't say I didn't warn you. The night after I was at your place?" At her nod, he continued, "My class noticed how tired I was and gave me grief about pulling an all-nighter."

"Oh." She felt an answering blush sweep up her cheeks. She glanced around to see if anyone had overheard. It didn't look like it. Relief washed over her. She recognized a few parents of students. She ducked behind the book again and pretended to read.

She had to go back a whole chapter and reread it before she remembered what the heck it was about. It didn't help that while Marcus was focusing on his own work, he was sitting right there. The breeze kept carrying the scent of his aftershave to her, taunting her.

Most of his work was on his laptop, but a few of the things were papers. He switched back and forth, occasionally stopping to take a drink from his own iced drink. Her gaze couldn't seem to stay away from him, and watching the muscles of his throat work as he swallowed drew her gaze down, over his broad shoulders, to the thick, muscular arms that had held her tight.

"Keep looking at me like that and I won't be responsible for your never finishing that book." His laugher sent her hastily looking at her page.

"I don't know what you mean." She refused to look at him again.

"Yes, you do." His warm hand settled on her knee beneath the table. Softly, gently, lightly caressing the overly sensitive skin. Who knew a knee could be such an erogenous zone? She sighed, then hastily sat up straighter. "You are a cruel man, Marcus Skylar."

"If you think that was cruel, you haven't seen nothing yet."

She looked up from the book then, despite the promise she'd made to herself that she would not give in. Their gazes met, and the heat pouring from him washed over her. She bit back a sigh—and he shot her a wink.

She was in trouble. Serious trouble. Lindy's laughter from the other day in the office seemed to surround Addie.

"So, can I assume from your good mood that your parents have left?"

"As of bright and early this morning, yes." His smile was relieved. "Don't get me wrong, I love my parents—"

"Even your dad?"

"Yeah, even my dad," he said on a sigh. "I'm thirty-five years old. I've been out of their house for almost as long as I was in it. But they just can't stop trying to tell me what to do."

She wished her parents were around to at least try to boss her around, but she didn't tell him that. "Your mother is worried about you. She really does care."

"I know. We talked quite a bit while she was here. I think we're in a good place." He leaned back in his seat, lifting his drink to take a sip. She tore her eyes away from the movement of his lips.

Silence, not uncomfortable, settled around them. A couple at the next table left, pushing chairs around loudly enough to make conversation a challenge. Two women settled in next.

"Oh, hello, Principal Hawkins," one of the women said, waving.

"Uh, hello. How are you?" She blanked on the woman's name, and her panic must have shown on her face.

Marcus turned to look at the women. He introduced himself. "My son is new this year. Do your kids go there?"

"Yes, yes." The woman smiled overly brightly at him. "I'm Bonnie Lasiter, and this is Marilyn Hill. Our girls are on the pep squad."

Addie loved parents who attached their own identities to their children's accomplishments. And she loved Marcus's last-minute save, though the speculation in both women's eyes wasn't good. "Marcus's son is Ryan Skylar."

Both women shook their heads as though indicating the name wasn't familiar. "We haven't been here long," Marcus explained. "Just moved from Chicago."

"Oh, is your wife involved with any of the parent groups?"

There was a moment of silence. "My wife

passed away a couple years ago." Marcus cleared his throat, and as the women expressed their condolences, he started to pack up his things. Every drop of heat had gone out of his gaze when he looked up again. "Thanks for the company." He looked at Addie and stood, shouldering the backpack. "Ladies, nice to meet you." He walked off in the direction of his house.

"Well, that was interesting," Bonnie said, sipping her coffee and staring at Marcus's retreating back.

"Why do you say that?" Addie asked.

"Oh, nothing important." She met Addie's gaze with a catty glare. "Just something Deidre Silvano said the other day now makes so much more sense."

Addie didn't like where this was going, and Marilyn's startled glare said she didn't, either. "Is there something you need to say, Bonnie?" Addie used her best in-detention/assembly voice.

"Oh, no. Just makes me curious is all." She went back to her coffee and didn't say anything more to Addie. Marilyn sat quietly finishing her own drink.

Addie turned her focus to the book she'd never finish, well aware of the other two women speaking just softly enough that she couldn't hear their words.

Would she never escape the drama and behavior of schoolkids? Did every parent revert to the stage their kids were in life? She sighed and pretended to read until the women left.

MARCUS SAT ON Addie's front step. He'd hoped she'd head back here after the coffee shop. They needed to talk. Finally, he saw her. Across the street, she caught sight of him and stopped, looking at him for a long moment. From this far away, he couldn't read her expression. He swallowed, not sure if he'd done the right thing.

Finally, she came to sit beside him. "Why did you leave?"

Marcus slowly closed his laptop. "I got the impression they were judging you. I never really thought about it. You're the principal at my son's school. Us—uh, dating— Is that a problem?"

"Are we dating?"

He paused for a brief second. Long enough to catch her gaze. "Considering the events in your kitchen the other night? We'd better be."

Addie laughed, a sweet blush slipping over her cheeks. "Um, I guess so." She fiddled with the edge of her book, looking away. "Since Ryan's only been here a couple months, and next year he'll be going to the high school, I don't think it'll be an issue."

"But it could be." He didn't want to cause her

any problems. Her job was important, to her and to the kids. She didn't deserve to lose it.

"Depends on the parents' response, I guess. To be honest, I've never done this before."

"Me, either."

"I've known teachers who've dated parents, but not of kids in their class, and I'm not sure about principals. I guess it could be seen as a conflict of interest. I'll do some checking."

Marcus loved her dedication to her job, her sense of right and wrong. "Do you know how badly I want to kiss you right now?"

"Then do," she whispered.

He glanced around, noting the neighborhood and the too many pairs of eyes that could potentially cause problems for her. "Not here. Too many witnesses."

"I do have an entire house here, private and all," she offered, pushing to her feet. "Would you like to come in?"

The silence of the evening stretched out between them. Finally, Marcus took his time shoving his laptop into his backpack. "Yes, I want to come in, but I'm not going to. Until school's out, we're going to be good."

Addie stopped in the doorway. "What do you mean, *be good*?"

"You know what I mean," he whispered.

"That's what I was afraid of."

TAKING A WALK seemed like the perfect solution to burn off the energy she felt. Addie's phone buzzed in her pocket as she turned the first corner, and she pulled it out. The screen seemed unusually bright in the twilight. "Hello?"

"Hey, sis." Wyatt's voice was loud in the quiet evening.

"Hey, yourself. What's up? How did the auction go?" She hadn't talked to her brothers since before the baby shower.

"Great. We bought some good stock. A couple cow ponies and a beautiful little filly for Dancer."

"So, you're picking out your horse's dates now, huh?"

"Hey, someone's gotta help the guys out."

"Uh-huh." The neighborhood was busy tonight. People out watering lawns, kids zipping by on bikes, dogs barking on the other side of the fences.

"You know Chet's retiring."

"Yeah." It didn't seem possible. Chet had been the ranch foreman since Granddad's day. He was a staple on the ranch. His wife, Juanita, had been the cook nearly as long. "It won't be the same without them." She already missed them.

"Yeah. I'm confident in his replacement. Patrick Thorne is a good man, but it won't be the same, you're right."

"Why are you calling me?"

"Emily and Tara are planning a barbecue to bid them goodbye."

"Sounds like a great idea."

"Yeah, and lots of work. We need everyone's help."

"Count me in." She smiled into the phone, looking forward to everyone being together. She liked Patrick, and she'd heard rumors that there was a new special lady in his life. Lindy's half-joking comment of the ranch being the land of everyone falling in love made her laugh.

"You want to come out for dinner on Sunday? You haven't been out in a while. They want to start planning."

Addie had been avoiding the big, boisterous family dinners lately. She'd wondered who would notice first. She still wasn't in the mood. But she couldn't avoid it forever, not without an explanation. "It has been a while," she admitted. "I've been busy."

There was a long pause before he said, "We'd really love you to come. I think almost everyone will be there. Usual time. Noon."

"Everyone?" That was an accomplishment.

"Yeah. Tara hasn't gotten Morgan out here for the whole-family experience yet. We need to initiate the boy."

Addie groaned. "They aren't married yet. Don't scare him away."

"We couldn't scare him away if we tried."

"Somehow, I think that means you tried."

"DJ did. Have you seen the size of the guy?" Wyatt laughed, admitting nothing and everything. "Besides, the boy's in love."

Things hadn't changed much over the years, even now that everyone was moving on with their lives. Addie laughed.

"What's funny?" Wyatt asked.

"Nothing." She wasn't really interested in talking about her siblings' love lives right now. As she walked another half block, she thought about the wand, and the box of scraps from Dad's garage. She'd take it and surprise them. "I'll bring cookies." She always brought cookies. Everyone got very grumpy if she didn't.

"Great. Make a double batch so there's leftovers."

"And I suppose you'd like them in a separate container so you can just set them aside for yourself."

"Well, that would be convenient."

Addie rolled her eyes. "Okay, I'll be there."

"With my cookies."

"With your cookies."

With only a few more comments, they ended the call, and as Addie pocketed her phone again, the quiet of the evening settled in. It felt good to let the peacefulness wrap around her, soothing her.

Her younger brothers and sisters would all be there. With their spouses and soon-to-be spouses, with their children and all the children that were attached to the people they'd come to love.

Addie looked up and realized that, without thinking, she'd managed to walk to Marcus's house.

CHAPTER THIRTEEN

MARCUS WAS DEFINITELY surprised to find Addie on his front step. A shiver of frustration shot through her when she heard Ryan's and Dex's voices behind him.

"I hope this isn't a bad time." She didn't step forward and give him a kiss, like she longed to do.

"The boys are having a game night." He pulled the door wider. "And yes, I made sure they had their homework done first." He grinned at her. "What are you doing here?"

"I was talking with my brother Wyatt, and I remembered the box of scrap wood from my dad. I want to show everyone the wand and see if there's anything else out there."

"Of course. Come on in." He led the way toward the back door.

"I hope I wasn't interrupting anything."

"Nothing stupendous. Just grading papers. Almost done."

Addie followed him out the back door. The yard looked better than when she'd been here last. The roses were leafing out with several buds threatening to open.

Mom always intended to go out and trim them off, so that a few could be rich and beautiful blooms. She'd never do it, though, loving the bunches of pretty, colorful roses more.

Addie glanced at the honeysuckle vine her mother had loved. Its blooms were full and beautiful, as well. "Mom would have loved that bush this year." She leaned into the leafy vines and inhaled. "Heaven."

The vines that covered the side of the garage were thick. She could barely see the window in the south wall. Dad used to trim them away so he'd have some natural light to work by.

She liked being here. It was like coming home. Shaking her head, she realized Marcus had asked her a question. "What? I'm sorry." She stopped and looked at him instead of the yard.

He smiled. He knew how she felt. They'd talked about it when she'd come by before. "I asked if you wanted me to bring the box into the house, or if out here's okay."

"Out here is fine." The new picnic table he'd put on the patio looked inviting.

"Have a seat, I'll get it."

"I can—" She shut her mouth, mentally reminding herself that she didn't live here anymore.

"Thanks." She sat on the bench and leaned her elbows on the tabletop.

Marcus looked right at home here, and she couldn't help but watch as he headed to the garage. Sunlight fell through the trees and landed on his thick, dark hair and broad shoulders. He wore his usual button-down shirt with jeans. The light blue color looked good on him. She laughed at herself. Whom was she kidding? Everything looked good on him.

"Here it is." He came out of the garage with the cardboard box. She knew it was heavy. She'd tried to move it the other day, finding it wouldn't budge. He carried it easily, but did let it thump down hard on his table.

Addie stood, peering over the edge, hoping she'd find something, afraid she wouldn't. She pulled out wood pieces, examining them, then setting them on the picnic table. Most were just scraps. She'd nearly given up when she reached the last layer of items. She paused.

"Did you find anything?" Marcus asked as he peered into the box, as well.

"I don't know." She pulled out the rough piece of wood. Turning it over, she gasped. A horse. It was undeniably a horse's head. The mane had been carved to follow the grain of the wood. She held it up to him. "It's beautiful."

Marcus nodded and smiled. "Anything else?"

"I hope so." The next piece wasn't finished, but she could tell it was a toy gun. Other pieces emerged, all of them clearly gifts for her siblings. A set of wooden spoons, certainly for Tara. She laughed when she pulled out the shape that resembled a book. Obviously for Jason.

She frowned, not sure what her dad had thought would fit Mandy. She pulled out a box. There were two pieces, not yet hooked together, but she could see where they would fit perfectly. A jewelry box? A treasure box? Either would fit Mandy.

Addie stared at the pieces scattered across the table. "He made something for each of us." She ran a hand over the horse's mane. "He didn't finish them, but he made them." She met Marcus's gaze. "The only one he had time to finish was mine. The wand."

Her eyes clouded, and she dashed the tears away. Dad wouldn't have liked her crying, not even happy tears. He was a man who, despite having daughters and a couple of sisters, hadn't ever been good at dealing with tears.

"He was very talented." Marcus picked up the box, taking it apart and putting it together, like puzzle pieces it fit so well.

"He loved to be in his workshop. We kids always wanted to go inside, but he said he didn't want us to get hurt." She smiled at the memory. "I think he just wanted peace and quiet."

Marcus nodded, picking up the toy gun. "For DJ, I assume."

"When he was little he wasn't sure if he wanted to be a cowboy or a soldier…they both had guns."

"I think this is more a soldier's gun than a six-shooter."

"Yeah. Dad had his opinions, too." She stared at the pieces. "They're going to love these."

"When are you going to tell them?"

She looked at him. "It should be something special. But Christmas is too far off, and their birthdays are too scattered."

"Does it have to be a holiday? Why not just make a normal day special?"

"I guess it doesn't have to be a holiday. I'm going out for Sunday dinner this weekend. That's what made me think of coming here tonight. Guess I'll take them with me."

The silence of the evening stretched out around them, and she savored the distant crickets singing in the bushes and the breeze in the tree branches overhead.

Another thought occurred to her. Should she tell him about Dex, and her conversation with Lindy. But that would ruin it all. She didn't want to, but he'd already been concerned about their relationship affecting her job. "Apparently, Ryan shared some of what's happened between us with Dex."

"What?" Marcus froze, looking at her with a frown.

"Don't get upset with Ryan. He needs to have a friend to talk to." She moved around the table, putting her hand on his arm. "But Dex—" She took a breath. "Has told pretty much everyone at school that you and I are, uh, involved."

Marcus cursed. "I'm sorry, Addie. I never meant to cause you any trouble."

"So far, it's not a problem." She didn't move her hand away from his. "I'm getting some interesting looks from my coworkers, though." Even now, she blushed.

"I'm so—"

She put her finger over his lips to stop his next sentence. "I'm not worried about it. It's more—" *Mortification* wasn't the right word, but she couldn't put another name to her discomfort. She felt her cheeks warm. "It seems kinda silly to be good, if they know anyway," she whispered. She looked into his eyes and saw the flash of desire. Had she just propositioned him? What would he think of her?

He smiled against her hand, and she moved her finger away—or rather down. The roughness of his whiskers tickled her fingertip. She traced the edge of his jaw.

"Addie," he whispered. "I—"

He didn't say any more. She stood on tiptoe

and put her lips to his. He grabbed her, hauling her close.

His kiss was different this time. Harder. Deeper. Hungry. She returned every ounce of the intensity. It seemed like forever since he'd touched her, since she'd been with him.

She leaned into him, grinding her hips into the evidence of his arousal. Her legs grew weak, and the only thing holding her up was him. She wound her arms around his neck, holding tight.

As if some semblance of sanity had returned, he leaned back ever so slightly, and slowed his touch. She whimpered, and he chuckled. "I'm not going anywhere," he whispered. "Except, maybe here." He pressed his lips to the side of her neck. "Or maybe here." He licked the hollow at the base of her throat where her pulse pounded. "Here." He pushed aside the collar of her blouse, his hot breath slipped into the valley between her breasts.

Her nipples tightened, and she gulpedhard. "Marcus, I want you. I need you."

"I know, babe." He gulped in air. "I'm dying here. The boys are in the house. This isn't the place." He cursed. "Any secret places you know about around here?"

She shook her head. "My place," she whispered, nuzzling his neck and kissing his heated skin. She knew as soon as she said it that he wouldn't leave

Ryan alone. And she wouldn't sneak back here after Ryan was asleep.

"I'm starting to understand why teenage boys are so insane." He held her, rubbing his hands up and down her back. "This could drive anyone crazy."

She laughed, and did her own fair share of touching him. "We'll figure something out. In the meantime—" She pulled away, taking the temptation away from them both. She picked up the box. It was lighter now that it was half-empty. "I'll take all this and my frustrated self home."

"Hey," he said softly.

She stopped and looked back. "Yeah?"

"We *will* figure this out. I want you." The words sounded strained and shivered over her nerve endings.

Addie watched as the late-day sunlight slipped through trees and fell over him. The breeze fingering through his hair made her fingers itch to do the same. She almost dropped the box and walked back to him.

"I—" What was she going to say? The words *I love you* nearly slipped past her lips. Did she? Could she? She took a step back, and away, from him. "I'll see you soon."

She turned and fled as quickly as the box would let her go.

SUNDAY LUNCH WAS INSANE. There were people everywhere, and barely enough seats to accommodate them. It was like being at a school assembly—except more chaotic. Addie loved them all, but she'd never felt so alone.

They'd spent the morning putting all the details of the barbecue together. It was a tradition at the ranch, going back to Granddad's day, so it was more assigning duties and picking dates and times than anything.

Addie breathed a sigh of relief when finally, the dishes were all cleared, and the kids headed down to see Tyler's pet pigs. Only the littlest ones were here, and they were down for naps.

It wasn't as if silence settled over the house, though. The adults were as noisy as the kids. The only one missing was Jason, and she'd come to accept that he would miss things, living in Los Angeles. This was as good as it was going to get anytime soon.

"I have something in my car," she leaned over and told Wyatt. "Can you help me bring it in?" She hadn't told anyone about the box she'd gotten from Marcus's garage. She'd wanted to surprise them.

She'd decided to wrap them, and that made carrying the box more awkward. Wyatt frowned but followed her. When he saw the bright wrapping paper, his frown deepened.

"Is there some holiday I forgot about?"

"No." She laughed, feeling just a little bit like it *was* a holiday. Marcus had been right, though she wasn't sure she'd tell him that. "You'll see. Come on." She grabbed the wooden box with her wand in it, and a couple of smaller packages, and let him get the others. She nearly skipped into the house.

"What's all that?" Mandy asked.

"Just sit down and you'll find out." DJ and Tammie shared a glance, as did Wyatt and Emily. She saw Tara shrug. This was fun.

She'd found tags similar to the ones Dad had put on her package, and she'd written each of their names on them. Now, like they'd done at multiple Christmases, she and Wyatt passed them out.

No one opened the packages, just looked at them curiously. Addie stood beside the captain's chair that was one of the originals. The spindles on the back matched.

"My…friend Marcus—the guy who bought Mom's house—found a couple boxes in the garage rafters."

"I thought we got everything," DJ said.

"Yeah. You sure they were ours?" Wyatt asked.

"Oh, yeah, they're ours." She grinned, then realized she had to get this done quickly, before she started crying. "These were Dad's." She put her box on the table, not opening it yet.

"When I was about twelve, I wished for a magic wand." Everyone laughed. "Dad promised he'd

make one for me. I didn't think he did. But—"
She opened the lid of the box. "Look. And it
matches my chair. Yours, too, Wyatt." She held it
up against the chair back.

Mandy gasped. "Oh, my gosh." Her eyes sparkled. "I'm guessing it doesn't really work."

Addie gave the wand a flourish in the air.
"Nope. None of you turned into toads." She looked
around at them all. "That's what I wanted the
wand for when I was twelve." They all laughed.

Then, as if everyone realized it at the same
time, they looked at their packages.

"He made something for all of us," she said.
"Not all of them are finished, though." Her voice
wavered on the end. "Go ahead. Open them."

The sound of paper ripping filled the room as
they each opened theirs. Gasps and laughter filled
the room.

"Oh, Addie, this is wonderful." Mandy did just
like Marcus had done, opening and closing her
treasure box while Tara looked at the little spoons
with tear-filled eyes.

"He did amazing work." Wyatt ran his thumb
over the horse's mane before showing it to Emily.

"Guess Dad didn't think I'd make much of a
cowboy." DJ laughed, looking at the definitely-
not-a-six-shooter gun.

"What about Jason?" Wyatt asked.

She decided she could rewrap it. She opened

the package, passing the wooden book around for them to all look at.

"How perfect." Tara fingered the detail of the pages. "He'll love it."

"Thank you, Addie." Mandy gave her a hug. "That was a really nice surprise."

"Marcus actually suggested it. I was going to save them for Christmas."

"I'm glad you didn't," Tara said. Morgan was seated beside her, and the dainty spoons looked so small in his big hands. He was nodding in agreement, his hand resting on Tara's shoulder. Addie smiled. Wyatt had been right. They hadn't been able to scare him away.

"Thank Marcus for us, would you?" DJ said. "He could have just as easily tossed these in the trash."

"He'd never do that." Just thinking about him brought a smile to her lips, and for the first time, the pleasure of being with her family dimmed. She wished he was here. Or she was there. It wouldn't matter.

Not for the first time, she was disappointed the wand didn't work. If it did, she'd wave it and take herself to him.

Just then, her phone rang, and she looked at the screen. Marcus's number. She looked at the narrow piece of wood. No. It was only coincidence. She thumbed the phone on. "Hello?"

"Addie? Thank God. I—" Marcus's voice wasn't happy. Near panic came loud and clear through the phone.

"What's the matter?" She stepped away from her overly observant family.

"Is Ryan by chance with you?"

"Uh, no." She looked around, catching Mandy's eye. "I'm at my brother's ranch. I came here last night."

"He said he was headed to Dex's." She could almost hear him shoving his fingers through his hair. "He said he'd be home by dinnertime."

Dinner was long past. "No. I—" She swallowed. Mandy stared, frowning as she listened to the one-sided conversation. "He's not at Dex's house?"

"I called. There was no answer. When I drove by, the house was dark. I took a shot and thought maybe he was with you." Marcus cursed softly.

"No. I'm sorry." She tried to think of where he could be. Had he said anything when she'd seen him at school in Friday? Nothing came to mind.

"I gotta go," Marcus said.

"Wait. What can I do?" Silence came over the line. Finally, his defeated sigh came through the line. "I—I don't know." Something like sadness weighed down his words. "I don't know. Carolyn always handled this type of stuff."

"I'll call some of the parents. I'll see what I can learn."

"Thank you." His relief was impossible to ignore. "I'll start with the guys on the team. Keep me posted."

"I will." Despite her panic, she realized he needed reassurance, too. She was good at that. She'd given plenty of that over the years. It was her forte.

She wasn't sure when he'd disconnected. But the screen was blank. She thumbed it back on and started to call. The best part of working for a small school was the close-knit community it created. Small-town closeness in a big city.

"Hello?" a woman's voice answered.

"Melissa? It's Addie. One of the kids is missing. Can you help?"

"Of course. Who?"

"Ryan Skylar. His dad hasn't seen him since this afternoon."

"I'll start the phone tree. We'll find him, Addie. Don't worry."

The reassurances Melissa sent through the phone were those of a parent who understood the fear, reassuring the principal of the school. It was appropriate. But Addie needed so much more.

While there was a lot of speculation at school, no one knew how she really felt. No one except Ryan and Marcus knew the truth of what was happening between her and Marcus. And did they even know? Heck, she hadn't a real clue. She looked at Mandy and watched her image waver. She hadn't told anyone in her family, either.

Several sets of eyes turned to her. Instead of explaining what she didn't understand herself, she left the room and went into the den. She had several calls to make.

Please, let him be okay. Or put real magic in this damned wand, she prayed.

CHAPTER FOURTEEN

MARCUS WANTED TO throw something. He wanted
to shove his fist through the nearest wall. Instead,
he calmly walked to the back door and stared out.
Maybe by staring at the impending darkness he'd
see his son coming home. Ryan wasn't at Dex's.
He wasn't at Addie's house. So where had he disappeared to?

Keeping busy helped as Marcus put his phone
on speaker and dialed. He started by calling the
Silvanos again. Still no answer. He left another
message, hoping they'd get it soon and call back.
It didn't mean Ryan wasn't with them. They just
weren't at their house.

Next, he called Ryan's baseball coach. Clint
Lawson was a good guy, if a bit hard on the kids
at practice.

"Yeah," the man answered.

"Clint. This is Marcus Skylar. Have you seen
Ryan this afternoon?"

"No. Sorry. Something wrong?'

"I'm not sure." Marcus took a deep breath,
sweeping toast crumbs off the counter to dis-

tract himself. He pulled open the dishwasher and started unloading the clean dishes Ryan was supposed to have put away. "He went to a friend's house earlier and hasn't come home."

"I'll call around to the boys. See what I can find out."

"Thanks." The silence of the room seemed heavy after he disconnected the call. Now what? Ryan's coach was calling the team. Addie was calling the parents at school. Marcus stood there, feeling nearly as helpless as he had the months Carolyn was sick.

He cursed and gave the cabinet a good kick. Thank God, they were sturdy old cabinets, not the cheap fiberboard they used in houses nowadays. He hung his head.

He finished the dishes, slowly, methodically, focusing. Should he call the police? He had no idea what to do. His gut twisted and hurt.

Finally, finished with cleaning the kitchen, he had his emotions somewhat under control. When his phone rang, he nearly dropped it in his haste to answer. He didn't recognize the number. Not Ryan's. "Hello?"

"D-Dad?"

Relief nearly sent Marcus to his knees. "Ryan. Thank God. Where are you?"

"I—I don't know." Thirteen-year-old boys caught between child and man didn't cry. At least they pretended not to. Marcus remembered being that age.

"What do you mean, you don't know?"

Ryan was silent for a long time. "I—I— Dex's cousin has some horses he said we could ride. We went out to see 'em and…and look around. But I took a shortcut home."

"Ryan, you don't know any shortcuts. We've only lived here a few months." Keeping his anger and frustration under control was a challenge. "Whose phone are you using? Is your battery dead again?"

"Yeah. I tried using the GPS. Musta used it too much. That's why I got lost."

Ryan was always running his phone battery down. Marcus took a deep breath, trying to beat back the angry panic. Ryan's voice was calmer now that they'd connected.

"Where are you now?" He heard Ryan talking to someone. Was Dex there? Marcus groaned and wished he could crawl through the phone. "Who are you talking to?"

"Charlie. My bike tire went flat. He was working on his truck, so I thought he'd probably know how to fix a flat tire.

"Put him on the phone, Ryan."

"Yello," a gruff voice came through the phone.

"Where is my son?"

"My place."

He was going to deck the man when he finally got to his son. He'd teach the SOB a lesson for being a smart-ass. "And that would be where?"

"Out on Blackthorne Road. Head out past the Equestrian Arena. I'm the house at the end of the dirt road. I'd bring your boy home, but my battery on my truck's out. I was working on it when he got here."

"Is there an address?" Marcus could put it in his phone and find the place. He didn't know this town any better than Ryan did.

"Nope. Not that I use. Got post office boxes out here. Big salmon-colored house—blame the missus for that. Can't miss it. Don't y'all worry. I'll keep your boy safe here with me and my missus."

How the hell had Ryan gotten all the way out there? That wasn't a shortcut home. Ryan had some serious explaining to do. Once he got him safely home. "And who are you?"

"Name's Charlie Ferguson."

"Can I call you back at this number?"

"Yep. Only one I got."

"I'm on my way." Marcus tried to hide his fear, tried to project strength and control through the phone. He let the man hang up, let go of the only connection he had to his son. His heart sank as his stomach turned. There hadn't been any threats. Nothing to make him this concerned.

Addie would know where this place was. He

wished she was here. He was halfway through dialing her number before he realized it. She answered on the first ring. "Did you find him?" She didn't bother with any greetings.

"I think so." Why did hearing her voice make it easier to breathe? "He just called. Said he took a shortcut home from some place Dex took him to see horses and got lost."

"Oh, thank God. I was imagining the worst." She sounded as out of breath as he felt. "Is he on the way home? Are you going to go get him? Where is he?"

"He's with someone named Charlie Ferguson who lives out past the equestrian arena? A salmon-colored house?"

Silence was the only answer.

"Addie, help me out here. I don't know where that is." His panic returned.

"If I were there, I could get him." Her voice was full of regret. "I'm too far away."

"Addie, I'm perfectly capable of doing it." He clenched his teeth, trying to swallow his frustration. He grabbed his keys and headed out to the garage. "Tell me how to get there."

"I—" She paused. "Head toward Main Street." He pulled out of the drive. "When you get to the railroad tracks, take a left." She sounded out of breath. Was she moving or just anxious? He ached to know. Needed to talk to her. Wanted her here.

He followed her directions. "Okay, just past the tracks. Now where?"

"Go past the apple orchard. There's a fork in the road, go right."

He kept driving, feeling like he was working a puzzle. Thank goodness, he wasn't having to do it alone. "Talk to me, Addie. I need to hear a voice."

"What about the radio?"

"It's not the same," he whispered. "Just tell me something. Anything."

She was silent for a long minute. "Are you worried or angry?" she asked.

"I'm not sure. What was he doing all the way out here? I know we moved to Texas, but he's never been interested in horses before."

"You'll have to ask him. Have you reached the fork yet?"

"Just getting there. Then what?"

"There's a dirt road up ahead. It shouldn't be far. The house is just a short way down the road."

"I see it. It's getting dark." He didn't see any lights, no outline of a house, nothing. Just trees that lined the road so close and tight that he couldn't see beyond them.

"You're almost there," she said, her voice a reassurance in the growing darkness.

He rounded the corner and saw the big house. "There it is!" The front light was on and lights were glowing in the front windows. "I'll call you later." He hung up and jumped out of the car almost before he'd put it in Park. "Ryan," he yelled. "Where are you?"

"I'm here, Dad." The boy came out the front door. An older man stepped out onto the worn porch behind him.

Ryan turned and smiled at the old man. "Thanks." The old man nodded and smiled at Ryan. Nothing to fear. No risk. No threat.

Why didn't Marcus's stomach stop churning? Why didn't his heart slow down? Maybe it would when he got Ryan home. Or maybe after he got done hugging him. It felt so good to feel his boy's thin shoulders under his arm.

Once they were in the car, and Marcus had put the now-fixed bike in the back, Ryan finished thanking the Fergusons. He handed Ryan the phone. "Call Addie. She helped me get here. I think you scared her as much as you did me."

"I'm sorry, Dad. Dex showed me where—"

"And where is Dex?" Marcus demanded.

"He stayed at his cousins' for dinner. That's why I took the shortcut home." Ryan made it all sound so logical.

"Why didn't you stay? All you had to do was call and ask."

"I told you my phone was dead. I thought I could get home in time."

Marcus's head hurt. "We aren't going to discuss

this now." He looked away from the road for an instant, his anger finally coming to the surface. "Was it Dex's idea or yours to lie to me about where you were going?"

Ryan sat silent. "It's not Dex's fault." He stuck up for his friend, which Marcus would normally admire, if he weren't so angry. "He suggested it, but I did it. I'm sorry." He looked out the window but didn't dial the phone.

"Call Addie," Marcus snapped.

Ryan lifted the phone and dialed. Even though the phone wasn't on speaker, the close quarters of the car made it so Marcus could hear her. Her voice was breathless when she answered, her worry apparent. He wanted to ease that for her.

"Did you find him, Marcus?"

"Hi, Addie," Ryan said.

"Oh, thank God." She took a deep breath. "Where were you?"

"I got lost coming home from seeing some horses with Dex. I'm sorry I scared you."

"I'm just glad you're okay." Her voice broke, and Marcus had the feeling she was crying. Damn it. His heart hurt. She was too far away, and he couldn't ease the pain for her.

"I'm okay."

"I'm glad. And Ryan?"

"Yeah."

"Don't ever do that again. I'm not sure who'd kill you first, me or your dad."

Marcus laughed. Dear God, he loved that woman.

He almost missed the next turn as that realization suddenly hit him.

THE NEXT DAY, Ryan came into her office slowly, and quietly. He didn't usually come to her office, though they saw each other nearly every school day. And on the weekends, if she counted the time she spent with his dad.

Normally, though, she'd take her afternoon stroll to the bus stop, and she'd talk with him there. She'd talked with Marcus the night before and had told him she'd do what she could to find out what was going on.

He was at a loss, and maybe Ryan would share information with her that he wouldn't his dad.

"You want to talk to me about something?" she asked Ryan, not really looking up from her work. She didn't want him to be overwhelmed and think he was getting extra attention for something that had scared his dad half to death.

"Maybe." He slumped in the chair across from her. Most kids didn't want to end up in the principal's office. She hid her smile. Their friendship had grown since that week in detention, and the times she'd been at his house outside of school.

"Go ahead. I'm listening." She crossed her arms over the paperwork and looked at him.

"My dad's mad at me."

She knew that. "Yeah. I think he has a pretty good reason."

"Yeah." Ryan sat quietly for a while. "I know you and my dad really like each other. And I like that—it's just, weird, you know."

"I understand that." It was weird for her, too. "Is there something you need, Ryan?"

"When dad was mad at me—you know, before—Mom used to talk to him, and you know, explain things."

Addie stared at Ryan, a bit worried about what he was asking. "You want me to talk to your dad so you don't get in trouble for what you did?"

"No. Well, yeah, sort of. I want you to make him feel better. He's happier when you're around. I know you've been avoiding him because of, well, because Dex has a big mouth." He leaned forward. "If he's happier with you, he won't be as unhappy with me."

She sat back, enjoying the idea that Marcus was happier when she was around, but uncomfortable with Ryan thinking she could be involved in his relationship with his father.

"Do you understand exactly what you're in trouble for?" She knew what Marcus thought. She was curious what Ryan thought he did.

He looked at his feet, reminding her of that first day when he'd refused to talk to her about the fight. He wasn't telling her everything. "I sorta lied to him."

"Uh-huh." She sat for a long minute, wondering how much she should push him. "And what did you lie to him about?" she asked, though she already knew.

"I didn't tell him Dex and I were going someplace else," he whispered.

"Why did you do that?"

Ryan tapped his foot. "I'm thirteen. And I know that because of Mom, he's—"

"He's what?" she prompted.

"He won't even let me stay home alone. He hovers. He checks on me. He doesn't trust me."

"Oh, Ryan. I don't think that's it." There was more, but Ryan wasn't sharing. Would he share if she talked to Marcus for him? Would she learn more?

What a mess. And a possible solution. Giving Ryan more freedom would give her a better chance at being with Marcus.

Suddenly, she figured out why it was a bad idea to date a student's parent. *A little late now.*

ADDIE CALLED MARCUS later that night. She'd debated about going to his house, about asking him to meet her at the coffee shop, but those were places her heart reserved for them. This was about Ryan.

She dialed and waited. He was in the middle of finals, so she knew he was busy. He'd had one hell of a week, and she hated adding to it.

"Hello?" His voice slid over her ear, and she shivered. He sounded relaxed compared with the pain and panic she'd heard yesterday. And he sounded tired.

"Hey, how are you?"

"Tired. Exhausted, actually." She heard him take a deep breath. "Better now that I'm talking to you."

She couldn't help but smile. "Me, too. I was wondering. Would you and Ryan like to come to dinner Friday night? You've cooked for me. And my family loved the gifts. Thanks for suggesting it."

"You're welcome. You don't have to make us dinner, though."

"I don't have to. I want to." And she did. She wanted to see him. Wanted to spend time with him. Normal time.

"I'm not going to turn down free food, if you're worried about that," he said. "What time?"

"Six?"

"Perfect. We can celebrate the end of finals." The relief was thick in his voice.

"Great."

"And Addie?" His voice had dropped an octave. "Yes?"

He was silent for a long minute. "I—" He cleared his throat. "Thanks. We'll be there at six sharp."

Why did she get the feeling that wasn't what he was going to say at first? She frowned, then shook her head. "Six sharp," she repeated. "Night, Marcus," she whispered.

"Night." He ended the call, and she stared at the phone for a long time afterward. She shivered, not sure if she was doing the right thing.

Ryan's request hung unspoken in the air. Was she overstepping her bounds? Was this too big of a risk to this new relationship? Maybe she shouldn't say anything.

She set her phone down. She had until Friday to figure it out.

By the end of the week, she had no better idea of what she was going to do. She focused instead on her cooking.

Between visiting her grandfather's ranch as a child and being the oldest of six, she'd learned the value of skills like canning, gardening and using fresh food to prepare meals. Oh, she wasn't nearly as good at cooking as her mother, or as Tara, but she could make a good home-cooked meal.

So why was she so nervous? She'd made this

recipe dozens of times. Her siblings had always enjoyed it.

This wasn't her family, though. This was Ryan and Marcus. This was their first impression of her life. This was important.

Putting the lid on the pot, she took a deep breath. Letting the aroma of the minestrone fill her, she relaxed a little. Then, putting the fresh loaf of French bread into the oven, she savored that scent, as well. Her tight muscles eased.

Setting the timer, she stepped back and relaxed. It would be perfect. She'd done her best, and that was all she could ask. That's what she told the kids, and what she lived by. She just needed to remind herself once in a while.

The doorbell rang, and every nerve she'd just relaxed jumped to attention.

She took one last glance in the mirror before pulling the door open. There they were. The man and the boy who meant so much to her. She swallowed. "Come in."

"Something smells delicious." Marcus smiled. He handed her a box. She looked inside. Cheesecake. "Hope this goes well with that."

"We'll make it work if it doesn't." She led the way into the kitchen. "You're just in time. Another ten minutes and we can eat." She set the cheesecake on the counter.

She turned to Ryan, who'd quietly followed them in. "How was your day today?"

He shrugged, something she'd discovered he did frequently. "Had a test in algebra." He frowned. "Did okay, I guess." She met Marcus's gaze.

"What would you like to drink?" she asked Ryan. "You can help yourself to anything in the fridge."

Decisions made, she put the finishing touches on the table. The timer went off, and she reached for the hot pads to pull out the crusty bread. Just like her mother had done, she rubbed the top with the butter. It glistened in the dim light, the yeasty steam filling the air around them.

"I hope that tastes as good as it looks and smells."

Marcus was there, just inches away, his body heat nearly as warm as what poured off the fresh loaf of bread.

"I—uh—hope so, too," she said, breathily, having trouble breathing with him so close. Their eyes met. Time stopped, and she didn't ever want to look away.

"Ahem." Ryan's voice broke through her thoughts. Hopefully, Marcus would think the flush on her cheeks was attributed to the warm oven.

Hastily, she put the bread on a board and handed it to Marcus along with a knife. She turned away and focused on serving up the soup while he took the bread to the table. She racked her brain for something else to discuss, to think about besides Marcus's proximity.

"Oh, I'd like to invite you both to my brother's ranch the week after next for a barbecue." She sat in her seat, trying not to enjoy their company too much. "The whole county is coming. It's a retirement party for our ranch manager."

"That'd be fun." Ryan dug into his soup.

"I guess." Marcus didn't look nearly as convinced. She bit her lip. He'd be meeting her whole family.

"Wyatt has lots of horses." She looked pointedly at Ryan. "Might be a better way for you to see some."

"Uh, yeah." Ryan looked away.

This time when she looked at Marcus, he was grinning at his son. "I think we can make it."

Relief washed over her. One mission accomplished.

ADDIE WAS NERVOUS. He'd never seen her like this before. What was the matter? Was it just the invitation, and prospect of his meeting her family? Or something else?

If Ryan hadn't been there, he'd have asked her straight out. Hell, whom was he kidding? If Ryan weren't here, they wouldn't be doing much talking at all.

Instead, he enjoyed the delicious food and watching her. At least one appetite was being satisfied.

Finally full, Marcus pushed his empty plate away. "That was delicious, Addie." He enjoyed the way her cheeks tinted pink.

"Thank you."

"Yeah, it's really good." Ryan was finishing his second helping. Marcus still hadn't figured out where his skinny son put all the food he ate. He remembered being like that at that age, though.

"I'm glad you liked it. I enjoyed cooking something for more than one person."

She didn't get up and rush around to start cleaning up dishes, which he was thankful for. He liked to enjoy his food before the chores started. He'd never understood his mother, and later Carolyn, jumping up before everyone was even finished.

"Since we're all here." Addie squared her shoulders and looked at Ryan as he finished his last bite. "I thought maybe we should talk."

Uh-oh. What was going on? He glanced at his son, who looked just as surprised as he felt.

"Now?" Ryan's voice squeaked.

"Yes, now. And we're all going to discuss it." She wiped her mouth daintily with her napkin, then took a sip of her water.

"Uh." Ryan gulped that last bite, his gaze darting to Marcus.

"What's going on?" Marcus didn't like the feeling he was on the outside.

Ryan just stared at him. Marcus looked at Addie. Her lips were pursed, and she frowned. "Okay, I'll start." She looked at Ryan.

"I'm not really a part of your family," she said. "But Ryan asked me to talk to you about something. I think he should discuss it with you himself."

"But—"

"This is the best way, Ryan." She told him. "Open honesty. It's the best way to deal with a problem. You've heard me say it at school, right?"

"Yeah," he begrudgingly admitted. Still, he stalled, taking a drink of his water and taking time to fold his napkin beside his plate.

"Would someone please share with me what's going on?" Marcus tried to be patient, really he did.

Ryan followed Addie's example and squared his shoulders, looking at Addie for encouragement. She nodded, and he faced Marcus.

"I wanted her to talk to you about the other day, when…when I, uh, lied about where I was going." He swallowed. "I'm sorry I lied, and I won't do it again."

Marcus waited. He was proud of Ryan for doing this, and he realized this was an important step for him. He'd listen to everything he had to say, not argue with him. His father had never listened, and he knew how hard that was. He'd always sworn to be different.

"But—" Ryan glanced at Addie, then back at Marcus. "But I did it, partly, 'cause you don't seem to think I can do things on my own."

This time Marcus looked at Addie. Her expression clearly told him to listen to his son. He tried. He really tried.

"Like what?" Marcus asked. "Give me an example."

"Well—" Ryan swallowed. "You're always there. I can stay by myself sometimes. I promise I won't trash the house or ruin anything. I'll do just like I do when you're there."

It sounded like Ryan didn't think Marcus trusted him. Marcus stared. Then cleared his throat. "I trust you, Ryan." He leaned forward, making sure his son could read the sincerity in his voice. "I'm—" He had to clear his throat again. "I guess, I—" Damn this was harder than he'd expected. "Since we lost your mom, I guess, I'm just a little overprotective, huh?" How did he explain that the idea of anything happening to Ryan gave Marcus nightmares?

"A little."

Marcus laughed. "And by that, I gather you

mean a lot." He reached over and squeezed his son's shoulder. "I'm sorry. Guess you're growing up." He swallowed. "Is it enough if I say I'll try to do better?"

Ryan nodded and smiled, his relief as strong as what Marcus felt.

"But promise me one thing."

Ryan frowned. "Uh, sure."

"I'll promise to try to be more lenient and open, if you promise to tell me what you want, and not lie to me. Sound fair?"

"Sounds fair." Ryan nodded and smiled at Addie. "Thanks, Addie."

"You're welcome." Now she got up and started doing the dishes. She didn't look at him, but he'd seen the smile she'd sent Ryan. Her pride was clear. She cared about Ryan, and he seemed to trust and care about her in return.

"So, to test this." Ryan stood and carried his plate to the sink. "How about I go home now? On my own. You can come home, uh, later."

Marcus stared at his son, not sure what was up, and pretty sure this part was a setup. Addie stared at them both, her beautiful wide eyes made the decision for him.

He reached into his pocket and handed Ryan the house keys. "I'll be home in an hour." At Ryan's frown, he said, "Baby steps, son. Give me time, okay?"

Ryan nodded and smiled. "See ya' later." Then he was gone.

Marcus looked at Addie.

And they were alone.

CHAPTER FIFTEEN

ADDIE WATCHED THE interaction between Marcus and his son, her heart alternately swelling with pride and skipping a beat in anticipation.

Had she done the right thing? Had she handled it right? She had no idea what Marcus was thinking, though Ryan's thoughts were painted all over his face as he raced out of her house with an hour of freedom.

If anything happened to him, she'd never forgive herself. Marcus would never forgive her. She almost turned to stop Ryan, but forced herself to focus on dishes instead.

Dear God, being a parent was not an easy job. When she'd helped with her siblings, she'd had backup from Wyatt and her mother. How did Marcus do it alone?

She'd have never succeeded if she'd made a different decision all those years ago—

Marcus came up behind her, startling her as he slipped his arms around her waist. She leaned against him. "Have I ever told you how smart you are?" he asked.

"Uh, no." She tried to keep things light. "But I'd happily take it in writing for later."

His laughter rumbled in his chest, and she felt it against her back. With his arms around her, he engulfed her, and she relished the sense of security.

Slowly, Marcus let go and reached out to take the dish from her hands. "I have only an hour with you," he whispered. Gently, he turned her to face him.

A lot could happen in an hour.

"Is this part of your plan to work things out?"

"Uh, no. I mean, yes. To help Ryan. And you. Not so that we can..." Her face flamed. She was so screwing this up.

"Addie, relax." He took her hands before she grabbed more dishes. "It's okay. You did fine."

"No." She tried to pull away, to put distance between them so she could at least think straight. He held her tight. "I'm not his mother." Though a big part of her wished... She stopped those thoughts dead in their tracks.

"I know that, Addie. He knows that." He tilted her chin up with his hand. "Thank you. I appreciate your caring about Ryan." He leaned in close. "Now stop thinking about him, or I might get jealous."

"What, um, exactly, should I think about?" She tried to let go of the tension that had been there since they'd arrived for dinner.

"Well, for one, you can relax." He tenderly kissed her forehead. "Since you didn't tell me we would have time alone tonight, I'm not any more prepared than I was last time we were alone in this kitchen."

"Oh." She looked at him, realizing exactly what he meant. "That isn't why I did all this." She should be angry, but she felt more like laughing.

"I know that, but damn, Addie. It's going to be another sleepless night." He leaned his forehead on hers.

Seconds ticked by as they looked at each other. Whatever this was between them, it burned hotter with each encounter. She bit her lip, debating with herself, with the desire that stayed banked inside her.

"Maybe," she whispered. "Maybe, not." She reached up, unable to stop from touching him. She traced the shape of his lips with her finger and gasped when his tongue slid out and returned the caress.

"I'm not sure—" she slid her hand lower, over the taut muscles of his chest "—how much more I can take," she whispered.

"You're going to drive me crazy, aren't you?"

"No. I'm going to help you sleep." This time, she pulled his head down so that she could kiss him, needing him more than ever before.

When they finally moved apart again, both of

them pulled in hard breaths. Her heart pounded in her chest, driving the heat through her entire system. "There are other ways…"

She couldn't stop touching him, and the way his big, strong hands held her made her feel safe in wanting him.

"Addie," he whispered against her lips. "This is too dangerous."

"Come with me." She pulled back, taking his hand in hers. "I have an idea."

Just like the last time, she took his hand and guided him out of the room. "I'm not taking you upstairs, though," she whispered, her voice husky with desire. "We'd never survive that." She led him into the darkened living room.

The drapes were already closed, and she moved slowly around, lighting the candles she'd lit when he was here that first time.

"Addie, you're testing my self-control."

She put a finger on his lips. "Shh, just let me do this. For both of us." Addie had never wanted anyone as much as she wanted Marcus right now, right here. They were adults, responsible adults. There were other ways to satisfy each other without the risks. Ways to take the edge off…before she went up in a ball of flame.

"I can't wait much more." She reached up and released the first button of his shirt. And then the next. "I don't know how you can, either." Opening his shirt, she leaned in and slid her arms around his bare waist, resting her cheek against his chest. So strong. So sexy.

When she slid the shirt off his shoulders, he didn't resist, instead he helped her remove it. His skin was hot beneath her touch.

Touching him turned her on even more, Marcus could tell. Her eyes sparked with desire as she looked at his bare chest, and when she touched him, her breath quickened, brushing warm against his skin.

Slowly, she nudged him to the couch, letting his shirt drop to the floor. "We're doing this together," he growled and, wrapping his hand behind her neck, he pulled her to him, taking her lips in a hard, demanding kiss. Soon, there would be no turning back. Hell, maybe they'd already crossed that line. He didn't know. He couldn't think straight anymore.

He'd waited too long to be with her, stopped too many times. He might not be able to do things all the way, but damned if he wasn't going to make it good for her. She tasted of dinner and joy and everything else Addie always tasted like. He couldn't get enough.

Rougher than he intended, he moved his trembling hands up to the thin straps of her shirt. He slid it off her shoulder and down her arm, dragging the fabric away from her breast. She wasn't wearing anything underneath. He groaned and cupped her in his hand. She filled his palm completely, the hard point of her nipple insistent against his fingertip. "Do you like that?"

She nodded vigorously. "Marcus," she whispered. "I need you."

"I'm here, honey." He picked her up and set her on the couch, stretching out and guiding her along the length of his whole body. He quickly got rid of her shirt. The dancing candlelight kissed her skin, and envious, he watched it touch her. Slowly, reverently, he eased her higher, closer until her breast was right at his lips. He suckled her, gently at first, then harder, deeper, until her cries of pleasure filled his ears.

He wanted her—his body ached for her. He'd have to find some relief tonight, but for now, this was as close to heaven as he'd been in a hell of a long time.

Panting, Addie finally slid back, bringing her face down to his. "My turn." Her husky voice made him groan. Was she—?

She slid along the length of him until her hand found the button of his slacks. The zipper's growl seemed loud in the silent room. "Mmm." She seemed to need to fill the silence as much as he did. She slipped her hand inside and grasped him.

Her small, soft hand was hot on his burning

skin. Slowly at first, then harder, faster. "Addie." He threw his head back and closed his eyes.

Addie moved closer, wanting to feel him so desperately she couldn't stand it any longer. She wasn't willing to risk unprotected sex, but this... this was wonderful.

"Come in me, Marcus," she whispered, hearing his painful groan shatter the air as she lowered her head and took him in her mouth.

His big strong hands burrowed in her hair, and she thought, at first, he would stop her. He didn't, and the way he held her there, the way he fingered through her hair as if mesmerized by the feel of her, nearly sent her over the edge. She'd never felt this way with another person. She'd never wanted anyone as badly as she did him.

His hips bucked against her, and her longing ratcheted up. Deeper, harder until finally, he reached the edge. She savored his release, knowing she'd given him that.

"Oh, baby." Marcus grabbed her and pulled her into his arms, holding her, hugging her tight.

She clung to him, struggling to stay calm, but the feel of his chest, hard against her bare breasts, was too much. She tried to move away, to control her own rushing libido. This wasn't about her—

"We're not finished," he whispered, pulling her back and kissing her. His hand slid over her back then came around to cup her breast again. She gasped. She didn't expect—

Marcus grasped her skirt, slowly gathering it, so that he could reach his hand beneath. He palmed her backside, squeezing until she sighed into his mouth.

The thin lace panties were no match for his questing hand, and she gasped when one big finger slid enticingly through the damp curls. Her cry of pleasure bounced off the walls. "Marcus, please."

"Please, what?" he whispered, his entire focus aimed at pleasing her, at watching her come in his arms. "This?" He slid his finger over her again, then gently slid that same finger inside.

"I'm going to…" she cried.

"Come for me. Let me watch you." He moved his finger deeper, faster, matching the rhythm her hips made. He felt her tighten, and the only regret he had was that he wasn't truly, deeply buried inside her. He would be. Soon. Just not tonight. His body burned in anticipation.

"Marcus!" Her voice tore from her throat as she shivered around him, falling over the edge of her release. He kissed her again, tasting the last of her cries. He didn't want to stop touching her, didn't want to end any of this. He wanted to do it again and again until the morning came.

But that wasn't to be. Not this time anyway.

Soon. Very soon. For a long time, he simply held her in his arms as they lay there on her couch.

Slowly, Addie came back to earth. Sated and tired, she struggled to sit up. At first, he held her tight, his body perfectly aligned with hers. He gently rubbed her back, his hands never straying any farther.

Relaxed, she nearly drifted off to sleep. "Marcus?"

"Hmm?"

She laughed. "Your hour's up," she whispered, knowing he had to leave and not wanting him to.

"Hmm."

"Such witty conversation." She pretended to complain. This time, his groan was not one of pleasure. Suddenly, he rolled her over, somehow managing not to push them off the narrow couch. His hard body pushed her deeper into the cushions, and in this position, she felt his hard arousal press at the juncture of her thighs. She moaned. "It didn't work."

"What?" He gazed at her, his hands on each side of her face, gently tracing the rise of her cheeks with his thumbs.

"I want you even more now," she admitted. "It didn't take the edge off."

His warm laughter rumbled through her. "Nice idea, though." He kissed her then, slowly, gently, holding back. "Very, nice idea."

Marcus reluctantly let her go, then reached for his shirt as he handed hers to her. She sat up and pulled it on, suddenly conscious of her messy hair and the rumpled state of her clothing.

He must have noticed her failed attempts to right her clothing and smooth her hair. He stilled her hands with his. "You look…beautiful," he reassured her. "Like you've just almost been made love to."

"The operative word there being *almost.*" She leaned against him and held on tight. "Almost—" she groaned and stepped away "—doesn't count except in—"

"Horseshoes and hand grenades," he finished with her. Then just before he left her, he whispered, "No more *almosts.* Promise."

Then he was gone, out the front door and into the night. She sank onto the couch and buried her face in her hands.

She hadn't taken the edge off anything. If anything, she'd added fuel to the fire.

THE NEXT WEEKEND, Addie came downstairs at Wyatt's ranch bright and early the morning of the barbecue, showered, dressed and anxious to help with any last-minute preparations. She should have known Tara and the retiring ranch cook, Juanita, would have everything handled.

"This is your party. You're not supposed to

work it." Addie gave Juanita a warm kiss on the cheek. "But with you two cooking, it's going to be the best barbecue ever."

They both laughed and continued with their work as Addie fixed herself a cup of the tea Juanita kept in the cupboard just for her and toast. She wasn't eating much, leaving room for all the amazing food ahead.

Wyatt came in then, pulling work gloves off his hands before fixing himself a cup of coffee. "Fire pit's ready and Patrick and the boys are getting the beef set up."

"Buckets are in the walk-in." Juanita waved toward the freezer that held enough food for the entire ranch—and then some. "We'll send 'em down as soon as you're ready."

Addie tried not to think about what lay ahead other than the food. Marcus and Ryan were coming out, and she'd arranged for them to stay tonight. She was hoping, but not planning, on dancing with Marcus under the stars.

And maybe more than dancing. Before anyone saw the heat sweep up her face at memories of last week's dinner, she hid behind her cup.

"Oh, what *are* you thinking about, sister dear?" Tara stood across the table from Addie grinning like she'd just read her diary.

"Nothing I'm sharing with you." She hastily bit into her toast and focused on chewing.

"Probably a safe idea." Tara laughed, returning to chopping veggies at lightning speed.

"Just tell me what I need to do to help," Addie said, putting her cup in the dishwasher.

And so, the insanity began. It felt like old times when they'd all come here for a holiday. Granddad was gone, but all the traditions, all the things he'd kept going at the ranch, were alive with Wyatt and his men.

An hour later, she carried the buckets of rub and sauce out to the fire pit. The sun was heading to the top of the sky, and already the heat was intense. The fire pit was far enough from the house that the flames and the smoke wouldn't be a risk to anything, but close enough that the rich aroma wafted around and made everyone hungry well before it was time to eat. She'd just set down the last of the buckets next to Wyatt when she saw a flash of red in the driveway.

Her breath caught as she recognized Marcus's Jeep. Ryan jumped out nearly as soon as Marcus pulled to a halt. She made her way up the hill, trying not to look like she was running.

"Hey." She waved at them. Ryan waved back while Marcus climbed out. He looked relaxed, his hair tousled from the drive, a pair of dark sunglasses hiding his gaze from her. He'd worn a blue button-down shirt and jeans that were faded, but not frayed. She liked the way they fit. His smile made her forget about everything else.

"This is quite a place." He walked up to her and leaned in to give her a kiss. Warm and short. Well, that answered that question. Guess they weren't going to keep everything a total secret.

"What's this place called?" Ryan looked around, his eyes wide with awe.

Addie shrugged. They didn't have an official name for the ranch. "We've always just called it *the ranch*." She shrugged. "The brand our cattle wear is the double rockin' J. Guess that's as official as it gets." She was proud of her family's history, and showing it to Ryan and Marcus only added to her joy. "Come on. Let's get you settled, and I'll show you around."

Both of them had packed backpacks, so it was easy to get everything inside. She led them upstairs. "This was the boys' room when they visited." She waved at the four bunks that filled the room. "You'll have the whole room, so pick whichever bed you'd like."

"I'll take the top one," Ryan offered with a smirk to his dad.

"Good choice. I'm not climbing up there." Marcus dropped his backpack on the opposite bunk. "And I'm not going to put up with your wiggling around, either."

Ryan laughed and flung his backpack up on

top. "Come on. Let's go see stuff." He headed to the door. "Do you have a lot of horses? Cows?"

Addie laughed at his enthusiasm—enjoying it and enjoying having them both here. "It's technically Wyatt's place. He's got tons of cattle, a jillion horses and two pigs."

That stopped Ryan in his tracks at the top of the stairs. "Two pigs?"

"Yep. They are my nephew Tyler's pets," she explained. "Though now there's a whole family of them, apparently. I haven't seen them." She was pretty sure a herd of pigs was not in Wyatt's business plan.

"This'll be interesting," Marcus said, following them downstairs.

Ryan wanted no part of what was indoors, and Addie couldn't think of any reason not to let him see the whole place. It was huge, and she'd already done her share of helping with the barbecue. Everyone else was in charge now.

She did take them to the fire pit first. Wyatt was the honorary pit boss—the real cook in charge was Juanita.

He was dressed just as Granddad had always dressed to oversee the fires. His summer Stetson, work shirt, jeans and boots that looked straight out of Granddad's closet. The white apron looked suspiciously like one from Tara's diner.

As they approached, she heard a metallic jingle and looked down. Wyatt was even wearing Granddad's spurs. He was pulling out all the stops on this one.

The grills were full of red-hot coals from local wood. Mesquite was Wyatt's favorite. The aroma wrapped around them. One of the buckets of barbecue sauce, which she'd carried down earlier, sat nearby with a big mop in it.

"What's the mop for?" Ryan asked as they walked closer.

"Once the meat starts cooking, Wyatt, or one of the men will mop it with sauce. It's the only way to do it with this much meat. That'll make it tender and totally messy to eat."

"Smells awesome." The boy was enthralled, and she liked his enthusiasm.

Cowboys stood around, leaning against pickup bumpers, or seated on hay bales that had been put there just for that purpose. A cooler of beers sat between the two piles, and everyone had one in hand. Nearly every head turned and watched the strangers who were with her. Addie ignored them. At least for now.

"Care for a beer?" Wyatt offered Marcus by way of introduction.

"No, thanks," Marcus said casually, and no one said anything more. Addie saw Ryan breathe a sigh of relief the same time she did, though they probably weren't for the same reason. She was just glad no one made an issue of it.

"Good to see you again, Wyatt." The two men shook hands.

"Oh, yeah." Addie blushed. She'd forgotten that Wyatt had been at the hospital when she'd gotten sick. But no one else knew her guests. Probably explained the curious glances going around the circle of cowboys. "You know my brothers Wyatt and DJ."

DJ stepped from his spot on the other end of the grill. "I'd shake hands, but I'm a bit messy." His big hands were covered in the spicy rub that Juanita had mixed up days ago. Only hand-rubbed meat went on Wyatt's grill.

She let Wyatt introduce the rest of the men. She'd given up a long time ago trying to remember all the men who worked here. An older man stepped forward. She knew him and gave Chet a warm hug. "This is Chet. He and his wife, Juanita, are the reason we're having this whole event."

"Good to meet you." Marcus smiled and shook the older man's hand. "Guess I should thank you for retiring, so I can try true Texas barbecue."

"Ah, now, you're welcome." Chet took a big swallow of his beer. "But if you want to know about true Texas barbecue—"

"Don't get started," Wyatt said, lifting the mop from the bucket.

"Whose party is this?" Chet winked at Addie. "Seems I should get to choose the topic of discussion."

"Not if it's to argue whose barbecue is better." Wyatt smeared a mopful of sauce over the briskets on one side of the grill.

"Well, there's no argument here. My father—"

"Run while you can, Addie." DJ laughed as he threw another hunk of brisket on the grill.

Marcus looked at her, confused, and she grabbed his arm, laughing. "We're outta here." To Marcus she said, "Come on. They'll be arguing about whose is better for hours now."

"There's a difference?"

"Oh, don't let them hear you. Yes, there's a difference, but no one agrees which is best."

Out of earshot, Ryan said, "Doesn't look like any barbecue I've ever seen."

"You've probably had St. Louis or Southern barbecue. That's more pork and baby-back ribs. Texas is where beef and brisket are king. Some Texas places don't even have sauce. It's about the grill and the rub." She shrugged.

"So, no pig roast, huh?"

"Shh…" She laughed. "Don't let Pork Chop or Hamlet hear you. Or my nephew Tyler."

Ryan rubbed his belly. "When do we eat?"

"Not soon enough. I've been smelling it all

morning. I'm starving." She led them to the horse barn. "I'll show you around, then we'll go and stuff ourselves."

CHAPTER SIXTEEN

SUNSET CAME WITH a fireball of orange in the west. Addie was disappointed the day was at an end— but the night ahead was just beginning.

Marcus sat across the picnic table from her. All through dinner, she'd been conscious of him. Twice, he'd caught her staring at him. Twice, he looked back and gave her a wink that made her stomach flip-flop.

She'd caught him watching her, too. When she'd been licking sticky barbecue sauce off her fingers, he'd watched every single movement. The heat in his eyes rivaled the fire pit that still glowed in the distance.

She'd resisted the urge to fan herself—barely.

Dozens of the wooden picnic tables had been set up around a large dance floor. Strings of lights hung over the floor and stretched out above the tables to poles the men had buried into the ground. "More posthole digging," her soon-to-be brother-in-law, Lane, complained. "Lord, I don't miss that."

He'd worked for Wyatt before deciding to become a hotshot firefighter. Addie hoped the fire season stayed slow so Mandy's wedding next month could go off without a hitch.

A local band was set up in one corner. She'd heard them before, and they were good. She couldn't remember when she'd last been to a dance, other than DJ and Tammie's wedding last year, which didn't count.

Addie was surprised to see Dutch and Elizabeth Ferguson seated at one of the picnic tables. "I need to say hello to someone," she said to Marcus after they'd tossed their empty plates into the trash.

He nodded and watched her walk through the crowd. She could feel his gaze follow her. She was sure he wondered who they were, and she knew that if things kept going the way they were, she'd need to explain at some point.

"Hello, Dutch, Elizabeth."

"Hey, sweetheart." Dutch gave her a hug then sat down. "Elizabeth, it's Addie." He didn't even bother to wait for Elizabeth to acknowledge her.

"Addie?" Elizabeth frowned as she looked at her.

Addie held her breath.

"Oh, yes. Addie. You're Cal's friend from school. I remember."

Addie looked at Dutch and saw the strain on his face. He looked tired and worn out. "Are you okay?" she asked him softly.

"I'm fine." He forced a smile. "Lots keeping me busy at the station these days." His eyes went to Elizabeth, who was focusing on her brisket, eyes that were distant and yet focused at the same time. It hurt to watch.

"I have some friends visiting from Austin. I'd like you to meet them." She waved to Marcus and Ryan. Dutch glanced over, then smiled up at her.

"Ah, hon. Looks like it might be more than a friend." He gave her hand a squeeze.

"I—I hope so." She put her hand on his shoulder and made the introductions.

MARCUS HAD WATCHED Addie in her natural habitat all afternoon. Surrounded by family, friends and traditions of time, she smiled and doled out hugs like she was related to everyone and hadn't seen them in years.

He couldn't keep his eyes off her. She was beautiful and warm. The older couple he'd just met were obviously dear to her, and he wished he could ease the pain he saw in her eyes when she looked at them.

The woman, Elizabeth, was definitely suffering from the effects of dementia. The wear and tear of being her caregiver showed on her husband's face. Marcus understood, remembering the long hours he'd spent at Carolyn's side.

"Dad!" Ryan came running up to where he sat

at a picnic table. He was obviously out of breath. Most of the kids in Addie's family were much younger than Ryan, but some of the ranch hands' kids were his age. They'd bonded over video games and, of all things, horses. Their knowledge and Ryan's suddenly insatiable interest in the animals made them click.

The ranch kids were more than willing to share their knowledge, and Ryan sucked it up like a hungry sponge.

"What?" He smiled at Ryan's flushed face.

"DJ and the ranch boss, Patrick, are taking us down to the corral. They said I could ride one of the horses. If it's okay with you."

Marcus paused, a shiver of apprehension making him pause.

"Please, Dad. I'll be careful. Some of the kids are sleeping in the hayloft. Can I? Please?"

Addie's brother had impressed him with his strength and knowledge before, plus his friendliness today. Ryan would be in good hands. He still paused before answering. "If DJ's there, I'm okay with it."

"Thanks, Dad."

"Just don't—"

"I know, Dad. I'll be careful." Ryan grinned, and with a lift of his hand, a gesture he'd seen the ranch hands use several times in the day, Ryan was heading toward the barn.

"That was nice of you, *Dad*," Addie whispered in his ear. He hadn't heard her return. She sat on the bench seat, her back against the tabletop. "He'll have a blast. You're getting better at letting go?"

"He's fallen in love with horses. And yes, I'm trying." Marcus watched Ryan run, enjoying his abandon. He hadn't seen him this carefree since—well, since before Carolyn got sick. He looked at Addie. "Thanks for inviting us. He's happier than I've seen him in a long time."

"You're welcome." She leaned closer. "But I didn't just invite him." Was that a blush on her cheeks? "You're here, too."

Their gazes met and held. So much danced in the air between them. As if on cue, the band that had been playing quiet background music stepped up to the microphones. "Ladies and gents. It's time to party!" The fiddle player stepped forward and launched into a fast riff. The crowd applauded and couples stood. Addie laughed and grabbed his hand.

"Oh, no. I don't know how to do this." He swallowed his panic.

"I'll teach you. It's easy. Come on." She tugged his hand, and the laughter in her voice pulled him to her. He'd try just about anything to please her—even make a fool of himself. What's the worst that could happen? It wasn't like he'd ever see most of these people again anyway.

He let her lead him to the edge of the dance floor. Most of the couples gravitated toward the center, specifically the area right in front of the band. Good. He'd stay back here.

"Watch me." She took his hands in hers, and that was pleasure enough.

Marcus looked at her feet that were moving way too fast. He shook his head and laughed.

She leaned closer, and, ignoring the beat of the music, she slowly demonstrated the individual steps. Then she made him repeat them, once, twice, then faster, then faster still. He laughed, and she took his hands and tugged him farther out onto the floor.

By the second song, he'd figured out those steps and could almost keep up with her.

Until she turned and looked at him again. He stumbled. Not because he didn't know the dance. He was knocked over by her, her smile, her enthusiasm. By how much he wanted her.

"Come on." She grabbed his hand again when the song ended. They headed toward the bar, and his heart sank.

When was the last time he'd been to a dance? These types of activities included alcohol. While he wasn't tempted, and he didn't need it—he knew about expectations.

Addie reached into a metal tub filled of ice. She yanked out two long-necked bottles and shoved them under the edge of the tub. "Handy can opener there," he commented. She nodded.

"Whatever works." She handed him the dark bottle and upended hers to her lips. He had to force himself to look away from the bottle, and her lips. He turned the label of his and smiled, chagrinned. He needed to trust her. The rich root beer tasted sweet and cool going down.

"I understand, Marcus." She leaned against him and tilted her face to his. The world faded away fast, leaving him alone with her, with the scent of her hair, the root beer and the night. Nothing more.

She froze, looking up at him. She didn't look away. She didn't move.

The music was the only thing that broke through the haze that had hold of him. It slowed, mellow and sweet. He touched her soft cheek. Dear God, he wanted to kiss her. Right here. Right now. In front of everyone.

"Dance with me," he said, softly.

Addie nodded, tossing their empty bottles into a barrel. Twining her fingers with his, she let him lead her to the dance floor. She moved in close, but not too close. She didn't lay her head on his shoulder or against him. Instead, she put an arm on his shoulder and leaned back to look at him.

She smiled. "So, how many people are staring at us?"

He didn't look around to find out. "Probably plenty. Most certainly your brothers. Does Addie Hawkins ever bring anyone home?"

"Nope. Not in a long time."

"Then there's even more than I thought giving me the eye."

She laughed and let him pull her close, his hand settling in the small of her back. This felt so good. Right.

"At least I won't embarrass us. I can do this step without your instruction," he said.

"Good, then maybe I'll let you lead." This time she leaned in closer, her cheek against his shoulder. Her breath skimmed against his neck, sending heat to every nerve ending in his body.

For the first time in years, he felt alive. Awake. Ready to take a chance.

The song ended, and the up-tempo beat of the next song startled them both. For an instant, they stood there, staring at each other.

"Come on," she said, though he didn't hear it. He saw her lips form the words. She tilted her head away from the dance floor. She didn't let go of his hand.

Outside the circle of light, the night quickly fell dark. Overhead, he could see the increasing number of stars.

Addie seemed to know where she was going, leading him along a well-worn path. He followed without question. And while the music still filled the distance, he heard other sounds. Crickets. A soft breeze in the grass. Their muffled footsteps. A short distance more, voices came out of the dark.

A few minutes later, they topped a ridge and looked down at a wide sandy area. Flames from a bonfire danced in the darkness. He made out some of the faces he'd met earlier, as well as several others.

"This is my favorite part," Addie told him as she halted and he came to stand beside her. "This is where we all retreat after the work is done."

"Addie's bringing company," a woman's voice came from the darkness around the fire circle.

"DJ's gotta behave now," another woman said.

"Since when?" DJ's voice held laughter.

In the firelight, Marcus saw her siblings—and the whole couple thing that was going on. Wyatt sat with his arm around a slim brunette. A blonde sat on the ground in front of the lawn chair DJ sat in. Two other couples sat together on a group of tree stumps.

"Where's Jason and Lauren?" the brunette asked, looking up the path they'd just come down.

"Jason's probably still trying to explain to her where we all disappeared to."

"Jason isn't explaining anything," another man's voice came out of the darkness. Jason and a tiny woman emerged out of the shadows—not from the path. Where had they come from?

"Please tell me I don't have to remember everyone's name." Marcus leaned close to Addie.

"Professor," she teased, "you know there's always the possibility of a pop quiz."

"Wonder what subject they're studying," DJ said, which got him a smack on the arm from the woman beside him.

"Okay, people. Enough." Addie stepped forward, using the voice he recognized from her dealings with the kids at school. "Fork over the marshmallows."

The activity broke up the speculation as everyone loaded big, fat marshmallows on long wires. "Here." She handed him one. He stared at it. He'd heard about marshmallow roasts.

Addie watched him. "You've never done this before." There was a hint of sadness in her voice.

"Nope." He took the metal wire—was that an old hanger?—and did as the others did. He could learn.

"I think the boy can figure it out," Wyatt said. "Sit down, Addie."

Surprisingly, she did as her brother instructed, and Marcus was struck by shock. "How'd you do that?" he asked Wyatt before thinking.

Laughter circled the fire ring. "*Lots* of practice," Wyatt admitted to more laughter.

Addie jumped up then. "Careful." She took the metal wire from Marcus and yanked his flaming marshmallow out of the fire. She puckered her lips and blew out the flames. He could only stare. She was beautiful, her lips in just the right position…

"Good thing she likes the burned ones," DJ offered.

"You eat them burned?" Marcus asked.

She looked at him then, and grinned. Their gazes locked and she slowly nodded. Opening her mouth, she took the whole marshmallow in between those luscious lips, her tongue licking the last of the white goo from the wire. She grinned and licked her lips—never once breaking the path of their gazes. "Yep."

The silence fell around them like a heavy blanket. Memories of the last time they'd been together rushed in. He broke out in a sweat that he prayed everyone assumed was because of his proximity to the fire.

Addie froze, then looked around, and he'd bet her cheeks were flaming. She'd obviously forgotten everyone was there. She hadn't forgotten the events in her living room.

Neither had he.

His ego enjoyed the fact that she was as affected

by what was going on between them as he was. He just wasn't sure where they went next.

The woman he was used to seemed so different here. Not bad—not weak—but different. Curiosity pushed him to save her.

"My turn." He took the wire and loaded another marshmallow that he held over the flames. He focused on cooking the thing this time. The simple, normal actions brought everyone—except him—back to earth. The conversations resumed, and Addie smiled her thanks.

"Don't let it burn." She leaned against him. "Or we'll be in serious trouble."

He laughed with her, and the easy camaraderie returned.

"That boy of yours is a natural with horses," DJ said a short while later. "They really took to him."

Marcus nodded. "He's never been around them before. Though I think that's about to change."

"Yeah, he even volunteered to help the boys rub them down and put them into their stalls for the night."

Marcus smiled, proud of his son. "Maybe that's why he wanted to come to Texas so badly."

DJ nodded. "Can't say as I blame him. The boys'll make sure he's back when the festivities wind down."

"Thanks." Marcus appreciated the way everyone watched out for each other here. Maybe Texas was the place for him and Ryan.

"Where are you from?" Wyatt's wife asked.

"Chicago, by way of half a dozen military bases. My dad was career military." He didn't want to think about his past. He didn't want to think about the world beyond this time and place.

"What made you leave?" Wyatt's wife asked.

The all-too-familiar grief shot through him. Silence, broken only by the fire's popping crack, stretched out. He looked at Addie. What had she told them? What did she want them to know? He shook his head. Secrets weren't his style. "My wife passed away a couple years ago. Ryan and I needed to start a new life."

The round of "I'm sorry" was heartfelt, but he didn't want to hear it. He didn't want his past to be a part of this. Addie was a part of his new life, his new beginning.

He didn't miss the glances that were aimed at her. What were they thinking? Worrying that she was getting involved with someone who had issues? He didn't owe them any explanations, but he didn't like the idea of his situation causing a rift between her and her family. They were obviously very important to her.

Suddenly, Addie stood and extended her hand. "Walk with me." He looked at her, seeing the firelight, and something else, reflected in her eyes.

Pity? Pain? What? She blinked and the emotion was gone.

He stood. "Sure." He'd never turn down an invitation to be alone with her. He faced the crowd. "Thanks for the marshmallows."

Addie walked quickly, and he had to race to keep up. What about those questions had upset her?

"Addie?" He hurried, finally catching her and grabbing her arm. She halted but didn't look at him. Finally, he cupped her chin in his palm.

He shifted to stand in front of her, and with little more than starlight and the wash of the moon, he was surprised by the pain in her eyes.

"Ah, babe." He swept her into his arms, and the way she held on, held on tight, made him think of suits of armor and thick heavy swords. He'd slay dragons for her. He'd do anything to protect her. "What's the matter?"

Addie stood on tiptoe, her lips hovering near his for an instant of indecision. He made the decision for her, kissing her hard. She tasted of marshmallow and root beer—and sweet, powerful woman.

And he was lost.

Her cry wasn't one of protest, but there was pain in it. She pulled back and looked into his eyes. "I don't deserve you," she whispered just before stepping away. She hurried down the narrow strip of sand.

He cursed. And followed her.

ADDIE DIDN'T SLOW her hurried steps until she topped the next rise. How had she gotten here? She bent over slightly, taking tiny steps, pacing the edge of the dune, trying to catch her breath. She stared across the moonlight-washed hills—at the river rushing through its newly carved banks.

Last spring's flooding had altered the river's path. The wildfire the year before had done its own sculpting of the land. White moonlight glistened on the waves that the current created as the water headed toward the sea.

Somehow, the difference was a comfort. Mother Nature's hand erased the part of the past that hurt the most.

From here, Addie could make out the shadowed arms of the old cottonwood that reached out over the waters. What was left of it.

It stood out scorched black even against the dark night sky, the remnants of the rope that had hung from the biggest branch over the water. Frayed. Charred, just as stark against the sky.

She could almost hear the echoes of childish voices, laughter, screams and howls of joy and fear at letting go of the rope. The thrill of the air rushing over bare skin. Flying through the bright blue Texas sky until finally hitting the cool water on a hot summer day.

She hadn't been out here in years. Too many years. She'd purposefully not come here.

Something hurt. Inside. Deep inside. She felt ready to shatter.

The bonfire had unhinged the door of her memory. The glances from everyone were a silent reminder of the past. Didn't they realize she needed to leave all that behind? The sadness in Marcus's eyes had echoed inside her loud and painful. Reminding her of his pain, his loss.

Of everything that still stood between them.

"Damn you," she yelled at the river. At the place she'd first met Cal, first loved him—where he'd drowned. "Damn you," she whispered.

"Addie?" Marcus's deep voice called from down the path. "Addie?" he called again. He was getting closer.

She'd left the fire, needing to get away from everyone but him. When he'd kissed her, she'd wanted nothing but him. But that level of want, that need, scared her.

Her brothers and sisters knew not to follow her when she was in a mood.

She'd asked Marcus to come with her. Invited him with the intention of telling him about her past. But now, she wasn't so sure.

Instead of waiting for him, she hurried her steps, sliding, half on her feet, half on her backside, down the sandy hill. Soon she found herself on the small stretch of beach that remained.

She was on Haymaker land now. But Pal was

gone now, too. Trey had run off, and Pal Jr. didn't care about this strip of land anymore, either. She'd be safe hiding here.

Marcus, though, wasn't going to leave her alone. Part of her loved him even more for that deep caring.

She froze. Love? Glancing over her shoulder, she saw his silhouette against the night sky. Could she love again? Could she let go and love him?

Right now, feeling like this, she didn't want to talk to him about Cal or about the past she'd worked so damned hard to escape. Her family's glances earlier said it all.

Thirteen years wasn't long enough. Halfway across Texas wasn't far enough.

A lifetime wouldn't take away the past.

"Addie?" he called again, this time from the top of the rise where she'd stood only a minute ago.

He was the dark shadow against the star-studded sky. He, though, wasn't a memory. He was real. And now. And—the future? Dare she hope?

The ever-present wind dried the tears and the sweat on her skin. That same breeze fingered through the branches of the tree, clicking the last few charred leaves together. Whom was she fooling? Certainly not herself.

She closed her eyes, seeing Cal's image behind her eyelids. The boy who'd stolen her heart. The boy who'd never become the man he could have been. He'd always be there.

Between them.

She'd lost so much on this beach. Oh, it wasn't anywhere near the ocean. But the rushing of the water, the feel of the wind, the sound of it in the trees, was like that shoreline down on the gulf. And eventually this water ended up there. Spilling into the sea somewhere far away.

This was the only beach she'd ever loved.

The sand was wet today, not from the river, but from the rain that had fallen this year. Since the flooding, few people looked forward to the rain.

Addie Hawkins wasn't a crier. She'd worked hard after Dad's death to be the grown-up, to be strong for her younger siblings. She'd taught herself to compartmentalize her feelings. About everything.

Closing her eyes, she could imagine the neat little boxes she'd mentally created to help herself do that. Dad's box was a deep, dark green, like the vines that grew over his workshop. Mom's was a bright sunny yellow, like the curtains in the kitchen where Addie had grown up. Cal's…she wasn't sure what color his was. She was afraid to look. She'd hidden those feelings away so far and deep she didn't even know where to look.

And her son's? That was the baby-blue box,

with the little elephants on it. She didn't know why elephants. It was what it was.

"Addie!" Marcus's alarmed voice broke through the night. The pain and worry in it tore at her heart. She couldn't hurt him anymore, but right now, she couldn't respond. There was nothing left of her. Nothing but the shell of a person whose head was full of odd little boxes she didn't know what to do with.

"Addie!" he yelled again. Was his voice farther away, or was she slipping away? Huddled there, on the beach, the sand sinking between her toes, she wrapped her arms around her knees and sank a little farther down. She could almost imagine it swallowing her up.

"Addie." This time relief filled his voice. It was closer now. Warm. Strong. She closed her eyes. Afraid to look at him, afraid of what she'd see there. Of the censure. Of the blame. Of the pity.

"Addie?" he whispered as he sank beside her. Instead of looking up, she leaned her head forward, resting it on her knees. She couldn't curl in any more. She couldn't hide from him—or herself, but oh, how she wanted to try.

He didn't speak. Instead, he settled beside her. He reached around her, encircling her with his legs, with his arms, and resting his chin on top of her head. A cocoon. Holding her, keeping her safe.

Warming her. And she hadn't even realized she
was cold. She shivered, and he absorbed that, too.

"I'm here," he whispered. And then he fell silent, simply holding her until she was ready to
emerge into the light. "I know that feeling. I know
that hurt. You can tell me. But don't shut me out,"
he whispered, holding her close, letting her rest
against him. He waited.

CHAPTER SEVENTEEN

ADDIE DIDN'T WANT to feel the grief anymore, and she certainly didn't want Marcus to feel it, either. She pulled away from him, turning to look into his eyes. She wished she could see him better. The moonlight was dim.

"I loved someone. Once. A very long time ago."

"What happened?" he whispered.

She held her breath. For so long, everyone she knew had known about Cal. She hadn't had to explain. She hadn't had to speak about him, about the events, or the pain.

She didn't even know what to say now, but somehow the words began. She glanced at him, gauging his reaction. "Cal Ferguson was my boyfriend in high school. I thought he was the one." She paused. She still did sometimes. She still loved that boy. Her heart hurt thinking about him.

"He was Dutch and Elizabeth's only child. The couple I introduced you to earlier? He was a bit spoiled, I think. He got everything he wanted. Which, since his dad was the sheriff, pretty much gave him star status."

Marcus rubbed her shoulders. She nearly purred it felt so good to let him take the tension away.

"I came out here to spend the summer on the ranch. And being the new girl—let's say it was a fun summer. Wyatt and Granddad had a heck of a time."

He laughed and kept massaging her shoulders. "Sounds like a lot of fun."

"It was." It had been the best summer of her life. "It's the only time in my life where I focused on what *I* wanted. What *I* needed. I had that one summer of wildness."

She couldn't hold back the hiccup of her tears. The massaging hands moved around her and pulled her up against him again. She let him comfort her.

"Cal was wild. Living on the edge. That day… we…we were all down here at the river. Someone had smuggled some beer in a cooler, and he was pretty drunk." She sobbed. "We were barely seventeen."

"You don't have to tell me. It's okay," Marcus whispered.

"I need to." As much to rid her soul of the pain, as to make sure this man who'd become more than just a neighbor or a friend knew exactly what he was getting into. She hadn't said the words aloud, barely even thought them in years.

"This used to be where we swam. All summer long." Addie's voice broke.

"Used to?" he asked.

She took a couple of steps, moving more carefully down the bluff this time. Now she stepped out in front of him, dipping her bare toes into the gentle current. "I haven't been here since..." She tilted her head back and stared at the sky. "Since Cal drowned."

Several minutes ticked by, the rush of the water filling the void.

"That's why Elizabeth says water's evil." Realization dawned on his face and in his voice. His arms tightened for an instant. "I'm so sorry, Addie." And she could tell he really was sorry, he felt for her. "So sorry."

She nodded, letting the rough fabric of his shirt against her cheek comfort her.

"Elizabeth never recovered from that night. I think I'll always hear her screams when Dutch told her." Why she'd been with him, she didn't remember. She didn't remember much else of that night beyond the pain and screams. She'd wondered if any of those screams had been hers.

Slowly, cautiously, Addie turned to face Marcus. "When Emily asked you tonight about why you left Chicago, I saw it."

"Saw what?"

"That flash of pain. That grief that I feel, that

follows me everywhere. I hated that you have that, too."

He nodded, and she saw the darkness creep into his gaze. She wanted to scream and chase it away. "I don't want them to be between us."

"Are they?" He pushed her hair behind her ear, letting his fingers linger on her curls.

"I feel like something is." She leaned her cheek into his hand, loving the warmth of his touch. "For so long, I was afraid to see anyone. Everyone kept warning me about rebounding." She looked down. "I don't want to be your rebound."

Even in the darkness, she could see his throat move as he swallowed. He didn't look away. "I never planned to find someone new," he said softly. "For a long time, I felt guilty even thinking about being with someone else."

"Me, too. I felt like I was betraying him. Betraying what we had."

Marcus nodded. "But if the tables were turned, I wouldn't want Carolyn to live the majority of her life alone. Cal wouldn't expect that of you, would he?"

She shrugged. "I don't know. We were too young to think about forever and death. We were invincible then."

"Carolyn and I never talked about it until she got sick. It doesn't usually come up." He shrugged.

She looked at him then, and he saw fresh tears

in her eyes. "I—" She stopped. She'd never told anyone what was on the tip of her tongue.

"You can tell me. What?" he asked gently.

Addie bit her lip, as if that would keep the words inside. She couldn't ignore the shame. "Looking back…" Deep breath. She focused on the button of his shirt. "I don't even know if we'd have been to-gether forever if he'd lived." She rushed her words. Another deep breath.

There, it was out there. She couldn't control what he thought of her now.

"You've tormented yourself too long with that guilt."

She looked at him again. "Maybe." She couldn't look away. "I don't know how else to feel."

For a long time, he sat there, holding her, not speaking, not moving. Finally, he spoke. "The day Carolyn died, I felt a huge relief. She was at peace. She wasn't in pain anymore and I wouldn't have to watch her suffer anymore."

"Oh, Marcus—" She reached up to soothe him, but he grabbed her hand and pulled it away from touching him.

"I'm not telling you this to get your sympathy. I want you to understand. The guilt I felt is why I drank. I was ashamed." He breathed in deep, his chest expanding and moving against her. "For being glad…she was gone." His voice hitched, and she knew it was from unshed tears.

Only the rush of the river nearby broke the quiet of the night. She didn't know what to say. She understood. "Marcus?"

"Yeah?" he whispered.

"Will you do something for me?"

"Anything."

She reached up and ran her fingertips along the rough line of his jaw, stopping to linger on his lips. "I know we won't ever forget." She didn't really want to. "For the first time, I'm ready to move on."

His smile was bittersweet. He leaned closer. "Let's make some new memories."

"Yes." She sighed, her breath fanning over his lips just before he settled them on hers. So warm. So firm. So right.

She kissed him back, parting her lips to silently ask for more. Marcus gladly complied, deepening the kiss.

Gently, he slid his big, strong hand into her hair, cupping the back of her head and holding her to him. His other arm slid around her waist. Somehow, they were stretched out on the cool sand, her curves snuggled against his solid angles.

Where her mind had been full of memories and words just a moment ago, it was now blessedly blank, filled with nothing but the sensation of his taste, his touch.

She couldn't get enough of him, and she reached up to the buttons of his shirt that she'd stared at earlier. The simple white pearl buttons slid easily through the worn buttonholes. The t-shirt he wore underneath held his body heat, and she savored the warmth as she slid her hand over the hard muscles of his chest.

"Addie," he whispered as his lips left hers and slid along the edge of her chin to the sensitive skin of her neck. "You feel so good."

He slid his hands along her shoulders and arms, finding the curve of her hip. Then, slowly, cautiously, he slid his hand up, over her ribs to the soft curve of her breast.

Surprised, she gasped. As if he took the sound for protest, he halted the movement of his hand—until she encircled his thick wrist with her hand and hesitantly guided his hand upward.

There was no mistaking his groan for a protest.

Heat washed through her veins, and her body tingled in places she'd nearly forgotten about, reminding her that they wanted more. Of him.

Arching her back, Addie begged him with her body for more. Much, much more.

Marcus moved, rolling over so that she was beneath him, the sand warm against her back, his body hot over hers. They were eye to eye now, and he looked at her, pushing her hair away from her face, giving him more access.

For an instant, he paused, staring at her. "The

moonlight suits you." Marcus lowered his head, kissing her with an intensity he hadn't before.

This man. His touch. His kindness. His smile. Everything about him fit into her heart. She gasped as she realized how much she wanted him. How much she cared for him.

Was it possible? Could she…?

She didn't know how, didn't really care how, but she knew she'd fallen in love with him. How could she have been so foolish as to confuse this with anything else?

"Marcus… Please…"

"What?" He lifted his head, giving her space, time to think, though she saw the strain on his face. She smiled, loving him even more for the restraint he was struggling with.

"Make love to me," she whispered. "Tonight. Now."

His gaze darkened, passion shadowing the eyes she knew were a rich, deep blue.

"I want you." He kissed her swiftly. "You're killing me." But instead of coming back to her and touching, kissing her, he pulled away.

She frowned, afraid she'd said too much, afraid he'd changed his mind. "I—" He didn't pull away.

"I did manage to get to a drugstore. Not a lot of good it will do us in my backpack at your brother's house."

And then she laughed. At first soft, sweet, almost a giggle. And then it grew, loud and hard. He joined her until his eyes shone with mirth. He rolled her over in the sand. "I still want you."

Her laughter melted away as quickly as it had come. An ache grew in her chest, spreading lower, deeper, to the hollow inside her that ached to have him.

"My room is across the hall from yours," she whispered. "It's already late."

"Late enough?"

She nodded slowly. "It will be by the time we get there." She reached up to pull his lips to hers. He didn't even bother to resist.

THE HOUSE WAS empty when they approached. That wouldn't last much longer, even though the party would last well into the night.

Addie hoped no one was sitting on the porch or relaxing in the kitchen. And no one was. She held Marcus's hand and led him in the front door.

The old house muffled the sound of outside. She didn't hear anyone even snoring, which was a good thing. They had the place to themselves. "This way." He followed her instructions as they climbed the stairs.

It was one thing to want to make love, it was another thing completely to sneak into the house and actually do it. Her entire body shivered at the realization she'd be as close as she could possibly be to Marcus. It wasn't soon enough.

She couldn't see much from the doorway, but when he went into his room, she saw him put something into his jean pocket.

The realization of what that was, and what was ahead, made her entire body ache with longing. Finally, he walked to her, silently closing the door.

They stood there. Staring at each other. Waiting for what? She felt smaller now that they were on solid ground. "Did you change your mind?" she whispered.

"Ah, babe." He ran a rough finger down her cheek. "I couldn't if I wanted to. You are so damned beautiful." He leaned in and kissed her. Slowly, she backed up, bringing him with her until she reached the door across the hall. She reached behind and turned the doorknob. It opened silently, and she mentally praised Wyatt for his maintenance skills.

Then all thought was gone as Marcus scooped her into his arms. She laughed softly, hiding her face against his neck to muffle the sound. He paused only long enough for her to close the door. "Lock it," he said.

She did.

MARCUS STRODE ACROSS the floor through the darkened room. The moonlight, falling in through the single window and landing in a square of white on the bed, was all the light he needed. He didn't stop until he reached the bed, where he laid Addie on top of the old-fashioned quilt.

The light fell over her, wanting to touch her as much as he did. The moonlight in her eyes, she smiled. "Marcus." She said his name. "Love me," she whispered.

"Ah, honey." He leaned in and joined her on top of that quilt. He put his lips on hers deep and hard, not even hesitating. There was no reason to hold back now. Nothing could interrupt them now.

But that didn't mean he intended to hurry. He was ready for this, and he was going to make sure it was special for them both.

Slowly, he pulled back, just wanting to look at her. He wanted to make sure he saw her in his mind's eye as well, and that she was seeing him. He needed to make sure.

Her hair, all those luscious curls, was tangled and scattered around her face. He pushed a few stray strands out of her eyes, loving the soft feel of them between his fingers.

Her cheek was smooth and warm against his fingers, and those lips. They tasted sweet and turned up so adorably when she smiled.

The shirt she wore was high necked, but that was an illusion as the lace showed him plenty of tanned skin through its design. He slid the tiny button through the collar, then kept following the row of matching buttons downward. The heavy fabric fell apart, exposing the gentle curve of her breast and the white cotton nothingness of her bra.

It didn't take much to move the fabric off her shoulders so that he could slide one narrow strap off her shoulder. And then the other. And then suddenly she was there in the moonlight, her shirt cast aside, the white strip of her undergarments scattered on the floor. He looked his full.

But he'd never been good at just looking. He wanted—needed—to touch her. And he did. Slowly, carefully palming the full curve of her breast and tweaking the tender nipple with his thumb.

Her sigh was pure pleasure. "Marcus," she whispered, reaching out to pull his head down to her kiss. "You're driving me crazy," she whispered just before her lips took his.

Marcus had been so focused on tasting and touching her, but Addie had been doing her own exploring. The sensation of her hand slipping beneath his shirt and gliding up his bare spine shot straight through him. He couldn't get that shirt off fast enough, needing to feel her touch everywhere.

She was happy to assist and oblige. "More," she whispered, those magical fingers finding the button of his jeans. "Now."

Marcus laughed and did his own finger dance

down her belly. Feeling her muscles contract in reaction made him want more, too. Lowering his head, he tasted the dark, round nipple that had been taunting him since he'd first started to undress her. Her moan of pleasure sent heat straight to his groin.

He was ready for her. More than ready. But he wanted to make sure she was right there with him. He ignored her plea to show her more. He wasn't sure how long he could hold out if there were no barriers between them.

Slowly, he undid her jeans. The thick denim was a rough contrast to the pure, soft skin he found beneath. His fingers brushed lace panties, and he felt her shiver and buck against his touch.

She reached down then and pulled off the jeans for him. "I need you closer. Much closer." Her breath came in quick, hot pants, and he wasn't going to deny her much longer.

Before he granted her wish to lay skin to skin with her, he made sure he grabbed the packet from his pocket. Holding one up, he grinned at her, enjoying her knowing smile in response. She plucked it from his hand and opened it for him.

He stared. He couldn't do anything else. His entire body froze in delight and desire. Waiting.

Addie nudged his shoulder, pushing him back so that she could touch him, gently, carefully sheathing him. Marcus groaned aloud. Anyone in the rest of the house might hear, but at this point, he didn't care, nor was he able to deny the pleasure this woman gave him.

"You amaze me," he whispered, reaching for her and pulling her lips to his. He deepened this kiss, lengthened it to the point of forgetting where he ended and she began.

As gently as she'd touched him, he slid his hand lower, finding the spot where he ached to be. Slowly, he slid his finger along the tender fold, testing, teasing.

She was as ready as he was. Maybe more.

Carefully, he slid over her, letting his body envelop her and hold her close. He kissed her, pouring all his want and need into that single kiss. Taking all her desire inside.

"Addie, are you sure?" he whispered at the last, as he was poised to take that next step.

She nodded. "Please," she whispered, as she lifted her legs and put gentle pressure on the small of his back. "Now!"

With a single thrust, he was inside her, moving slowly, wanting to prolong this moment. Passion took over and she was moving with him. Taking him deeper, harder, more.

Addie let herself experience it all, tasting Marcus's kisses and the wonder of his heat inside her. She felt herself flying higher, closer to the joy she knew lay ahead. She let it overwhelm her. Throwing her head back, she pressed her breasts against the wide expanse of Marcus's chest, increasing the pleasure, sending her higher.

Finally, she tumbled over, taking him with her. She rode it, savored it, wrapped her arms tight around him and prolonged it.

Catching her breath, she held on to Marcus's shoulders and tried to calm her thoughts. Nothing had prepared her for that. Nothing.

His chest rose and fell in the same rhythm as hers. He looked at her. "You okay?"

She couldn't hold back the smile. "Oh, yeah. More than okay." Leaning up, she kissed him softly, quickly, half-afraid to do anything else yet…yet.

Marcus reluctantly rolled away, returning to pull her against his side and settle them beneath the covers. Something hitched in her chest. He planned to stay with her. Not sneak off like this was some kind of secret.

She snuggled against his shoulder, knowing, hoping that the night was still long ahead of them. She kissed his shoulder and closed her eyes, not so much to sleep as to savor the memories of tonight.

"What are you thinking about?" Marcus asked softly, pulling her tighter into his arms.

"Us. You." Heat washed up her cheeks. "About just now."

"Good thoughts, I hope."

"Oh, definitely." She looked at him. "Most definitely." Their gazes caught, and the heat in his eyes ignited the fire in her.

His lips met hers just as a loud pounding echoed throughout the house. At first, she thought it was Wyatt or one of her other brothers at the door. Then she realized it was downstairs.

It came again, this time with the sound of hurrying footsteps in the hall.

"Wyatt? Addie?" Dutch Ferguson's voice cut through the night.

What did the sheriff want this time of night?

CHAPTER EIGHTEEN

BY THE TIME Wyatt had Dutch settled at the kitchen table, the entire family had come in. Everyone was there, but Addie was the one who pushed her way to the front. "Dutch."

Dutch was the rock that this community relied on. Right now, he was broken.

"I... She just wouldn't listen," he whispered. He ran his hand down his weathered face. "I tried to stop her."

"Elizabeth?"

He nodded, looking only at Addie. "She's gone. I've looked everywhere."

"We'll find her, Dutch." Wyatt's voice was that of reason and determination. Addie had relied on that voice, on his broad shoulders, so many times in her life. But was he going too far? Was he promising something they couldn't do?

Dutch looked toward the window, and Addie followed his gaze to the inky black beyond the yard lights. What was he thinking? Imagining? Remembering?

"I should have known what to do," he whispered. "I'm trained. I know not to push her, I know to just go with her, not try to make her see reality."

Addie put her hand on his shoulder, hoping to comfort him. "You said yourself she was upset."

"Yeah. Something set her off. She said she saw Cal." His voice broke. "She kept screaming at me that I was keeping him away from her." Dutch's shoulders shook. "I'd never do that to her."

"We know better." Addie tried to reassure him, but the memories of Cal hurt them all too much. The idea of Elizabeth out in the night, searching for what she'd never find, hurt.

Dutch looked defeated. "I gotta find her. I thought because we were here earlier, maybe she came back. She swore she saw him tonight."

"I'm sorry, we haven't seen her." Wyatt grabbed his jacket. "But we'll help you look for her."

Everyone moved then. No one even thought twice about jumping into action. Dutch stared at them, wiping his eyes with his big, weathered hand.

"What if...what if she goes back home? I didn't think of that. No one's there." Panic filled his voice.

"I'll go over to your place and wait," Emily volunteered.

"She might not recognize you."

"Maybe. We have to take that chance. I don't

know what choice we have. I'll call you if she shows up."

Dutch slowly nodded and headed to his cruiser. Wyatt called the bunkhouse to get the men involved while Emily grabbed her car keys.

This was a search everyone wanted to help with.

Marcus stood at the edge of the kitchen, watching the commotion, watching the family kick into gear. Addie approached him then.

"What's going on?" Marcus put his arms around her, letting her lean into him.

"It's bad," she said, holding on to him, needing someone to lean on. Needing him.

"What happened?"

"Elizabeth thought she saw Cal. I told you how she never recovered from his death. And lately, her dementia's been getting worse. She took off this evening, and Dutch can't find her." Addie finally pulled away. "We're going to help look for her."

The sound of footsteps on the stairs broke through the night's quiet, reminding Addie that she needed to pull herself together and get changed. Everyone would be leaving soon, and she intended to join the search. "I—"

"What can I do to help?" Marcus asked, his offer smoothing some of the rough edges of her sorrow.

"You don't have to—"

"I know that." He hugged her. "I want to help. When Ryan was gone those few hours." He swallowed hard.

Addie remembered the panic in Marcus's voice over the phone that night. Empathy for Dutch covered his face.

"Thank you." She wanted to kiss him and go back upstairs. "Later," she whispered before letting all the commotion engulf her.

In the yard, the men had mounted the varied ranch horses. They'd go over the hills. Wyatt and DJ sat behind the wheel of the trucks. They'd drive the roads, paved and dirt. Mandy was on her phone calling neighbors.

Elizabeth would be home by morning. Addie was confident of it.

Addie led Marcus across the ranch—to all the places people had partied, danced, ate, walked. The dance floor was deserted. The bonfire had been put out, though the circle was still warm.

"Do you really think she came back here?" Marcus asked as they headed toward the barn. The kids were still sacked out, so they were moving around quietly.

"I don't know. She's familiar with the ranch. With our family."

"Because of you and Cal?"

She had to think about that answer. "Some. But she was friends with the family long before us.

I remember her when I was a kid. She was fun." She hadn't known Cal then. Addie laughed softly with a memory. "The bonfire was her idea originally." She kept walking. "Except back then it was over by—"

Suddenly, Addie knew where Elizabeth was. She didn't want to know, didn't want to even think about her there. But it was the only answer. The memories overwhelmed her. She fought to clear her mind. No. She had to focus. Had to...go there.

"Where are you going?" Marcus called after her. She heard him, but couldn't take the time to explain. She ran. Across the lawn, down the hard-packed dirt track she hadn't followed in years.

Her sandals slapped loud against the dirt. It was strange wearing shoes here. Barefoot was the norm back then. The sand and soon the mud oozed up between her toes. She swallowed the ache inside her throat.

Addie heard thudding steps behind her. Knowing it was Marcus. And probably Wyatt. And half the ranch. She didn't care. If she waited, she might never get the nerve to face it again. She hadn't managed it in fourteen years.

She heard the water rushing over its banks. So familiar and beautiful. And painful. *Oh, Cal.* She almost thought she heard his laughter. The call of his deep, sweet voice. The boy who'd never had the chance to grow into the man. The ghost she couldn't manage to leave behind.

ELIZABETH STOOD ON the edge of the river. Even from here, on the bluff just a few yards away, Addie saw her eyes. Her stare was that distant blank that only a person whose mind had faded could display. Addie's heart hurt. Sad for Dutch. For Elizabeth. Who was that with her?

The boy standing beside Elizabeth turned, and the relief that washed over his familiar face nearly tore Addie's heart in two. "Ryan?" Addie called.

Elizabeth turned as well, her eyes suddenly coming to life. "No, you stay right here with me, young man." The authoritative voice grated on Addie's nerves. It was so unlike the Elizabeth she remembered.

"Elizabeth," Addie called, slip-sliding down the side of the sandy bluff. Finally, she halted at the bottom, sand under her feet and clinging to her legs. She ignored the discomfort. "He's not Cal." She said it firmly, but not without an edge of her own fear.

"He's my son." Elizabeth bit out the words.

"No, he's not." Addie lifted her chin, struggling to stay calm, to stay firm. "This is Ryan."

Elizabeth's gaze wavered as she looked at the boy, a frown on her brow. "No. It's…" Elizabeth stared, looking at Ryan. Then at Addie. Then

Ryan again. "Addie?" she whispered. Her confusion was strong, but Addie couldn't worry about her now. She needed to protect Ryan. Get him away. Then she'd deal with Elizabeth.

"You need to let him go home to his dad." Addie spoke carefully, clearly. "He's got school tomorrow." Maybe that would help. God, she hoped so.

"No!" Elizabeth reached out and curled her hand around Ryan's arm. "He's... He has to stay with me."

"No!" Ryan tried to pull his arm away from Elizabeth. "I gotta go home." He sounded panicked.

"Ryan, just hold still," Addie told him. All his reacting and struggling would only make Elizabeth worse. The older woman's adrenaline had to be high.

And Addie almost understood. Elizabeth thought this was Cal. Her son. Her only child.

Addie didn't think she'd ever let go, either. She looked at Ryan—wishing. Not now. She pushed those thoughts away.

"Elizabeth." Addie stepped closer, trying to get the older woman to look at her, away from Ryan. "We all need to go home." For once, she wished it would start raining. That type of clue wouldn't be lost even on Elizabeth, but the sun was coming up, bright gold.

"Why?"

"It's time." She kept her answer short on purpose.

The men who'd been running behind her crested the hill just then. Addie groaned. Elizabeth looked up, startled. Her grip on Ryan tightened. "Make them go away," she screeched.

"They won't go away until you let go of him," Addie told her, hating the pain that blanketed Elizabeth's face, but knowing there was no choice.

"He's my baby," Elizabeth cried, and Addie didn't have the heart to hurt her any more. Instead, she stepped even closer.

"It's okay, Elizabeth," she whispered. "I'm here. I'll help you." The vague reassurance seemed to calm the older woman.

Elizabeth's confusion grew, and Addie had to use it to her advantage. Once Ryan was gone, she could soothe Cal's mother.

"You need to take him with you." Elizabeth reached out and took Addie's hand. She put it on Ryan's shoulder. "He likes you."

Addie took the opportunity to get Ryan away. As they crested the hill, flashing red and blue lights cut through the night. Dutch's cruiser came down the dirt road. He'd take care of her now.

THEY WALKED TO the house in silence. The only sounds were the breeze and the whisper of their footsteps in the dirt. Marcus had his arm around Ryan's shoulders, and they spoke softly.

Addie didn't have anything to say. She was exhausted and just wanted to sleep for a week. Relief stole the adrenaline that had kept her going the past couple of hours.

"Go on up to bed," Marcus told him. "I'll be up in a minute."

When Ryan turned, but didn't leave, Addie looked over at him. The frown on his face told her something was wrong. What had Elizabeth said or done to him tonight? His face was pale and his eyes wide.

"Ryan?" She looked at Marcus. He looked as surprised as she felt that Ryan was still here. "What's the matter?"

"I didn't mean to cause any problems."

She frowned. "Tonight wasn't your fault."

"What are you talking about, son?" Marcus walked over to the boy. "What's the matter?"

Ryan crossed the floor and flung his arms around his father. Addie watched the pure pleasure on Marcus's face as he returned his son's hug.

"You know you can talk to me." After several long minutes of silence, Marcus pulled back. "I think you need to tell us what's going on. What happened that you aren't telling us?"

"I'll be right back." Ryan turned and ran up the stairs.

"Do you know what's going on?" Marcus asked her.

She shook her head. The long day, the long night, Elizabeth and now this— She wasn't sure how much longer she could function.

It took several minutes before Ryan returned. He had a folded piece of paper clutched in his hand.

Instead of walking to Marcus, he stopped in front of Addie. "I…" He rubbed his nose with the back of his hand. His eyes glistened with unshed tears. He extended the paper toward her. "Here."

"What's this?"

"Look."

Slowly, she opened the much-folded and unfolded paper. "What—"

The world around her spun. Her heart pounded so hard against her ribs she thought it would knock her over. *Oh, God.*

Then, as if her brain kicked into gear, something else dawned on her. Slowly, too scared of what she wouldn't see, what she would see. "Ryan…" She looked at Ryan. Then at the paper. Then back at Ryan. At the copy of an all-too-familiar birth certificate.

Marcus was behind her. When had he moved? Did it matter?

"What's this?" He reached for the paper. His

frown grew. His glare turned to her. "Someone better start explaining." He shook the paper at her.

Why hadn't she seen it? She took a step. And then another. Those eyes. She blinked hers to keep them clear. That chin. They were so familiar.

"How—" She could barely think, much less compose sentences.

"At computer camp last summer." Ryan glanced sideways, warily, at his father. "One of the guys who'd been there before. He showed me how to hack into places."

"Like sealed court records?" she whispered.

He simply nodded.

"After Mom died—" Ryan looked at her then "—I wanted to find you."

"What's going on?" Marcus yelled, though she saw the realization in his eyes.

Marcus stared at the paper. She didn't need to see it. She'd seen it too many times—every time she opened the blue box on her bedroom closet.

"You knew about this?" He shook the page at her again.

"I—" She shook her head. What was he asking? Of course she knew about her child. "Yes."

No one else here knew about—this. Mom had been the only one she'd ever confided in. Addie thought her secret had died with Mom.

Anger contorted Marcus's handsome features. "I don't know what you're up to." His voice was deep and menacing. "But Ryan is *my* son. You have no rights to him. You gave them up."

"Dad!" The confusion and hurt in Ryan's voice cut through her. She'd hurt him enough. Dear God. This was—she turned and took a step toward him—her son.

All this time she'd remembered the baby, mourned the infant. She'd never thought of him as growing up. That would have made it unbearable. Would have driven her slowly crazy.

"Don't even think about it." Marcus stepped forward, between her and Ryan, his broad frame blocking the boy from her view. "Ryan, get your things. We're leaving."

"But Dad—"

"No *buts*. Now!" His voice echoed through the house.

Ryan stood there a long minute, then turned, and the sound of his slow steps on the stairs told her he'd left.

She didn't move. She couldn't. Her body was frozen in place. She looked at Marcus and, like a kaleidoscope, every last detail of tonight spun around her. She loved him. Her heart hurt for him, for Ryan, for herself. For all of them.

His eyes filled with anger and so much more. Pain. Betrayal. Fear. He'd never believe her now if she told him how she felt. Anything she'd say now would seem like a desperate excuse to get to

Ryan. And while she wanted that desperately, she wanted—needed—Marcus, too. A sharp ache hit her deep in the chest. "Marcus, please—"

"I don't want or need to hear it. I've had enough of lies and secrets. Save it, Addie."

His anger was justified, she knew that. But it also hit a nerve she didn't know she had. He wasn't the only one surprised here. "No, I'm not going to *save it*." She stepped closer to him, her own anger loosening the pain's grip. "You don't get to be the only one angry here."

"Don't I?" He threw his hands in the air, then stepped closer, menacingly close. "What was last night all about, then?" His eyes sparked with pain and anger. "All that sharing? Where was this little secret in all that?"

Memories washed over her like sandpaper, rough and painful. "Last night was about common ground. About you and I connecting. You lost Carolyn. I lost Cal. Shared grief."

He had the grace not to say anything. Maybe he was actually listening and considering her words.

She took a deep breath, trying to contain her own hurt and anger and think straight. "Your having a son isn't a part of common ground. I don't have that."

"Apparently, you do." She saw the anger, but she also saw the pain in his eyes.

His mother's warnings rang in her mind. Donna

had said Skylar men were lousy at relationships. She'd warned her they always walked away.

No, she'd been wrong.

She'd been—Addie mentally cursed—too right.

Marcus came out of the house then, taking Ryan to the Jeep—and away.

CHAPTER NINETEEN

ADDIE HUDDLED ON the porch swing. She didn't know how long she'd been there. No one had come near her all morning, and she'd noticed only a few things around her. The creak of the swing's ancient chain. The whisper of the breeze. The movement of the sun.

Finally, the screen door squawked open. She didn't look up. She barely moved, except to breathe. The familiar, confident footsteps told her it was Wyatt. Her heart sank. What must he think of her? She curled her arms even tighter around her knees and leaned her head against the swing back.

The silence hurt to listen to. "What...what do you want?" she whispered.

Her big brother cleared his throat. "Are you okay?"

God, she loved him. Looking over at him, not lifting her head, she said, "I don't know."

The silence returned. Wyatt pulled one of the old wooden chairs closer to the swing and sat. He leaned forward, resting his elbows on his knees.

Finally, he asked the question that hurt. "How come you never told us?"

Addie closed her eyes, fighting the burn. "Mom knew." Right now, her heart hurt, missing her mother, missing the hug that Mom would have gladly given her. "We talked endlessly about what to do." She remembered the barrage of tears her mother had mopped up. About Cal's death. About his never knowing. About her decisions to give the baby up for adoption.

"Until today, he— He was just a baby in my mind." She knew she wasn't answering his questions. She didn't know why she hadn't told her family.

"I'm glad Mom knew. That you weren't alone."

He was being too nice. Afraid she'd lose it? She looked at her brother again, and then the hurt and anger inside her exploded. "No. I— Don't you see?" She swung her legs off the edge of the wooden seat and sat up. "I was selfish. I was ashamed for not being responsible like Dad told me to be," she yelled.

Tears streamed from her eyes, and she noticed only enough to shove them away with the back of her hand. "Until today, it never crossed my mind that I'd given up Elizabeth and Dutch's grandchild. I never thought of them. Or Mom. All I thought of was me." She practically spat out the last word.

"Dad never meant for you to sacrifice for anyone, especially us." Wyatt wasn't angry, though there was a note of confusion in his voice that she managed to notice.

"Dad told me I was the oldest. I had to be responsible. He didn't ask much. But what he did ask, I failed him."

"No, you didn't." Wyatt's anger finally surfaced and brightened his eyes.

She welcomed it. She was spoiling for a fight, a release to her pain. "Denying it won't make it less true. I failed." She shot to her feet.

"Addie, stop it!" Wyatt barked out the words, startling her. "You are not a failure, and you made a choice. It was the right choice for you. My God, you were what? Eighteen? Nineteen? You were still a kid."

"Yeah. A kid who thought she was so grown up."

"Real or not, is this why you've always put others' needs before yours? Why you don't take care of yourself, but mother the rest of to death?"

She simply stared at him. He and the others were all she had. And they didn't want her—need her. Shocked by what he said, she stepped back, the swing hitting the back of her knees. She plopped down with a thud that the wooden roof protested. "I—I don't…"

"Yes, you do." Mandy came through the screen

door with Tara, DJ and Jason trailing hot on her heels.

"It's why we keep telling you to go find your own life. To stop worrying about all of us. We want you to be as happy as you've helped us to be." Tara walked over and did what Addie had wished Mom could do. She slipped her arms around Addie's trembling shoulders.

Their words were meant to soothe and calm her pain. But how could they understand? Her life, as they kept referring to it, was gone. Over. Forever. Cal was dead. She'd tossed Ryan away almost callously, and Marcus—she ached with the sob that got stuck in her throat.

Images of last night returned, with the impact of a jackhammer, to taunt her. The firelight on his features. The way his lips moved into just that right position to kiss when she'd yanked the flaming marshmallow from the fire to blow on it. The way his arms held her on the dance floor. Of the taste of that singed marshmallow in his kiss. "Oh, God," she whispered, her hand instinctively reaching up to touch her lips.

She didn't dare tell them that she'd fallen in love with Marcus. It was too new for her, and maybe the feeling would go away if she didn't ever say it out loud. She didn't need their pity or the platitudes they'd spout to try to ease her broken heart.

Looking through her damp gaze, she saw the

contentment they'd all found. The love they felt was strong around each one of them, for their lives and the families they were building.

She didn't want a pity seat at any of their tables.

"She's doing it again," DJ said to Wyatt, like he was that little kid tattling on her.

"I know." Wyatt sighed. "Addie. Stop worrying about us." He tried to make it sound like an order, but failed miserably.

Didn't they understand? They were all she had left to worry about. There wasn't anyone else now.

ADDIE NORMALLY FOUND solace in baking. Over the past two weeks since school let out, since the barbecue at the ranch, since Marcus and Ryan left, she'd filled half her freezer with cookies. She'd be good for months.

Still, she couldn't shake the sense of loss and emptiness that followed her. The cookies everyone loved, though, didn't hold the normal comfort.

Standing at the counter, the familiar ingredients scattered around her, she didn't move. She just stared. Now what?

The battered recipe card had faded to yellow. and, to be honest, she made the recipe from memory anyhow. Leaning forward, she looked at the words. Stains, worn paper and torn edges obliterated half of them.

Carefully, she touched the card. Peanut butter

chocolate chip cookies were a staple in her family, a bridge to the past. But what about the future? She shook her head, banishing that train of thought.

With a sigh, she gathered all the items and put them back. She did not need to make any more cookies. What she needed to do was get on with life.

Just then, the doorbell rang. Her heart skipped a beat. After a deep breath, she reminded herself it wasn't going to be Marcus. She ignored the wave of sadness as she opened the door.

Ryan stood there.

"Hi," she said softly. She hadn't seen him since the last day of school.

"Hi." He gripped the strap of his backpack hard and scuffed a foot against the walk. "How...how are you?"

"I'm okay. You?"

He shrugged. "You're really my mom," he whispered, though it wasn't a question.

"I am." She waited for him, drinking in the sight of him,

Silence filled with the sound of the breeze and the late afternoon. She'd wait for him to ask the questions she saw in his eyes.

"Why did you give me away?"

She'd spent fourteen years dreading that question. She'd come up with at least a million answers to it. Now that she was faced with the inquiry, all those answers vanished.

"I know I owe you an answer," she whispered and pulled the door farther open. "Come in, and I'll try to answer. It's not easy," she admitted.

Her palms were suddenly damp, and she tried to calm her heart. She could totally screw this up.

"That's okay." He wasn't angry, which was one of the responses she'd always expected. But he wasn't happy, either. She led the way to the kitchen. "Are you makin' cookies?"

"I decided not to." Addie smiled. "Want some to take home? I've got plenty." She opened the freezer and pulled out a plastic bag full. She knew she was stalling.

"Does your dad know you're here?" She realized she should have asked that earlier.

"No." Ryan didn't meet her eyes. "He's—"

"He's what?" she prodded, wanting to hear about Marcus more than she dared admit.

"He's grumpy." Ryan shrugged. "He won't like me being here."

That wasn't what she'd expected to hear, and her heart sank. She missed him. Missed both of them. She knew it, and she'd stopped denying it.

"Call him." When Ryan glared mutinously at her, she glared right back. "I'm not arguing. I'm happy to talk to you. But I won't do it behind his back."

Ryan frowned but pulled his phone out. He thumbed the screen on and she heard it ring. She waited, slowly using the dishcloth to wipe down the counters as something to distract herself.

"Hey, Ryan." Marcus's voice filled the kitchen, and Addie's breath hitched. She closed her eyes for a moment, taking it inside. Savoring.

"Dad," Ryan said. "I'm over at Addie's house. She—" He looked over at her. "She said I had to call you and let you know I'm here."

The silence was stunned. Finally, he spoke. "You should have asked first."

"You'd have said no."

"Maybe. But you should have still asked." The anger was strong in Marcus's voice. She wanted to ease his pain, but her own anger responded.

"We're only going to talk." She spoke loud enough for Marcus to hear. Ryan responded by hitting the speaker button on his phone.

"I just want to ask some questions."

"You can always ask me," Marcus offered.

"You don't know the answers." Ryan was growing angry himself.

"Okay, that'll do," Addie cut in. "He'll be home in a few minutes," she promised, not wanting to be the one to send Ryan away.

"That's acceptable."

He was so distant, so stiff. She missed the man

who'd been so sweet and wonderful, whom she'd talked with, laughed with, enjoyed so much with.

"Bye, Dad." Ryan didn't wait for his father to respond before pocketing the phone. Addie took her time rinsing out the dishcloth and stretching it over the faucet to dry.

"He's not very happy," Ryan whispered. "But I needed to come see you."

"I'm glad you came over." She tried to smile.

"Will you tell me? About you? About my— about my father?"

Addie took a deep breath before stepping closer. She froze for an instant, looking at the boy she'd helped create. "Wait here," she whispered. Hurrying upstairs, before she could change her mind, she headed to her room. To the closet.

The box. It was exactly where she'd left it. Clutching it tight, she went back downstairs.

She forced herself to slow down and consider Ryan, who was leaning against her counter. She owed him an explanation. "Cal Ferguson was your father." She purposefully didn't use *dad*, the term he used for Marcus. It wasn't appropriate, or fair to Marcus, who really was Ryan's dad.

Cal had never even known about Ryan, so he'd never had a relationship with him. "He died before I even knew I was pregnant with you." She'd never get over the hurt of his not knowing. Still clutching the box, she stopped beside him.

"I thought about keeping you. I really tried to figure out how I could do it." Her voice cracked as she remembered the agony of making the biggest decision of her life—at all of eighteen years of age. Sounds of shuffling steps made her look up, and she found Ryan had moved closer, just inches away.

"Why didn't you?"

"I finally realized I couldn't do a good job for you." Her fingers itched to reach out and touch him. She didn't dare. She'd promised Marcus she'd send him home soon. "I was too broken. I hurt too much. I was too young—eighteen, only four years older than you are now."

She set the pretty blue box on the counter between them. "I've kept so many memories in here," she said softly. Every item in the box was whole in her mind. "Maybe this will help." She pushed it toward him.

Ryan nodded, a frown still on his face, though, as he stared at the box. Time stretched out while she waited, holding her breath. Finally, he opened the lid and stared at the contents. He didn't do anything more than look.

"So that lady, Elizabeth, is my grandma?" he whispered.

Addie nodded, wishing Elizabeth were better. "She's had a rough time. When Cal died, I think she lost a little bit of her mind.

"Elizabeth's heart broke when Cal died." Addie cleared her throat and spoke a bit louder. "She didn't mean to hurt you. She just misses him so much." And Addie understood all too well.

"So... I have another grandpa?"

That's when Addie lost it. Her shoulders shook as she fought the sob that burned up from her heart. Dutch. The man who'd been like a second father to her would be thrilled. He'd love Ryan. He'd—

Ryan's phone went off just then.

Disappointment washed over Ryan's face. "Bet that's Dad."

"You're probably right." She took a deep breath, fighting to control the disappointment that threatened to overwhelm her. "Come on." She forced herself to shift into principal gear. "I promised you'd head home." With her hand on Ryan's shoulder, she nudged him toward the front door.

"What about...this?" He put his hand on the box.

"It's yours now." The decision felt right. "I don't think your dad's ready for it yet."

Ryan nodded and headed toward the door. "Yeah." His voice was full of reluctance. "I can come back?"

"Any time."

Silently, Ryan stepped outside and headed down the walk. She watched him leave.

And then she saw him. Marcus. Standing across the street, his phone in his hand. Her heart and breath caught.

She moved down the steps and across the walk. She stopped only when she reached Ryan's side. She squared her shoulders and faced them both. "I don't owe your father or anyone an explanation," she said. "But I, we, owe you the truth. You want that, don't you?"

Marcus could hear her. He didn't move, but she knew she'd hit a nerve. She could tell, using his words against him. She turned to his—her—their son. "I gave you up because it was the best thing for you. And I'd do it again if I had to."

Ryan's eyes shone, and she prayed she could put the right words together. "I didn't want to. Now that you're back in my life, I don't want you to ever go away again. But Marcus is your dad, Ryan. He loves you. You love him. I see it. I know it."

She couldn't hold back anymore. She reached out and engulfed the boy she'd last held as a baby in her arms. Ryan's arms went around her, holding on.

"I've come to love you so much." She didn't analyze whom she was talking to right then. Finally, she pulled away and put space between them. "I'd never do anything to hurt you." She met Marcus's cold stare. "Either of you. I'll never take Ryan from you." She wanted to say it over and over again until Marcus believed her.

"But I hope you'll at least let me have a piece of his life to be a part of." She backed up, afraid she'd never be able to let go if she didn't.

When she reached the steps, she spun around and hurried inside. The door slammed behind her. She didn't open it again.

And no one came to knock.

MARCUS OPENED THE BOOK. Ryan hadn't said anything about his visit with Addie and Marcus hadn't asked. Not because he was angry or upset. They'd both grown in the last month. But he'd asked for time.

And Marcus had given it to him.

He'd needed some himself, especially after seeing Addie today.

He needed a distraction. So, he'd decided tonight was the night to start reading the book.

Except the words kept blurring in front of his eyes. He hadn't slept much lately, and he rubbed his tired eyes now. Maybe tonight he'd sleep.

Not if he read this book, he wouldn't. He closed the cover and shot to his feet. He paced over to the dining room window that overlooked the backyard. Ryan had come in a short while ago, leaving the back lights on. The big floodlights up under the eaves cast pools of gold over the lawn. Fairy lights scattered along the walk, and in the flower beds, softened their glow.

It was an inviting place, and he wondered for the millionth time what it must have been like growing up here, crowded into this four-bedroom house with seven other people.

Memories bombarded him as he gazed out at the detached garage where Addie's father's shop had been. The day he'd found her long-lost birthday present returned to haunt him.

So sweet. So wonderful. A lifetime ago.

He'd thought he'd found love again. *Fool*. And maybe... No, if there was one thing Marcus hated, it was secrets. He turned around and stared at the book. Wasn't that what had started him on his entire career? His curiosity? All his father's secrets?

His father had seldom been home, and they'd never known where he was or when he'd come back. If he'd come back. He remembered the tears his mother had shed when he'd been small. She'd missed him. Missed sharing a life with the man she loved. Lord, Marcus certainly understood that pain.

But eventually she'd stopped crying. She'd never told them why, and he'd hated that wall she'd built around herself.

His father's secrets had driven him crazy. And he got the feeling that if Elizabeth hadn't taken Ryan, if Ryan hadn't decided to share the birth certificate, Addie wouldn't have ever told him about her past, about the child she'd given up.

He smacked a palm against the counter. It wasn't as if she'd lied to him. She'd been totally honest when he'd asked. But the sin of omission was just as bad as a lie, wasn't it?

To him, it was. Perhaps worse because you intentionally hurt someone.

He stared out the window again, reaching over and turning off the lights, plunging the backyard into darkness. There was so much about Addie that he didn't know, and he didn't think he'd ever know.

But there was one secret he *could* solve.

His father hadn't told him anything about his military life. That curiosity had driven Marcus to study all the events his father had been involved in. Vietnam had to be the biggest event.

As Marcus met vets and became involved in the academic piece of his father's world, he heard rumblings of a mission. A mission gone horribly wrong. He had more questions than answers, and the one person who could give him those answers refused to discuss it.

Stalling, and knowing it could be a late night, he opened the cupboard where the coffee was stored. He'd make a pot. The bottle of wine Addie had innocently brought that first night he'd invited her over sat there. Had he put it there? He didn't remember doing so. Had Ryan? Did it matter?

He stared at the dark bottle. It didn't call his name. It didn't even look enticing. He smiled and, with one swift move, grabbed it by the neck. He had a corkscrew around here somewhere. He remembered unpacking it. He didn't remember putting it in any of the drawers.

He opened a couple where he thought it might be. Nope. He looked in the pantry. Nope, not much there anyway.

With the bottleneck fisted in his hand, Marcus moved through the kitchen. No luck finding the blasted thing. Finally, angry and frustrated, he stopped in the middle of the floor. Looking around. Did he have any other options?

"Dad?" Ryan's voice was quiet, higher-pitched than normal. "What are you doing?"

Marcus laughed and looked down. He cursed. "Sorry," he mumbled. "Didn't mean to upset you."

"What's that bottle for?"

"It's the one Addie brought that night we grilled."

"What…" Ryan swallowed hard. "What are you gonna do with it?"

"Well, I was going to do this civilized." He looked at the hurt in his son's eyes and knew he'd put it there. "Guess you'll just have to help me."

"Drink it?" The face he made almost made

Marcus laugh, and while he was pretty sure that someday they'd be able to look back at this moment and laugh—not now.

"No. Come on. Come over here." He walked to the sink, waiting until Ryan was right there beside him. "Put your hand here." He pointed to the bottom of the bottle. Ryan grasped the thick glass. Marcus had his hand over the label. "Ready?"

"I—I guess." Though the look on his face said he had no idea what he was ready for, he trusted his father. Marcus's heart swelled with pride that he'd built a good relationship with his son. Nothing, absolutely nothing, was more important right now.

"Okay. And don't ever do anything like this without me, okay?"

"Uh, sure?"

Marcus lifted his hand—Ryan's and the bottle rising with it. He brought the neck of the bottle down hard on the corner of the marble counter. The top did exactly what he expected, sending droplets of wine over them both, a hunk of glass and some slivers fell into the sink. He upended the broken bottle and poured it straight down the drain.

Ryan's laughter rang out, filling the bright warm kitchen. When the last drop had fallen down the drain, the acrid scent wafting up around them, Marcus turned on the water. There might be a few glass slivers, but if he had to replace anything, he'd gladly do it. That sound was worth it.

Marcus took the hunk of broken bottle and tossed it into the trash. He carefully grabbed the other broken pieces and they followed into the can. They stood there, silently staring at the sink.

Finally, Ryan stepped back. "You okay, Dad?"

"Yeah." Marcus looked up from the sink where the water still ran. He turned it off. "I am. I'm better than I've been in a long time."

"I'm glad."

"Me, too." The silence stretched out. That was one down. He turned and looked back at the other. The book that he'd told himself he was going to read—eventually—sat there, the cover still closed.

"You going to read the book?" Ryan asked, his voice once again soft and higher-pitched, stressed.

"I need to." He knew the information inside was important to him for his field of study—at least that's what he'd told himself. And it was the key to who his father had become. Would he truly understand the older man once he'd read it? Once he knew the truth of the horrors his father had faced, and possibly done, in Vietnam?

"Maybe we could do the same thing."

Marcus looked over at Ryan and frowned. "Do what?"

"Maybe we should do it together. You know, read it. Break it like we did the bottle."

A shot of pain cut into Marcus's chest. Addie's reassurances that he'd raised a good kid echoed in his mind. Suddenly, he missed her, missed the woman his heart believed her to be. The one he knew he couldn't face until he'd slayed all the demons.

"Are you sure you're up to it?" Marcus wasn't going to have Ryan do anything that would harm him in any way, physically or emotionally.

"Yeah. If you're there."

"Okay. Let's give this a shot."

Slowly, Marcus walked over to the big kitchen table, thinking vaguely of the old wooden chairs that had sat there at one time. The one that sat in Addie's kitchen where… He yanked his mind back from that path. He pulled out one of the new, straight-back chairs he'd bought.

The book hadn't changed. The cover was still the hand-tooled leather that Sam had spent months creating. The hand-cut and printed pages were rough on the edges.

Ryan stood next to him and reached out his young hand. Instead of caressing the cover and appreciating its beauty, he did what Marcus hadn't. He flipped it open. And started to read aloud. "Vietnam was a hell of a place." Sam's words filled the kitchen.

The words were stilted for the first chapter. The detailed descriptions of getting the draft notice, of the conversations Sam had had with his buddies and his family about going. About the idea of running to Canada. Of the details of boot camp and the long flight over the massive ocean that were distant and safe. After he'd gotten past the initial shock that Ryan was actually reading the book, Marcus sat back and listened.

"You want me to keep reading?" Ryan looked up at the end of the chapter.

Marcus smiled at his son. So damned proud. "If you don't mind. But how about we go find a more comfortable seat in the living room?"

"Cool. Can I grab a soda?"

"Yeah, get me one, too."

They settled in the big overstuffed couch that had taken nearly six months for Carolyn to talk him into buying. Now he felt her support in the room. Ryan flopped down beside him, kicking his tennis shoes off and propping his feet up on the coffee table. Carolyn definitely wouldn't have liked that, but Marcus didn't mind.

"You ready to hear more?"

"As ready as I'll ever be." Marcus took a swig of his cola, hoping caffeine had the same protective powers alcohol had once had for him.

"The worst part of each day was the waking up." Ryan read Sam's description of the military jungle. "Waking up and remembering where you were and how far you were from home." Ryan stopped and frowned. He looked over at Marcus. "That'd really suck."

"Yeah, it would." Marcus wasn't seeing Sam's face in his mind. He imagined his father's face. The face he remembered from when he was a kid. The one that was in the black-and-white photos his mom still had.

Ryan turned the page. "Hey, listen to this. 'I met a bunch of great guys in that first week. We were all from Chicago, and here that makes us neighbors, even though back home we were from totally different worlds. There was Timothy Harden. Matt Sutter and a guy from up on Lake Shore Drive. Never thought I'd meet anyone from up in that hoity-toity area. But here we were sharing beers every Friday night. James Skylar turned out to be a man I'm mighty glad I shared a jungle with.' That's Grandpa, ain't it?"

"It…it is." Marcus tried to swallow the fear in his throat. The soda just got lodged somewhere near his Adam's apple, and he set it aside.

"Cool!"

Marcus's heart hurt. What if the grandfather Ryan was so proud of turned out to be the evil monster Marcus was afraid he was? Would Marcus be able to see through his own pain to help his son deal with it? Dread settled over him.

Ryan kept reading for a while, with no further mention of James, though. The room grew darker as the sun set, and Marcus turned on the lights. At the midway point, he stopped and they ordered a pizza. While they waited for the delivery, Ryan read another chapter. The battalion Sam was with was moving location and the Chicago crew was splitting up. They were sad to leave each other and the connection to home behind, but the months had made them into responsible, hardened soldiers. "We'd become men without even realizing it." Sam ended the chapter and they left off to answer the door for the pizza.

Halfway through the pepperoni, Marcus decided he needed to talk to his son, prepare him for where they were going with this story, that it might not be the hero-worship-worthy place he was expecting. "You know this book is about a war, right?" Marcus asked.

"Yeah. I know." Ryan ran into the kitchen and grabbed another soda. "Wars suck. But Sam survived. Grandpa survived." He shrugged and opened the book again. Before he read again, he looked at Marcus. "You should make us some popcorn."

"You just had half a pizza."

"Yeah, but there's no crunch. We need crunch."

Marcus shook his head and took the opening his son gave him. The familiar, modern hum of the microwave was a welcome respite from the images the book filled his head with of his father's oddly black-and-white image, the jungle and—what was that feeling in his chest? Anticipation? Anxiety? Curiosity?

"Dad, you coming back anytime soon?" Ryan yelled.

"Hey, microwaves are fast, but not instantaneous." Just then, the familiar ding sounded and, after a few stray pops, the snack was done. He took his time splitting the popcorn into two bowls before returning to his side of the couch. "Okay, read on. Unless you want me to."

"No. I'm good." He paused and looked at Marcus. "I like doing this." Then he turned back to the book and turned the next page. The paper scraped on the edge of Ryan's jeans, loud in the quiet room. Quiet until Ryan dug into the popcorn and munched.

"We headed north. We didn't know where we were headed, just followed the directions. Just followed orders."

Marcus listened as Ryan read, enjoying the sound of his voice. He closed his eyes, picturing the jungles. For the first time since they'd started reading, Marcus felt the change in Sam's writing. It grew more vivid. More emotional. "We were on the edge of the delta. We had no idea what people at home were hearing, though later I learned what Mom and Dad were hearing each night on the news. Sometimes I think they had it worse.

We were there, just getting through each minute. They were in the kitchen back home, worrying, unable to do anything but worry."

Ryan looked up and fell silent. "Did you know Grandpa's parents? Were they like that?"

"I do remember them." Marcus cast his mind back to his own grandparents. They suddenly seemed so distant, so old-fashioned in comparison from this world, even the world Marcus knew of before he was born. "We'll have to ask Dad about them."

Ryan nodded and returned to reading. From here, Marcus could see they were nearing the end of the book. Nothing in this book answered the questions Marcus had always lived with. And then Ryan started the next page.

"We were pinned down in those rice paddies. I'll never want to step in standing water again as long as I live." Sam's grimace came through in the words. "But that day, we were sure we were standing in our watery graves. Bullets flew at us from every direction. The enemy was close, and we weren't sure where to turn. Then we saw the bellies of those flyboys and started cheering. We were gonna make it. We were gonna see another Friday night beer. But then those bombs came too close. Butch and Hack were hit first— by our guys."

Ryan stopped reading. He looked over at Marcus, his eyes wide. "How does that happen?"

Marcus didn't want to explain friendly fire right now. He'd studied it plenty, how it happened and how it affected those who faced it, and who lived with the haunting. There was a long silence.

Ryan turned the page and resumed reading. "And then it stopped. Suddenly, steered around us like the hand of God was guiding that plane. It was a sight to see. We didn't know what happened until we got back to the base.

"That first day, we saw all of them Chicago boys. Only a couple were missing. We didn't do much talking about them. But we drank a beer to each one. And then that Lake Shore Drive fella came strolling in. When he saw us, he came over and pert'near hugged us all. And then he told us about that day in the rice paddy."

Marcus stood and paced the room. He couldn't sit. Did he want to listen?

"Dad, you okay?" Ryan looked up, a frown on his face. "I can stop reading."

"No. We've come this far." He was committed. If he didn't read it now, he wasn't sure he'd ever be able to do it again.

"Okay, but if it's too rough, let me know." Ryan's eyes sparkled, similar to when Marcus used to read bedtime stories to Ryan.

"Yeah, I'll be sure and do that."

Ryan laughed and looked down at the book. "Here we go. We're finishing this tonight. 'Skylar was up in that bird. He told us about the surveillance they were doing, and as he talked, some other guy stepped up and let us know that Skylar was the reason we were able to drink those beers that night. He'd realized the coordinates were off. From what this other fella was telling us, he saved our sorry asses that day."

Ryan laughed and continued reading. "He did everything in his power to get word up the chain that they were firing on us. He couldn't save us all. We all had another beer for the guys. And then we bought him another beer because it was all we had to say thanks. We couldn't give him a medal or any money or much more than a handshake. But we could buy him a beer, and danged if that isn't what we did. By midnight, we were all so polluted, I'm still amazed we got up the next morning." Ryan paused reading for a few moments, pondering what he'd just read. He turned to Marcus.

"Is that why you and Grandpa argue? Because he drank like you did?"

"No." Marcus's gut tightened. He'd always argued with his father, and he thought, perhaps, they always would.

MARCUS STOOD ON the front step of the town house where he'd grown up. He reached up and knocked on the door. He waited, shoving his hands into the pockets of his coat. Texas was already full of summer, but here rain fell heavy and hard.

The door opened. "Marcus?" His mother stood on the other side, staring at him. "What are you doing here?"

"I—" His throat went dry. "I came to see Dad."

She shivered. "You know you don't have to knock. Come on in. He's in the den. Did you bring a suitcase?" She looked past him. "Is Ryan with you?"

Marcus stepped inside. "No. He's got summer baseball and a big tournament. His team is depending on him. He's staying with his friend Dex's family."

The den. Marcus smiled and shook his head. After he and his sister had moved out, his mother had converted his sister's bedroom into a room with a desk, bookshelves and a couch. It was the den. It always seemed strange to him to go in there. He'd been banned from her room the instant she'd hit puberty and presumably had teenage girl secrets he, the younger brother, would never understand. The never-understanding part he still didn't get.

"James?" she called, leading the way down the hall. "Marcus is here." Even as she called her husband's name, it sounded curious, unsure.

James looked up from the paper he'd been reading. He hastily set it aside and stood. "Is something wrong?"

"No, no." Marcus waved his father to take his seat. "I just—" He looked at his father, then at his mother and then turned away to move over to the window. It looked out over the backyard, and he looked over at the fence he'd helped build, begrudgingly one summer, at the lawn he'd hated mowing, at the back patio he'd cleaned leaves and snow and other assorted bits of nature from. All under protest. "I'm sorry," he whispered, surprised when his breath fogged the glass. "I came to talk to you about—"

He took a couple of steps, finally facing his father again. "I read the book." His voice shook. "Actually, Ryan and I read it together."

"I see." James settled back in the big chair he'd been lounging in. He wasn't relaxed now, though. He didn't meet his son's gaze.

"I'm curious." Marcus sat on the couch, at the end nearest his father. He perched on the edge of the cushion, clasping his hands together, surprised at how cold his own fingers were. "Why did you let me believe that what you did in Vietnam was bad?"

Donna gasped. The silence that followed stretched out thick and heavy. Long minutes ticked by as no one spoke. Marcus waited. He figured he'd waited twenty years to find out the truth. Surely, he could wait a few more moments.

Finally, James looked up. His eyes were deep. Filled with something that Marcus wasn't sure he wanted to know. "I don't have to explain myself to anyone." His defiance almost surprised Marcus.

"Not even your son?"

"Especially not my son!" James shot to his feet, smacking the paper on the seat. Ryan stood, as well. He did not want to argue with his father. He'd come here hoping to fill in the blanks Sam's book created. The details of the heroism his father hid. He'd hoped, maybe, he could connect with the man who'd been gone so much of his growing up. The man he'd always wanted to have more of.

"And why is that?"

James spun around, halfway to the door. He seemed to chew on the words before letting them go. "You have a son. I thought maybe you'd understand."

Maybe he did. Maybe he didn't. But Marcus wanted—needed—his father to explain his piece. "Tell me what I'm supposed to know." For the first time, Marcus noticed the age settling over his father's features. He noticed the evidence of time. The signs of the harsh world his father had lived in.

"Tell you what?"

"About that flight. About why you noticed

something no one else did? Tell me your side of Sam's story." Silence once again stretched out. "Dad. Please."

"Hrumpf." James didn't explain, but he didn't leave the room either, which is what he'd clearly intended. "I don't care what Sam said. I'm no hero."

Marcus knew better than to speak at this point, though the questions swirled around in his brain. Slowly, finally, James took a few steps and plopped back down in the chair. The newspaper crackled under him, but he didn't seem to notice. "I was just doin' my job." He looked up, the damp red in his eyes surprising Marcus.

"I don't know why I noticed it. I don't know." James rubbed his brow, looking up at Marcus. "I don't know why it didn't happen ten minutes earlier. I don't know." He stared down at the floor, the vacant stare telling Marcus that James was a long way from the small den.

"But you did notice," Marcus whispered, almost afraid of breaking the spell.

It didn't matter that Marcus spoke softly. James reacted the same. "Too damned late. There were already half a dozen men dead." His voice was soft but intense. "I couldn't save them."

Marcus had read the accounts. The rest of the company had survived because of James's realization that they were firing on their own men the same time they were killing Viet Cong. He'd tried to convince his superiors to call a cease-fire. He hadn't been able to do that. But they had changed their attack. No more friendly fire.

"Six boys came home in body bags," James whispered. "Six men lost. That was too many. Just too many." He looked up at Marcus then. "I know they gave me those medals. I know they patted me on the back, but…" His voice cracked.

Donna moved farther into the room then. She reached out and squeezed Marcus's shoulder, then she walked around to put her hand on James's arm. "Tell him the rest." She nodded. "He should know. I'll bet Sam didn't write about that."

"Sam didn't know."

"Yes, he did." She leaned her head sideways, forcing her husband to look at her. "He went to see every one of those families, too. He talked to me. I wrote you about it."

"Guess I forgot."

"You chose to forget," she chastised him. But despite her urging, James didn't explain. "Well, fine. You won't, I will." She turned to face Marcus.

"Your father went to see every one of those wives, mothers, families. Remember when we'd pack you kids up in the car and we'd go visit some distant cousin? They lived near one of those families. He'd go see them."

James still didn't speak.

"Why didn't you ever explain to me? Why didn't you share that piece of it?"

James looked up then. "I wasn't doing it for you. Or for me." He finally spoke. "I did it for them. They needed to know the truth. Lord knows the government wasn't going to fill them in. They deserved that."

Marcus sat back, staring at the old man who'd been that young soldier, quietly traveling all over the US with his small family to make amends for some debt he didn't owe. What did you say to a man who did that? What did you do?

"You're a good man, Dad."

James glared at him. "Now you notice?" His laughter held no humor. "Why the hell do you think I didn't share all this before? I'm your father. I don't have to impress you."

Marcus cursed. "You think that's what this is about? You think that my opinion has changed?" He cursed again. "I love you. I wanted to be like you. All that time growing up, when you left, it sucked. Everyone else had their dad around. I wanted you there. Or at least I wanted a legitimate excuse as to why you weren't there." He took a breath, shoving his fingers through his hair in frustration. "You gave me nothing. Nothing." He didn't want to be angry. He didn't want to argue. He'd just wanted the truth.

James shot to his feet, nearly knocking Donna over. "You don't understand."

"Then help me understand. Explain it to me."

James stalked to the door, his back straighter than it had been in years, nearly at attention stance. He didn't stop until he reached the doorway. He stopped, looking over his shoulder. "Some memories—hurt too much to revisit." And then he was gone, his footsteps slow and heavy down the hall.

Donna stared after her husband. "He had nightmares for years. Don't judge him too harshly."

"That's the problem." Marcus stared at the empty doorway. "I'm not judging him. I'm not disappointed. I'm not—" He sighed. "I don't know."

"You're still acting like a boy." She walked over to him. "You know how a parent feels. When Carolyn was sick, I know you kept things from Ryan. You did it so he could stay a boy. You protected him. James did the same with you."

Marcus didn't know what to say. "I'm grown now. He doesn't need to protect me anymore."

"You're probably right." She moved in close. "But old habits are hard to break. You're still his son. And maybe you're not the one who'll be hurt when he remembers."

"How'd you get so smart, Mom?"

"Practice. Lots of practice." She reached out and hugged him. They laughed, though the subdued nature of it was strange. "Are you at least staying for dinner?"

"I'll stay tonight. But I'm going home tomorrow."

"It's better than nothing, I guess." She patted his cheek. "I'm glad you came home today."

"Me, too." He smiled. "Think Dad's wishing I'd leave tonight?"

"No. He'll never admit it, but he missed you, too." She frowned. "I think I've got some things you should take with you."

He frowned. "What?"

"You'll see." She looped her arm through his. "So, tell me. How's that young woman we saw you with?"

His father's words echoed around him. Some secrets aren't secrets because of humiliation or pride or ego. No, they were secrets because of pain. It hurt too much to even tell about it.

Addie's face appeared in his mind. Dear God, he was a fool. He'd let her, his father, and himself down.

He froze, knowing he'd never hide anything

from his mother. "Not good, Mom." He hung his head. "I screwed up. Big time."

"Something you can fix I hope."

"I hope so, too." Lord he hoped so.

CHAPTER TWENTY

ADDIE OPENED THE door to find Marcus standing on her doorstep. She hadn't expected anyone, least of all him. A part of her wanted to slam the door in his face. The polite school principal said, "Hello." She didn't smile, though another part of her, the part she chose to ignore, was jumping up and down for joy.

Stifling a gasp, she curled her hands tighter around the precious piece of carved wood, instinctively holding it tight against her chest.

"Hope you're not practicing your incantations to turn me into a toad," he said.

She stared at him for a long minute, then realized he was referring to the wand. "Uh, maybe just—" She waved it absently. "Making a couple wishes," she whispered.

"Do you have a minute?" He stood there, his hands in his pockets, his shoulders hunched a bit, reminding her of Ryan.

She nodded and slipped back, opening the door wider. Was that relief on his face? She led the way into the living room, perching on the wing-backed chair. He didn't sit, choosing to pace in front of the fireplace instead.

Silence stretched out. Finally, Marcus cleared his throat. "There's a pretty awesome kid at my house who would really like to have a relationship with his mother."

She gasped, her fingers suddenly aching as she gripped the wood. She looked down at it and made herself let go before she broke it. Carefully, she set the wand on the end table before turning to face him again. Without something to hold on to, she twined her fingers together, gripping so hard her knuckles turned white. She ached to touch him.

Oh, how she wanted to touch him. Memories of that last night they'd spent together came back, taunting and teasing.

"How do *you* feel about that?" She had to ask, had to know how he really felt.

"I won't stand in the way of that." He didn't look at her, simply stared at the empty fireplace. "He's afraid of losing you."

"I won't—"

"I know you'd never hurt him." He looked at her then. The pain in his eyes was so deep she actually felt the brunt of the hurt. "Addie, I'm sorry."

"S-sorry for what?" Why was he here? Just for Ryan? Or was there more?

"For everything." He turned to face her. "For you losing Cal, and having to give up Ryan. But to be honest, I have to thank you, too. Your sacrifice allowed Carolyn to have her dream of being a mom."

Addie's eyes burned. This wasn't what she'd thought they'd talk about if they ever saw each other again, which she'd seriously doubted would ever happen. "I'd say you're welcome, but—" She shrugged, trying, and failing, to keep control of her hurt.

"Yeah, a little weird, I know." He rubbed a hand over his face. "Ryan deserves to have you in his life, and you deserve to watch him grow up."

She stood there, letting time slip away, afraid to rock this precarious boat. "What...what do you deserve?" she finally asked.

Marcus looked at her then, the fire in his eyes causing her to take a step back. She swallowed.

"I don't deserve anything." He turned and paced away. "I read the book. Ryan and I did it together." He paused. "Then I went and saw my folks." He spoke quickly, as if forcing himself to focus, needing to get the words out.

"How are they?"

"Good. Better now." He shoved his hands into his back pockets, and she wished he'd reach for her instead.

"I finally understand, Addie."

His voice broke, and she couldn't stand it anymore. She walked over to him. "Marcus, I'm confused. What's going on?"

He didn't speak, but he didn't push her away, either. Progress or just a lull in the storm? Her heart beat loud in her ears, hard against her ribs.

"The memories—" He pulled away from her, shoving his fingers through his hair as he paced away. "I pushed you to remember, just like I did with my dad." He paused. "I had no right to hurt you like that."

She ached to hug him. His understanding warmed her heart, and scared her just a little bit. Something big, something unexpected loomed over them. Dare she hope? "You had no way of knowing." She followed him. "If I'd told you, you might have. But I didn't. I didn't tell anyone, and I'm sorry for that."

"You don't have anything to be sorry for." Suddenly, he was there, right beside her. As if he couldn't resist any longer, he reached out.

"Ah, sweet Addie." He gently cupped her chin with his hand. "So sweet."

"Marcus—"

He laughed, a warm sound she'd missed so very much. He stepped even closer, bracketing her face with both hands. "I came here to apologize and leave. I thought I could do that, but I can't. I can't let you go, Addie." His voice deepened. "I need you. I love you."

She'd hoped, but she hadn't expected that. "Marcus?" His image wavered, and she blinked away the damp. "You do? I was afraid to hope—" She threw her arms around him. "I love you, too. So, so much."

He swooped in then, pulling her tight and kissing her with a wildness she'd never felt before. She returned his kiss, finally free from the secrets and pain of the past.

EPILOGUE

FOR SIX MONTHS, Addie had been given the chance to get used to being a mother. So far, it was just as wonderful as it had been the first day.

While she hadn't technically moved in here with Ryan and Marcus yet—she was here more than her place. Glancing out the kitchen window, toward the garage that had been Dad's workshop, to the rich green vines from what had been Mom's garden, she felt at home.

"Dad, Mom's crying again." Ryan laughed, reaching past her to grab a hot cookie from the pan.

"I am not." She used the hem of the apron she'd borrowed from Tara's kitchen to wipe her eyes. "Watch you don't burn yourself."

"You're never going to have enough cookies if you keep letting him steal them." Marcus strolled into the kitchen as Ryan ran out, and grabbed a cup from the cupboard. He filled it with fresh coffee before turning back to lean on the counter and watch her.

She sighed and scooped more dough from the

big mixing bowl. "I only have a few more dozen to make." She pressed the fork on top of the neat balls before sliding the cookie sheet into the oven.

"The wedding is in a week." He lifted his cup toward the calendar on the kitchen wall. "You do remember Tara's pastry chef is making us a cake, right?"

She smacked him with the towel. "How could I forget? She calls every day to make some change."

They were silent for a long moment as the kitchen filled with the sweet aroma of her now-familiar cookies. "You know that no one expects you to make cookies for your own wedding."

"Yes, they do." She stared at him. "It's what I do."

He smiled and set his coffee cup down. Slowly, he moved over to her and took her hands in his. He made sure she met his gaze. "They love you. With or without your cookies." He pulled her into his arms. "Just like I do."

She leaned into him, lifting her face for his kiss. He was happy to oblige. While she still wasn't a coffee drinker, it tasted good on him.

"Uh, guys?" Ryan came back into the kitchen and slid to a halt. "Really? Again?" He'd gotten into the habit of complaining about all the PDA—public displays of affection—a term he'd learned his first year in high school. He enjoyed the blush on Addie's cheeks almost as much as Marcus did.

Marcus sighed, resting his forehead on hers. "He will move out someday, right?"

She laughed. "Don't rush it. I just got him back."

Marcus sighed an exaggerated sigh. "I guess he can stay."

"Think positive," she whispered. "He'll have a girlfriend someday. Paybacks." She pulled open the oven door. "Did you need something, Ryan?" More cookies hit the cooling rack.

"I think another wedding present is being delivered." They'd been getting presents, primarily from Marcus's scattered family, all week.

"Put it in the living room." Marcus retrieved his coffee.

"I…uh… I don't think it'll fit." Ryan stood in the hallway, staring toward the front door.

Now that they weren't talking, and Marcus wasn't distracting her, she heard noises and voices. Several voices. "What the…"

"Do I smell cookies?" DJ's voice was the first one she heard, and an instant later, he came through the doorway.

Addie stared. He was carrying the dining room chair he'd strapped on the back of his motorcycle after Mom's funeral all those months ago.

Without another word, without asking, he walked over to the big table and set it down where it used to sit when Mom lived here. Tammie came in an instant later, with little Rachel Ann and Tyler beside her.

Mandy was right behind her. She was holding Lucas, and Lane carried her chair. Tara had her chair, too. Morgan and his daughter, Brooke, were with her.

How the heck had Jason gotten his chair here? He and Lauren had to have driven from California. Finally, Emily came in slowly. She'd managed to stay so trim—except for the rounded bump that would soon be Wyatt's son. She smiled as he followed her into the room, with the big captain's chair. He set it at the head of the table.

Exactly where Dad had always sat. He guided Emily into it, and she breathed a sigh of relief.

"What's going on?" Frowning, Addie reached out and caressed each of the chairs. They looked right here, together again.

Wyatt grinned, walking over to Marcus and extending his hand. "Welcome to the family."

Marcus nodded and accepted the handshake. At his nod, Ryan, who'd somehow snuck out of the room, returned, carrying the final chair that Addie had thought was still back at her house. Instead, it was here, and Ryan put it in the final empty place.

"What are you all doing?" she asked again, and no one answered her this time, either.

Instead, Tara went to the cabinet beside the

fridge and pulled out the cookie plate that had always been there, and that she knew was back there again. "We came for cookies." She nudged Addie aside with a laugh, and scooped hot cookies onto the plate.

Handing it to Mandy, she pulled down glasses, not even having to ask where they were, either. "Milk and cookies, right, kids?"

Everyone's cheers drowned out any answer she might have gotten. She stared at the table.

All the kids were anxiously waiting for their snack. Brooke was in Tara's chair. Tyler was leaning against the chair where Rachel Anne's carrier was perched. Emily sat in Wyatt's chair. Lucas stood on Mandy's chair, and the look on his face said he was thinking about climbing up on top if they didn't hurry.

Lastly, Ryan took his seat—in her chair—grinning like a boy who'd kept a secret—a good secret—from his mother.

Wyatt put his hand on her shoulder. "We want you to know that we're thrilled you're having the wedding here. Mom got her wish, you know." He whispered the last.

At his words, she couldn't speak, feeling Mom's presence there with them. With a smile, she cleared her throat and lifted the cookie plate. "Who's ready for cookies?" She moved over to the table. "Tyler, you can sit in Jason's seat. We aren't saving it for anyone."

The boy grinned and shook his head. He and Ryan shared a glance. They'd become fast friends, and she liked the closeness that was growing between the cousins.

Addie saw a movement, and she turned just as Lauren slipped into the seat. Her cheeks were a bright red, and she had eyes only for Jason. All the adults stared. The kids all cracked up.

"You?" Addie pointed at Lauren, then made the sign for pregnant. They'd all gotten plenty of practice in sign language the past few months with Emily's pregnancy and wanting to include Lauren in the discussions.

Lauren's response was to sign back, "Yes. A baby." Her smile didn't need any translation.

The big kitchen table, with its mismatched chairs, overflowed with kids, cookies and milk. Laughter and conversation filled the room as Addie leaned against the counter beside Marcus. She tilted her head to rest on his shoulder.

"Happy?" he asked, softly.

She nodded, overwhelmed by the joy she felt. If the wedding were right this minute, she couldn't be happier. She turned to look at him. "You know you're stuck with us?" Was he ready for this big boisterous family of hers?

"Stop thinking, Addie," he whispered against

her ear. "I love you. I will always love you. There's nothing you can say or do now that will scare me away."

She stared at him long and hard. "Nothing?"

"Nothing."

*****